house of
SCARLETT

MEGHAN

NEW YORK TIMES BESTSELLING AUTHOR

MARCH

Visit my website at www.meghanmarch.com.

ABOUT HOUSE OF SCARLETT

Gabriel Legend is unlike any other man I've ever met.
He came into my life like a hurricane, shattering all my
assumptions and preconceived notions.
I wasn't prepared for him. I wasn't prepared for any of it.
But life doesn't wait until you're ready.
Whatever happens next, I know one thing for certain.
I will never be the same Scarlett I was before I met him.

House of Scarlett is the second book of the Legend Trilogy and
should be read following *The Fall of Legend.* Scarlett and
Legend's story concludes in *The Fight for Forever.*

CONTENTS

HOUSE OF SCARLETT

Book Two of the Legend Trilogy

Meghan March

ONE

Gabe

T*wenty-five years earlier*
The storm siren screamed in the distance as I shook Ma awake. "We gotta go. They said we gotta get to the shelter."

Ma must have found a bottle she hid, because I'd already poured out everything I could find. But there she was, passed out on the couch again.

"Just a few more minutes," she murmured. "I'll go to work."

If I wasn't so worried about the storm coming, I would have snorted. She hadn't had a job in over a year, and the little money she did get . . . I swallowed hard. *Don't wanna think about that.*

"The whole park's evacuating. We gotta go."

Living in the middle of a bunch of tin cans in Biloxi meant that when the winds got to whipping up and the TV was sending reporters down to video stuff, we had to go somewhere safer.

"Go without me. I'll be there later." She patted my hand

absently from the couch, and I clenched my teeth. "Good boy."

Being nine sucked. I wasn't strong enough to get her off the couch and out of the trailer; not yet, anyway. Someday I would be, though. Then no one would be able to tell me what to do, and those kids who stole my stuff on the way home from school wouldn't be able to touch me.

I balled my hands into fists and dropped onto one knee. "Ma, wake up. We'll get you another bottle at the shelter."

Both bloodshot eyes popped open, just like I knew they would. "There's a hurricane party?"

"Yeah. Something like that."

There wasn't, but I'd say whatever I needed to say to get her moving. She wasn't the best mom in the world, but she was all I had. And she loved me. She did. If it came right down to it, she'd pick me over the booze. I knew it.

"Okay, okay. I'm coming. Let me freshen up first. Need to fix my lipstick."

She rolled off the broken couch, but there was no way I could let her look in a mirror. We'd never get out of the house. Her lipstick was smeared halfway up her cheek, her eyes were doing a good impression of a raccoon, and I didn't want to think about the man who dropped her off last night with black tears streaming down her face. The second she stepped foot in the trailer, she was tearing it apart, looking for liquor. I went to bed, thankful she was home safe. I'd learned to block out the noise to get some sleep, but no one could sleep through the sirens. They were way too loud.

"You look great, Ma. Let's go." I hoped she'd forgive the lie, because we didn't have time.

"Okay, okay. I'll get my handbag."

I grabbed it off the coffee table, which was piled with unpaid bills and ads for groceries we couldn't afford because Ma drank the check that came from the government, and handed the purse to her. It was a miracle she actually paid our rent this month. I hated it when Tony, the park manager, came and threatened to kick us out and called us white trash.

I shouldered the backpack I'd loaded with all our important stuff—eighty-seven dollars she didn't know I had from weeding and doing odd jobs for the neighbors, her inhaler that was down to its last few puffs, our birth certificates, and the pocketknife I found when the couple from Lot 18 ran off in the middle of the night without paying their rent.

It wasn't much, but it was enough for now.

Someday, things will be different . . .

One day, I'd be old enough to get a job and pay the bills. No one would be able to throw us out because the rent would never be late. There would be food in the fridge, and maybe even some Nutter Butters in the cupboard.

Before I got lost in my head, thinking about all the ways things were going to change when I was the one taking care of us, Ma tucked her handbag under her arm and straightened her shoulders. She was still pretty for a mom. Long blondish-brown hair—same as me. Bright blue eyes that were the color of mine. But hers were *too pretty*. Because she got herself in trouble every time a man noticed her.

"Let's go, kiddo. Time to party."

There was going to be hell to pay when she realized there was no liquor at the shelter, just people who were terrified of losing everything if the storm got worse like they said it could. But I'd deal with that later.

As soon as we stepped out of the broken screen door, all I heard was yelling. Mary Jo, the nice lady from next door who always made sure to save me a cookie and paid me for chores, was hollering at Carl, her boyfriend, to hurry. She jammed her hands into her hair, messing up all the black waves. But when she saw me, she smiled.

"Make sure you get Gabe to the high school, Lauralee," Mary Jo called out.

"Mind your own fucking business, bitch."

Ma flipped her off as we walked by, and my stomach twisted into a knot. I gave Mary Jo a weak smile to apologize for my ma, but she was already shouting at Carl again.

"That fucking cunt thinks she knows everything. Well, she don't have no kids. She's got a man to take care of her. She don't know shit."

Ma wasn't really talking to me, but I threaded my fingers through hers anyway and squeezed.

She glanced down at me and looked at our hands. "You're too old to be holding my hand, aren't you, boy?"

Something burned behind my eyes, but I shook my head. "I'm the man of the house. I can hold your hand if it means keeping you safe."

Her face softened, and she blinked a few times. "You're a good kid. I did a damn fine job with you."

Around us, trailer doors slapped in the gusty wind while people rushed out to cars and pickup trucks, and shoved armloads of stuff inside them. But we kept walking. We'd get to the shelter before the storm hit, and if I was lucky, there'd be sandwiches and juice boxes like last year when they said we were getting hit with a hurricane but didn't. Those sandwiches were even better than my school lunches, which were about as good as it got.

Even with the storm, today is a good day.

We were out of the trailer park and cutting through an empty lot across the street when I heard glass breaking.

"Shit. Looters are out," Ma said, dropping my hand and looking around to see where the mob was.

I'd only seen looters once before, and it was on TV. They burned cars in the street and the police had to stop them. But the only siren I heard was the one warning us about the storm.

"Hopefully, the police will get them," I said, moving toward the sidewalk that would take us up to the crossroad that led to the high school where we could take shelter. *And hopefully get sandwiches.*

My stomach growled. I hadn't eaten since lunch at school yesterday.

Weekends were the worst. I usually tried to save the bun from my Friday burger to eat on Saturday before I sneaked into the church up the street and stole doughnuts and juice to get me through Sunday. But this week, stupid Pat and his crew knocked the bun out of my hands as I was leaving the cafeteria, and it rolled under the trash cans. I couldn't get it without Mrs. Evert seeing me, and she already asked too many questions about Ma and how things were going at home as it was.

I took a few steps before I stopped and looked behind me. Ma wasn't following me anymore. She was heading the other way. *Toward the mob tearing apart Charlie's Liquor.*

Crap.

I changed direction and broke into a run. "Ma, no. Wrong way. We gotta go this way. The storm's coming."

She looked over her shoulder at me. "And it's bad manners to show up to a party empty-handed."

"There's no party! Ma!" The whipping wind stole my voice and sent her blond hair flying around her head. "Ma! Please!"

I reached out and grabbed her hand, yanking her to a stop.

Her face was completely different the second time she turned around. "You think you're big enough to boss me around? Not yet." She shook off my hand. "You want to go to

5

the shelter so bad because you're scared of the storm? Then take your own ass up there, and I'll see you when I see you."

I stood there, frozen in place, as she spun around and jogged toward the chaos.

She left me. To loot Charlie's. With a mob.

I looked up at the sky, which was a wall of angry black-and-gray clouds. The wind swiped at my face, and something wet hit my cheeks. I didn't know if it was rain or tears, and I didn't care.

She left me.

In that empty lot, my eyes stayed locked on her until she disappeared inside.

Then the other sirens started. The police ones.

No! I have to warn her!

But I couldn't. As soon as the mob heard the sound, they spilled out of Charlie's into the parking lot. People were running every which way, with as many bottles as they could carry. A woman clutching something to her chest collided with a man, and they both went down.

The first police car pulled up, blocking one entrance to the street. The crowd shifted and went another way. Everyone was yelling. The police were pouring out of their cars.

Where is Ma?

Not even aware I moved, I fought through the crowd, getting whacked and shoved with every step.

More cops. More screaming. Bullhorns.

I couldn't see. Someone ran into me and shoved me to the ground. I wrapped my arms over my head as someone's shoe whacked my forearm hard enough to leave a mark.

"Ma!" I screamed for help, but rain lashed me from the sky and the wind screamed.

I crawled away, until someone grabbed me by the back-pack and lifted me to my feet. I turned around, relief rushing through me, but when I saw the face in front of mine, the relief disappeared just as quickly.

It wasn't my mom. It was a cop.

"Come on, kid. You need to get out of here."

"But my ma—"

"She in the store?" he asked, reaching for the radio hooked to his shirt.

"I don't know. We were going to the shelter. We . . . got separated."

"Go sit by the car. I'll come back for you. Don't go anywhere." He shoved me toward the front of a squad car as a SWAT truck rolled up with a paddy wagon behind it, just like in the freaking movies.

I huddled against the bumper, getting pelted by rain, as the SWAT team controlled the crowd and handcuffed one person on their knees after another.

Ma was nowhere to be seen.

Until I heard the screeching.

Oh God. No. My stomach dropped to the oil-stained concrete below me, and I thought for sure that I would puke.

Ma held a broken bottle, jabbing it toward a cop while hugging more booze to her chest. He jerked back, narrowly missing her swipe at him with the broken glass.

No, Ma! No!

That's when I realized the screeching was coming from me.

But no one could hear me over the wind. And no one could stop Ma from getting her liquor.

At least, not until a second cop grabbed her from behind, knocked the broken bottle out of her hand, and yanked her arms around her back to cuff her. The other bottles shattered as they hit the cement. She wiggled and squirmed, trying to get free, spitting at anyone within range as they marched her toward the line of people sitting on the ground.

I knew right then that my life would never be the same.

My ma was going to jail. Which meant I was going to foster care.

She promised me this would never happen. She promised she'd never let me get taken away.

She lied.

I sat there, huddled against the bumper of a cop car with a nasty storm bearing down, and tears slid down my face. I was glad for the rain, because at least no one could tell I was crying.

As they led her and the others toward the paddy wagon, I watched her, expecting her to look around frantically to see where I was. Worried about me. Her only son.

But I shouldn't have bothered.

She never looked back.

TWO

Scarlett

resent day

P I stare at Gabriel Legend, a man who was *inside me* only a few minutes ago, and watch as he strides out of his office like demons from hell are chasing him.

But there are no demons in this room.

Just me.

My knees weaken, and I stumble toward the desk for something stable. My entire body, still languid from the toe-curling sex, is turning to ice, and I'm afraid I might shatter into a thousand tiny pieces all over this rug.

This fucking rug.

My fingers slip off the desk as I slide to my ass on the stupid freaking oriental rug that started it all.

Except it wasn't the rug's fault that I was falling apart. It was his.

"You'll always be what I want most. But I can't have you."

"How could he say that?" I whisper to the empty room. "How could he just . . . leave?" There's no answer.

"You should go. And don't come back, Scarlett. This isn't

happening." His harsh words from only minutes before play on a loop in my chaotic mind.

My head drops to my knees as I picture his face as it went from tortured to just . . . blank.

He shut me out. Shut me down. Shut everything down.

Someone knocks on the door a fraction of a second before it opens. I don't have enough time to scramble to my feet, so Q sees me sitting here on the floor like a stupid girl who was dumb enough to fall for the wrong guy.

I jump up and nearly lose my balance on my heels. He holds out a hand, like he's going to try to steady me, but I jump back and slam my hip into the desk. Pain radiates from where the wood cracks into bone, and I suck in a sharp breath.

With my eyes squeezed shut, I focus on the physical pain. At least that I understand. But what just happened in this office, I will never comprehend.

Q is silent for a long moment, and I assume he's probably waiting for me to open my eyes. I take another beat to pull myself together and straighten my posture, pinning my shoulders back.

My dignity may be in shreds on the rug where I once came to, after I was kidnapped, but I'm not going to let this man see me cry. I'm not going to let any of them see me cry.

I've worn armor all my life. The kind you strap on every time you leave the house, because the gossip columns will dissect your outfit, and they won't be kind if they decide your fashion-forward ensemble is really a fail.

Q is easy compared to that public humiliation. At least, that's what I tell myself.

"I need to go," I say, my voice steady as I pray the tears stay where they are—burning behind my eyes.

"Of course, Ms. Priest. Whatever you need."

I'm proud of the measured steps I take toward him, even as pain emanates from both my hip and my heart.

"Tell my friends something came up. Tell them . . ." I glance toward the door before I finally force myself to meet his gaze. "Tell them I'll see them tomorrow."

It's the apologetic, yet perceptive look in his eyes that almost undoes me.

"You knew this was going to happen. Didn't you?"

Q's face shutters. "I don't know what you're referring to, Ms. Priest."

"Bullshit," I say, spitting the word out. "But, don't worry, his precious club is safe. I hope it was worth it."

I stride toward the door, but Q reaches out to slow me with a gentle hand to my upper arm.

"I don't know exactly what happened here, but I can guess. The club didn't have a fucking thing to do with it. Any of it."

I turn my head slowly to study his face. "Then what the hell was that?"

My voice wavers on the last word, and I know my time is ticking down. The tears will come whether I'm out of here or not. For some reason, though, I wait for a reply. *I have a right to know why Legend would do this.*

Q's lips press together in a flat line. "It's better this way. Trust me."

If I were a different kind of woman, I would have slapped him across the face.

"I don't trust any of you." With what little pride I have left, I lift my chin and march out of Legend for the last time.

Screw all of you.

As soon as I slide into the car waiting for me at the curb, I dissolve into tears.

THREE

"Where the hell is she?"

I turn away from the column I was standing behind. Yes, I fucking watched her walk out like a princess who faced the villain, lost her crown, and regretted every moment of it. And yes, I'm still standing here, even though she's been gone for twenty minutes. No one notices me, until the shorter black-haired woman who came with Scarlett jabs me in the shoulder with a pissed-off finger.

Kelsey. The hair and makeup artist. The one who Scarlett said is one of her closest, most loyal friends.

I should have gone back inside. I should have gone anywhere but here.

I stare down at Kelsey, wondering what the fuck I'm supposed to say.

She doesn't wait. She jabs me again and repeats the question. "Where the hell is she, Legend? She left with you and now I can't find her, but Q said you were out here and I should ask you."

Fucking Q. Isn't it enough that I followed his advice? I'm keeping my circle small. Not taking any chances.

And yet you still managed to fuck everything up. The voice in my head is savage tonight. *Is it any wonder she got into that SUV and didn't look back? Because you're not worth fucking looking back for.*

My jaw tenses, and I grit my teeth against the truth. The voice is right.

If my own mother didn't turn around to see what happened to me, why the hell would Scarlett Priest? Especially after I all but kicked her out of the club. I'm a piece of shit, and the woman in front of me is next in line to make sure I'm aware of it.

"She's gone," I bite back. The words come out of my throat with a sharp edge, like they were clawed out.

Kelsey's hands go to her hips, and her expression turns militant. "What do you mean, she's gone? She wouldn't just leave without telling—" She cuts herself off as her face blooms into a violent shade of red. "Oh no. No, you fucking didn't."

Yeah. Yeah, I fucking did, I answer silently. But she doesn't wait for an answer from me before diving in to threaten me.

"If you hurt a single hair on her precious fucking head, I swear to Christ . . ."

"What's going on, Kels?" The brunette who Bump had his eye on joins us, with a tall, built guy next to her. I recognize him instantly as a major league baseball player. "Did you find Scarlett?" Her gaze flicks to me, and her eyes narrow.

"Scarlett left," Kelsey says through clenched teeth. "Something happened between them, and she *left*."

"Nate, I know your hands are super important, but can you please punch him in the face for me? Because if he fucked my girl and then tossed her ass out of the club like she was yesterday's trash instead of the queen she fucking is, he needs his ass beat, and now."

Monroe Grafton. That's who the brunette is. Married to Nate Grafton, who is eying me like he knows I deserve it, but he won't take a swing without backup. Smart man. I'd hate to take the team out of playoff contention by having to break something. I might fucking deserve it, but there's no way I'll offer him a free shot. He's not Scarlett's protector.

Yeah, and who is? Because you sure as fuck aren't.

I tell the voice to shut up as I grasp for something to say. But my mind is blank. I have no excuses. These people aren't the ones who deserve an explanation, anyway.

"You've got nothing to say?" Kelsey jabs me one more time. "You're a piece of shit, Legend. I told her to steer clear of you. I told her you were bad news. I love being right, but not this time. You fucked up. Whatever happened here tonight, one thing is for sure—you just lost your shot at the best thing that has ever happened to you. Go fuck yourself."

I take the onslaught. They care about her, and I'm responsible for what happened. I can't deny it, and I have no defense that anyone would understand.

Kelsey spins around and grabs Monroe's hand. "Let's get the fuck out of this place. I don't want to breathe his air, or I'll stab him."

"The only person who gets to stab him is Scarlett," Monroe says, shooting me a look with enough acid to kill. "Let's get Harlow. Then we're out of here."

She drops her husband's hand and the two women march into the club, leaving me facing Nate Grafton.

"I don't know what happened, man, but those women . . . they aren't the ones you want to piss off." From the tone of his voice, I have a feeling he's seen their brand of crazy in full Technicolor.

I glance down at my watch for no other reason than I'm

too raw to make eye contact. "No offense, man, but I've got bigger problems than worrying about them slashing my tires."

Nate Grafton huffs out a laugh. "That'd be minor. They'll ruin your life."

I think of the club that just rose from the dead, and wonder how long it will last once they start their crusade to destroy me.

Shouldn't have fucking touched her. She wasn't for you. You should have known better. This time, it's not the voice in my head, but me tearing a strip off my own hide for fucking this up so badly.

Everyone I love gets hurt, killed, or walks away from me. I should have known better than to reach so far above my station.

"They won't have to try too hard. I'm doing a hell of a job of it myself," I tell Nate before I turn and stride through the crowd, with absolutely no destination in mind other than *away.*

FOUR

Scarlett

The moment I walk through my front door, my cell starts buzzing with texts and calls. I figured it would take them a while to realize I was gone, and once they did . . . yeah.

It's safe to say I have great friends. But I can't handle them right now. Not when . . .

A tear drops onto the screen of my phone, blurring the words I was trying to type to the group message I'm being interrogated in. My fingers shake so much that I keep hitting the wrong letters, messing the word up so badly that not even autocorrect knows what I'm trying to say.

I snuffle in a breath, sop up the tears with a tissue, and start over.

SCARLETT: *I had to go. Things happened. Long story. I'm fine, though.*
KELSEY: *You are not fine. We're coming over.*
MONROE: *Nate didn't hit him, but we can hit him with a car. Just say the word, and I'll have a beater with no tags ready to go.*

A watery laugh escapes my lips as I imagine Monroe stealing a car to run down Legend. The laugh dries up the minute I think about him being hurt.

SCARLETT: *No. Please. Don't do ANYTHING at all. Not to the club. Not to him. Don't say anything either. This is double-vault material, and I don't want to see it in the papers.*

Harlow, Monroe, Kelsey, and I instituted the concept of the double vault back after Harlow accidentally leaked something about Monroe and Nate to the papers, and their friendship took years to recover.

HARLOW: *I'm not saying shit, so don't look at me. Double vault is secured. Bolt is thrown. But we're still coming over. I need to see for myself that he didn't hurt you.*

My body twinges and muscles protest in places they didn't before I walked into his office, but my friends don't need to know I got dumped after the best sex of my life.

No. Not even dumped. I got *fucked and ducked.* I think that was Kelsey's term for the time she had a one-night stand disappear when she went into the bathroom to clean up after sex.

No matter what you call it, it freaking hurts. My pride, my ego, my dignity . . . they all took a massive hit.

Yeah, and what about your heart?

The part of me that was worried about getting involved is

17

smug and self-righteous, but I'm not thinking about my heart. If I don't see blood, there's nothing wrong with it. *Right?*

I'm so full of shit that I don't even believe my own lies.

My lower lip wobbles when I picture his tortured expression. *It hurt him to push me away.* Part of me wants to cling to that as hope, but I can't. *Because he did it anyway.*

Whatever reason Gabriel Legend had, I don't know, and I can't allow myself to care.

But, first . . . I need to cry it out in the shower. Tears cried in the shower don't count, because you can't see them fall.

I wrap the towel around my hair, tighten the belt on my robe, and hurry toward the intercom that won't stop buzzing.

I want to believe it's *him*. That he regrets pushing me away. Sending me away. *Throwing me away.* But I know it won't be when I touch the button. My friends are relentless.

"Yes?"

"Ms. Scarlett?" The voice that comes from the speaker doesn't belong to Harlow, Monroe, or Kelsey.

"Who is this?"

"It's me. *Bump*. I saw Gabe leave, and Roux and I didn't know where else he might go. Is he here?"

I drop my head against the wall and close my eyes. I have no idea how he knows where I live, but I have to assume he either googled my address or followed me that time he kidnapped me. "He's not here, Bump. You should go."

The speaker crackles, and then he asks, "Do you know where he is?"

"No. I don't."

"Okay, we'll leave you alone."

The intercom goes silent, and I rush to the window to

look out at the sidewalk. Sure enough, it's Bump with Gabriel's dog. Alone. In the dark. *Hell.*

I wrench the crank until the night air hits my face, thankful I had the windows replaced a few years ago, and yell down to him. "Hey! You shouldn't be walking around at night by yourself. It's not safe."

He spins around, trying to figure out where my voice is coming from, and it takes him a second before he finds me at the window above him.

Given his uniqueness, there's no way I can just let him walk off into the night. If something happened to him, it would crush Gabriel and Q and Zoe, and I'm not going to be the reason it happens.

"Wait, Bump. Come around the side and I'll buzz you in. We'll call you a taxi that'll give you a ride home."

"I can walk back to the club."

"It's not safe."

He shrugs. "Roux is a tough girl. She won't let anything happen to me."

I want to believe him, but I can't risk it. "Around the side, there's a brown door. Open it when it buzzes and come up to the fourth floor."

Bump tilts his head from side to side, as if weighing the decision. When he nods and trots down the path, I wonder what the hell I'm doing.

Am I trying to get Gabriel to come to me?

Oh, hell no. I'm not that manipulative or desperate to use his friend to get his attention. I'm legitimately worried about the kid, and I don't want it on my head if something else goes wrong tonight.

When Bump knocks on my door, I open it, and Roux nudges her way inside. I've never had a dog in my space, but she doesn't jump on the furniture or knock anything over.

She just quietly pads around the room, sniffing things, before she comes back to my side.

"Gabe left and isn't answering his phone. I hate when he does that. He's my brother, and I can't lose him."

The admission is so raw and frantic that I feel sorry for the kid, even though he's *not* a kid. He's the *man* who *kidnapped me*.

"Does he do this often?" The question pops out before I can stop it.

"Sometimes. He likes to walk. Says it helps him clear his head. And since he likes you and you left the club, I thought he'd be here."

There are so many things I want to say, like, *he doesn't like me and he doesn't want to be anywhere near me*, but this isn't the time, place, or audience.

Roux bumps against my leg, and I reach down to pet her instead of spilling my guts to my one-night stand's sidekick.

"Where do you live, Bump? What should I tell the taxi driver?"

He frowns. "You don't want to help me find Gabe? I thought you would want to help."

Jesus Christ. How to handle this? "I don't think he'd be very happy to see me right now," I say for lack of a better explanation.

Bump studies my face. "You look pretty with no makeup on. Q says I should only look for girls who look pretty without makeup, because otherwise you could go to bed with a ten and wake up with a two. You're still a ten."

God, this kid.

I swipe at a lock of wet hair that's escaped from the towel on my head. "Thank you, Bump."

"Gabe shouldn't have gone walking tonight. He should be here with you. Even Jorie would agree."

"Who's Jorie?" I ask, mostly just to be polite, but also

because I'm still pathetic and desperate to know anything about Gabriel—even though I just promised myself I was putting him out of my head and life. But, unfortunately, the musical *South Pacific* was wrong, and you can't wash a man right out of your hair.

He frowns, running a finger absently along the streak of missing hair on his head. "My sister. She's dead."

I jerk back and stare at him. "I'm so sorry for your loss."

He shakes his head. "It's been a long time. That's why we came to New York. She and Gabe were going to get married and have babies, but . . ."

When he trails off, I can fill in the rest myself. *But they couldn't because she's dead.*

Jesus. Hell.

Gabriel was in love with Bump's sister, and then *she died.*

Right there, when I thought it was already broken, my heart cracks again. He lost the woman he loved, and the pain of that revelation socks me hard. For Gabriel first, but then also for me. *Even if I wanted to, I couldn't compete with a dead woman.*

"I'm so sorry, Bump," I tell him again as I reach out to bury my hand in Roux's rough coat.

"You don't need to be sorry. That's only if something happens to Gabe. He's the closest family I got."

"He's a tough guy. I'm sure he can take care of himself."

Bump shrugs. "People are looking for him. Bad things will happen if they find him."

The matter-of-fact nature in which he delivers this news rattles me to the core. "What people? What bad things?"

Another shrug, but it's easy to see whatever he's got going on in his mind is agitating him. He scratches his bicep under the wrinkled sleeve of his T-shirt. "I should go. Roux and I need to find him."

"Just . . . wait." I grab my phone and find Zoe's number. She answers on the second ring.

"Scarlett? Are you okay? Your friends left and they were . . . upset."

"I'm fine. Bump's here, though, and I think you or Q need to come get him."

"Bump is where?" She's rightfully confused.

I explain, trying to keep my tone upbeat, so I don't make Bump feel awkward. "He's petting Roux in my living room."

"Oh my God. I'm so sorry. I'll send a car over right away. Text me your address."

Bump is standing close enough to me now to hear every word we say. Almost shouting, he says, "I don't need a car, Zoe. I need to find Gabe."

I change the call to speakerphone so Zoe can speak directly to Bump.

"Bud, don't leave. Q was looking for you. He has something to tell you."

"What?"

"Come back to the club, and he'll tell you."

Bump kicks at my rug like a sullen child. "I don't want to go back to the club. I need to find Gabe. What if they find him first, Zoe?"

"Bump! Stop. The car will be there in fifteen minutes. I'll see you when you get back to the club."

"Fine," he says with a sigh.

I switch the phone off speaker and bring it back to my ear. "Is everything okay? Who wants to hurt Gabriel?" I ask her, praying she'll give me an answer that will quell the nervous twisting of my stomach.

"Everything's fine, Scarlett. Thank you for what you did for the club. We'll never be able to thank you enough. I don't know what happened between you and Gabriel, but if you ever need anything, call me. I'll always answer. Send me your address, and I'll have Bump picked up as soon as possible."

Before I can ask again, the call drops, and I'm staring at the lock screen of my phone. The lock screen that has a picture of me and the girls from tonight because we looked so damn good before we left, and I had to save it where I could see it.

The girls whose text messages pop up as soon as Zoe and I hang up.

HARLOW: If you don't answer, we're coming over.
KELSEY: I will kill him.

I tap to open my texts and send Zoe my address before typing out a message to my friends.

SCARLETT: I'm fine. He only bruised my ego. I'm heading to bed. Love you, girls.
KELSEY: I want to believe you.
HARLOW: She's full of shit.
MONROE: Meet us at Dolly's for brunch tomorrow. Noon. I won't even be late. I promise.
MONROE: If you don't show, I'll send a stripper-gram to the store on Friday while you have customers.

Brutal bitch.

. . .

SCARLETT: *I'll be there. Love you. Night.*

"Who are you talking to?" Bump leans over my phone and tries to read the messages.

I shove it in the pocket of my robe and give the belt another tug to tighten the knot. "My friends."

"The one with the pretty brown hair? Because she is *hot.*"

He has to be talking about Monroe. "Yeah, the pretty brunette is one of them."

"I like her, but Q says she's married, so I have to keep looking. I think Gabe should stop looking, though. He found you. He should be here and not walking the streets."

"Can we talk about something else?" I ask him quietly. "I don't think Gabriel would like us talking about him."

Bump looks at me with a pensive expression on his face and shifts his weight from side to side. "You should come home with me and Q. Then you can see Gabe and tell him he shouldn't go walking in the night. He might listen to you."

I sigh, accepting he couldn't be more wrong. "No, Bump. He wouldn't."

His head jerks back. "But he *likes you* likes you. A lot. More than any girl I've ever seen. If you told him whatever he did made you sad, he won't do it anymore. I don't like driving over the bridges, so we take the tunnels instead if we can. I don't like water. It makes me sad. I bet he wouldn't want to make you sad either."

I think of the way Gabriel's voice sounded when he told me he couldn't have me. It was gut-wrenching. "I don't think Gabriel and I will be seeing each other again."

Bump's eyes go wide. "But why? You don't like him?"

A lump the size of a Volkswagen rises in my throat. "Right this second, I'm not super happy with him, but no. That's not why."

"He probably thinks Jorie would be mad that he found you, but she wouldn't. She'd like you. You could've been mean to me after what I did, but you weren't. You're good people, Ms. Scarlett. I hope you see Gabe again. You make him smile when no one else does."

A horn honks out front.

Bump's head jerks toward the window, and the dog stands from where she's been lounging at our feet. "Is that for me and Roux?"

I walk to the pane and see a black SUV out front. "Yeah, that's for you and Roux. Do you want me to walk down with you?"

He shakes his head. "No, I'm not a kid. I just act like it because I got shot in the head. See you around, Ms. Scarlett. I hope you stop crying soon. It makes me sad."

Damn, he noticed. I guess shower tears aren't so stealthy after all.

He offers me a weak smile before giving Roux's leash a tug, and they disappear out the door the same way they came.

FIVE

There aren't enough miles of street in Manhattan for me to walk off the guilt of what I did tonight, so I walk all the way home to Jersey. Q is dropping Bump off at the service station when I finally show up.

Bump drops Roux's leash and runs toward me to clobber me with a hug. "Thank God you're okay, Gabe. I was worried about you. You went walking in the dark and you didn't take Roux. You always gotta take Roux. She keeps you safe."

I didn't know it was possible to feel any worse than I do already, but Bump's actions and outburst are another kick to the gut.

"I'm sorry, bud. I'm fine. I promise. Nothing got me."

Bump holds on for a few more beats before finally letting go. When he looks up, tears shine in his eyes, reflecting light from the streetlights hitting his face. "Promise me you won't do it again."

Bump takes promises seriously, so I'm wary of giving them to him. He will hold me to them for years, and I'd hate to disappoint him for the rest of my life if something prevented me from keeping it.

"Only if I really, really need to and Roux is busy, okay?"

He shakes his head and swipes at the moisture in his eyes. "Okay. I can handle that. I'm going to bed now. Can Roux come with me?"

"Yeah, bud. She can stay with you tonight."

He nods and pats Roux's head. "He's okay, girl. He won't leave us too."

It's a sucker punch, but I deserve it, and so I stand silent as Bump leads my dog to the door and disappears.

"What the fuck happened tonight?" Q asks as soon as Bump and Roux are gone.

I stare at my best friend. "I fucked up."

His black eyes rake over my face. "You fucked her."

When I nod and say nothing, Q pushes for more info.

"So, what happened?"

Under any other circumstances, I'd ignore the question or brush it off with a bullshit answer, but I can't this time.

"She's different, Q. She's . . . fuck, she's everything I never knew existed. It wasn't just sex, it was—"

Q holds out a hand. "Stop right the fuck there. I don't know what you're telling yourself, but you need to get your head out of your ass, and remember who you are and what you're trying to accomplish. A woman like that is nothing but trouble for a guy like you. I love you like a brother, Gabe. You're the most driven man I know. Don't let some princess from the Upper East Side take you off that path. She can't walk it with you."

Q's words are the common sense I need to hear, but that doesn't mean they're easy to swallow. I stand in the night air, still warm enough with the heat of the fading summer, and shake my head.

"What the hell am I supposed to do? Let something I know is fucking amazing walk away? You should've seen her when I told her to go. I might as well have slapped her across the face." I rake my hands through my hair for the thousandth time since I left my office.

"I don't know about that. But I *do* remember the look on your face when you showed up at my folks' door, interrupting dinner all those years ago. You had a bleeding kid with you and your world was gone. We picked up those pieces once. I don't ever want to see you like that again, man."

Q's memory is right on point. I can still smell the mac and cheese coming from Mrs. Quinterro's dining room table. I'd smelled nothing but blood and filth for the days it took to drive to New Jersey, switching cars every couple of states just in case Moses's boys were tailing us. I'd look over at Bump every few minutes to make sure he was still breathing. I kept thinking he'd be dead before I could get him the help he needed, but I was too afraid to stop. We left Jorie behind, and it still tears me apart to this day.

The idea of something happening to Scarlett, like it did Jorie, makes me want to puke my guts out on the pavement beneath my feet.

No. She'll live a long and happy life . . . without me. It's better for her this way.

I'm not a noble man. I don't know the first thing about selflessness, but . . . I know I shouldn't drag her into my mess.

The sound of her voice as she came on the desk in my office sneaks into my head, but I block it out.

She's better off without me.

SIX

Scarlett

"Someone called you?" I ask Flynn, who is the only familiar face at Dolly's Diner when I walk in the door at a quarter to twelve.

"Kelsey did. What happened?" my former stepsister asks, dressed more like the college senior she is in white jean shorts and a gray T-shirt, compared to the badass street-racer getup she wore the other night.

I glance around the diner, scanning past the mural on the wall of the busty cowgirl, but I don't see the rest of the crew yet.

Flynn crosses her legs and pats the open spot beside her. "If you're looking for your friends, you know they'll never be early. On time is a stretch. I already put your name in for a table, though."

I plop down on the bench. "Thank you, Flynn."

She nudges me with an elbow. "You're not answering my question. From what Kelsey said, it sounds like I need a getaway car or a hit man. Possibly both. She was really vague on details, but all I got was that last night, you went for it, and now Legend needs to die. So . . . you're going to have to fill me in here, because I'm coming up with way too many scenarios by myself."

"If I say it's a story I really only want to tell once, will you understand?" I turn sideways to see if her expression confirms I'm off the hook. At least for a few minutes. I knew coming to brunch was going to mean rehashing last night, but I've only got it in me to do it one time.

"Fair enough. I'll tell you about the car I picked up last night then. She's a beauty." Flynn dives into a description of the back-country roads in Pennsylvania where she, and some guys she has no business dealing with, raced for pinks. Thankfully, the story ends with her winning and the guys not killing her.

Just then Kelsey walks in the door, ahead of Monroe and Harlow.

"We're only two minutes late. That has to be a record," Harlow says, checking her diamond-encrusted Rolex.

"I'm going to need a bloody mary, stat. Spicy, and a double," Monroe replies, walking up to the hostess stand.

Thankfully, our table is ready for us and everyone is too busy ordering drinks to interrogate me. At least, until the server walks away. Now all eyes are on me.

"Are you okay?" Kelsey asks first.

"Yeah, I'm fine. It's . . . whatever." I flip my hair, like that's somehow going to get my friends to buy my lame reply.

"Did you bang him?" Monroe goes right for the kill, and Flynn elbows her in the side.

"Give her a few softball questions to warm her up, why don't you?"

Kelsey reaches diagonally across the table to cover my hand with hers and squeeze. "I'm so sorry we—"

"Stop. All of you." I slowly scan around the table and make eye contact with each of my girls. "I'm fine. He's just a guy. Things didn't work out the way I wanted. Shit happens.

I'll move on with my life and barely remember him tomorrow." The lies taste bitter on my tongue because they should be the truth.

"You fucked him, and he said that was all it would ever be, right?" Monroe is like a dog with a bone. She's not going to let this go until I give her the dirty details. Thankfully, the restaurant is packed and noisy, and no one can overhear our conversation.

"In a nutshell, yeah. I said I wanted more, and he told me he couldn't have me."

Every woman winces in unison.

"That's harsh," Flynn says, glancing at Kelsey. "Now the hit-man comment makes sense."

"Wait, wait." It's Harlow who interrupts. "He said he *can't have you*? Like he wants you but there's something stopping him? Tell us more about that."

I shake my head, my attention dropping to the busty cowgirl salt shaker and her pepper cowboy husband. "I don't know what to tell you. His friend showed up at my house last night and dropped a bomb about him being in love with a girl who died. I just . . . I can't compete with that."

"Dead girlfriend? Oh no, that's the worst," Monroe says with a grimace. "I've been down that road. College boyfriend. He was a total asshole about it too. Did Legend tell you he could never replace her?"

"No. He never mentioned her. Only Bump did. It was his sister."

"The dude with the missing strip of hair on his head? They call him Bump?" Monroe asks.

"He was shot in the head. I'm guessing that's his scar," I reply, fiddling with the straw wrapper from my water.

"But he said he couldn't have you. That means he wants you, but he's afraid to give himself permission," Harlow says, going back to the subject of Legend. "That means there's something there. I don't know, Scarlett. Maybe you shouldn't give up just yet."

I think of how I felt the moment his expression turned to anguish after I said I wanted to make it real between us. "I want to hate him. He gave me the best sex of my life and then . . . he shut down. And he told me to go."

"He has to die," Kelsey says, gripping her butter knife like a dagger. "No one treats you like that and lives."

"Whoa, street fighter," Flynn says, pulling the knife out of Kelsey's fist. "I can't believe I'm going to say this, but I think I agree with Harlow. There's something there. Not that you should be the one to work out his issues with the dead girlfriend, but . . . I wouldn't kill him yet either. He's a good guy, from the research I've done."

My gaze cuts to Flynn. "You've done research?"

She lays the knife on the Formica table and shrugs. "You're practically still family. Of course I was going to look into the guy."

Monroe leans forward, her boobs almost spilling out of her off-the-shoulder top. "What did you find out?"

"Gabriel Legend didn't really exist before fifteen years ago. He popped up in New Jersey, and that's when videos started surfacing of him fighting. He was smart with his money and ruthless with his opponents. He kept at it until he had the funds to open his own place—an illegal club called Urban Legend. It didn't have a liquor license and the cage fights were unsanctioned, but it did extremely well. Then one day, he just closed it and announced the grand opening of Legend." Flynn sits back and crosses her arms. "No one can figure out why he cut off the spigot to his cash cow. Then there was the shooting at the club, and you know the rest. Basically, he had it made, and then he tried to level up and it all fell apart—until you saved Legend."

"We can still take the club down," Kelsey says, and I shake my head while trying to process everything Flynn said.

"I told you last night. We're not going public with any of it. We're not going to do anything to the club. I'm not that kind of person, and none of you are going to be either."

"I agree with that. Because I think he still wants you, and he's just afraid he doesn't deserve you," Harlow says, and my attention locks on her.

"What the hell does that mean? He's afraid of me?"

Harlow's blond waves dance when she shakes her head. "No, he's afraid he doesn't deserve you. And if he has a dead ex, maybe he's got guilt tied up with her too. Do we know how she died? Was it his fault?"

The questions are relevant, but I don't want to think about the possible answers. Speculating makes me shiver. "I don't know. I don't want to know."

"So, what are you going to do now?" Monroe asks after she drains her bloody mary. "Do we have a plan?"

"Nothing," I tell all of them. "I'm going to do exactly *nothing.*"

"Oh fuck, he really did a number on you. You . . . were you falling for him?" Monroe's eyebrows, which normally barely move from the Botox, actually jump as her face contorts in horror.

"She wasn't. No way," Kelsey whispers, her jaw dropping as she stares at me. "It was just a walk on the wild side, right?"

"Yeah." I smile weakly and nod. "That's all it was. A walk on the wild side. Now, back to my regularly scheduled predictable life."

All the girls at the table study me, and I can almost guess their thoughts.

KELSEY: She's full of shit. This is bad. We need the bomb squad.

MONROE: Fuck. We're going to need more booze for this.

HARLOW: I don't believe her, but I'm not going to push.

FLYNN: Do I know any hit men?

When we leave brunch two hours later, we're standing on the sidewalk, trading hugs, and I feel Flynn slip something into my purse. I look down and see the salt and pepper shakers I was eyeing at breakfast and wondering if they were for sale.

"What? I saw you looking at them. Besides, you need a pick-me-up."

"But—"

Flynn puts her finger to her mouth. "Shhh . . . Don't get me arrested. You'll just have to bail me out."

I bite my lip and smile at her. "Thanks," I whisper as I let it go. "I appreciate that."

She wraps me in another hug. "I think Harlow is right about Legend. You could still have him . . . if you want him. So . . . do you?"

Piercing blue eyes appear in my head, and a shudder of awareness washes over my body. I whip around to look behind me, like he's standing across the street watching us.

Spoiler, he's not.

"It was really good to see you again, Flynn," I say instead, squeezing her tight. "Don't be a stranger."

"Invite me to brunch more often, and I won't be. Legendary Brunch Club. Or . . . maybe just the Brunch Club."

The word *legendary* is more than I can handle right now.

Anger and hurt have been thrumming through me all morning as memories of last night creep in. There's too much about Legend and his past that I don't know or understand.

What was I thinking? That somehow we could come from completely different worlds and have a fairy-tale romance, complete with a happily-ever-after?

Clearly, that's not how things work.

It was only good sex, I tell myself. *I just need to get me some more of that, and I'll be fine. I'll forget about him by next week.*

All lies. Especially that last part.

It was more than sex. We had a connection. And it wasn't just *good* sex either. It was *amazing.* No man has ever made me feel like that before, and now that I know it can be that good, I don't know if I can live without it.

Something about Legend unleashed a part of me I've kept caged my entire life because I didn't know it existed. He helped me see myself differently, and I loved it.

I release a long breath. There's no way around the truth.

I want more. More of him. More of us.

So, what am I going to do about it?

SEVEN

Two weeks later

The days that follow bleed together. Work, inventory selection, client consultations, meetings with Amy, makeup and hair with Kelsey, public appearances, dinners at the hottest new and old restaurants with the girls.

Through it all, no one mentions *him*. It's like those two weeks of my life, the two weeks I felt the most *alive*, didn't even happen. Like it was some alternate reality never to be discussed again.

But I can't stop thinking about it. About him. About Bump. Roux. Q. Zoe. The club. Any of it.

I keep reliving it over and over. The way he touched me. The way I felt. Then . . . the aftermath. A million thoughts I can't speak bounce around in my brain like pinballs gone wild.

It all comes to a head one morning when Kelsey is dabbing a bit of concealer on the awesome pimple that popped up last night along my jawline.

"I saw him."

Her statement requires no context for me to know

exactly who the *him* is that she's referring to. My questions come rapid fire.

"Where? When? How?"

"A few days ago. At a sandwich shop a few blocks from the club."

I jerk my head around to stare at her, not caring that the concealer is now everywhere. "You had dinner with me last night. Why didn't you say anything?"

"I didn't think you wanted to talk about him. Especially not around everyone."

She holds the blending sponge in midair, and I grab her wrist before she can fix the concealer mess.

"I think about him a million times every day. What the hell am I supposed to do, Kelsey? It's been two weeks. That's the same amount of time I even knew he existed. I shouldn't care anymore, but I can't stop thinking about him."

"I know, babe. I know."

I shake my head and slide off the stool, taking a step to my bathroom counter where all Kelsey's supplies are laid out. I pick up the tubes and pots and compacts one by one and space them out evenly on the towel.

"You don't know. You don't know what it's like to think you're broken and can't enjoy sex, and then you meet the one guy who lights you up like a goddamned Christmas tree, and then he *throws you out* instead of asking how soon you can do it again." My voice is rough with tears by the end, but I blink them back, not wanting to ruin her hard work.

"Oh, honey," Kelsey whispers from behind me. "I had no idea. You never said anything . . ."

I spin around and lose my battle with my emotions. A drop tips over my lids. "Chadwick destroyed my self-confidence when it came to sex. *He sent me to a sex therapist, Kelsey!*"

Her head jerks back, and her features crease with rage.

"Oh no, he didn't."

"He did! Because he told me there was something wrong with me. But, let me tell you, there wasn't a damn thing wrong with me when Gabriel touched me. Not a fucking thing. I felt like I was going to lose my mind, in the best way possible. What if I never find that again?"

She reaches for a tissue and carefully dabs beneath my eyes. "So, it *was* just the sex then? That's why you're hung up on him?"

I wait for her to pull the tissue back before I shake my head. "He took me go-karting. He held my hand. He made me laugh. He—"

"Oh shit," Kelsey whispers, her lower lip wobbling. "You were really, really into him."

The threat of more tears is strong. "I told him I wanted to make it real. To give us a serious try."

Her hand covers her mouth. "And that's when he pushed you away."

"If by *pushed me away*, you mean told me to leave and said we couldn't see each other again? Then yes, exactly."

"I want to kill him, but I also want to go kidnap him and tie him to a chair in your living room until he listens to reason and realizes that you're the best thing that could happen to any man, especially him."

I choke out a watery laugh, because kidnapping is what started this whole thing in the beginning. But I can't tell Kelsey that. She'd definitely want to kill him then, even more than she already does.

"How can I chase him after that? What about my pride? My self-worth?" I finally voice the questions I've been grappling with for weeks.

"I don't know, baby girl, but . . . he looked awful. Like he hasn't slept in days."

"What?" My head jerks in her direction.

Kelsey nods slowly. "He looked like shit. If it's any comfort, I'm pretty sure he knows he made a hell of a mistake."

"Then why wouldn't he tell me? Text? Call? Smoke signals? Anything? Why let us both suffer?"

"Men are stupid. That's pretty much the only thing I know for sure. Now, let me finish your makeup so you can slay this photo op, and then you can sweat it all off in your self-defense class. Maybe you could pretend he's the pad you're hitting?"

I try Kelsey's advice, envisioning Gabriel's face on the pad Bodhi is holding out for me, and it's not working.

"You're pulling all your punches. You're supposed to try to punch *through* the target, but you're barely hitting the pad. You need a break?" Bodhi lowers the pads and scans my face with concern.

"I'm sorry. My head's not in the game today."

He opens his mouth to start preaching, and I guess what he's going to say next, so I wave him off before he even gets started.

"I know that I always need to be ready to defend myself, trust me." I think of the nasty comments that came in last night. I saw them before they could be deleted. My troll has a new profile and his threats are escalating. I screenshotted them and sent them to the detective on the case this morning. "But sometimes, life is a bitch, and you have to work shit out before you can concentrate."

Thankfully, Bodhi doesn't try to lecture me. He unhooks the pads from his hands and tosses them in the footlocker near the wall. When he reaches down to unstrap the ones from his legs, I ask, "Are you firing me as a client?"

He glances up and shakes his head. "No. But you're not going to do yourself any favors trying to work out right now. It's a great way to get hurt, and I'm not going to be responsible for that happening."

"So you're kicking me out?" I hate that I care, but I do, and I feel like a total loser.

"Yeah, but I'm going with you. We're going to work out this shit of yours so you don't waste another session. Come on."

Twenty minutes later, Bodhi and I sit at a rough-hewn wooden table in the café on street level, protein shakes between us.

"Whatever you tell me isn't going anywhere. I signed that NDA your finance chick sent me."

I dip my head and swirl the straw around in the thick liquid. "It's complicated."

"So it's about a dude."

My gaze lifts to stare at his face. "How did you know?"

"Lucky guess. So, what the fuck are we dealing with?"

I don't know why I'm going to tell him anything. I shouldn't. But sometimes you need to unload on someone who's pretty close to a perfect stranger—and yet bound by the restrictions of a confidentiality agreement.

"I fell for a guy. We're from different worlds, though."

Bodhi's shoulders lift. "And here I thought we were all from Earth."

I shake my head. "No, I mean socially. He's not from the trust-fund or family-money set."

"Is that a problem for you? Because you didn't seem like a snob before."

I shrug, but I'm glad I didn't come off snotty and stuck-up. That's something.

When I don't reply, he keeps pushing. "So you're worried

that because the guy doesn't have money like you, you can't make it work?"

"No, that's the problem. I think we can, but he doesn't think so."

Bodhi leans back in his chair, his chin rising. "So you went for it, but he shut you down."

"He said he couldn't have me."

Bodhi's big arms cross over his chest, and he looks forbidding as hell. "He trying to be noble and save you from himself or some shit?"

"I don't need to be saved," I say, slapping the table. Bodhi chuckles, and it pisses me off. "And he needs to pull his head out of his ass. Typical man."

"Maybe he's doing you a favor. Could be a good thing."

"I refuse to believe that Gabriel Legend is that awful of a person that he needs to save me from himself."

As soon as I say his name, Bodhi's chair squeals against the concrete as he shoves it back and stands.

"Who the hell did you say?"

I stare up at the mountain of a man, and for the first time since our initial training session, apprehension fills me. Did I really just tell him Gabriel's name?

"Why?" I lower my voice.

Bodhi must realize he's freaking me out, because he lowers himself back into his chair, but his expression is stormy. "You said Gabriel Legend." He says the name like a curse.

My mouth goes dry. "Yes. Why are you reacting like that?"

"You need to stay the fuck away from him. Nothing good can come from that."

"What are you talking about? Why would you say that?"

Bodhi's lips press into a thin line. "Because I almost killed him once, and if we get back into the cage again, I still might."

EIGHT

Scarlett

I stare up at my trainer, but my jaw is in the vicinity of the floor. "How . . . how could you say that?"

Bodhi bristles like a beast held back by only a very delicate chain. "Because it's the truth. Stay the hell away from him. A guy like that can't give you what you need. Find someone from your own world."

"But you said—"

Bodhi shakes his head. "Forget what I said. You and Legend are never going to happen. He's trash. Stay the fuck away from him before he destroys your perfect life."

The protein shake in front of me has lost all appeal. I pick it up and nod at Bodhi as a dull pain thrums in my belly.

"I appreciate your input, but you don't know him."

"And you do?"

Do I? How well can you know someone after only two weeks? *Well enough to know I want to know him better.*

"Thanks for the protein shake, Bodhi. I'll see you next session." With freezing fingers wrapped around the cup, I ignore the hurt welling up inside me, grab my bag, and walk out of the café. Bodhi's words chase after me all the way home.

"Find someone from your own world . . . You and Legend are never going to happen."

"What does he know?" I mumble, clutching my bag to my middle after I slide into the back seat of a cab.

My phone slips onto my lap, and I can't help but wonder if it's a sign from the universe telling me to text him.

I could send him a message. Keep it casual. Ask him if the club attendance is still up. Ask him if Bump and Roux are doing okay. Just . . . keep the lines of communication open.

Right. I could just act like he didn't fuck me and tell me to leave.

Somehow, the phone finds its way into my hand, and the text window is open to his name. I scroll back and read through some of our messages before that awful night.

SCARLETT: *How can you not have a favorite color? Everyone has a favorite color.*
GABRIEL: *I don't know . . . I never thought about it. I don't like orange, though.*
SCARLETT: *Well, if I had to guess, I'd say your favorite color is black.*
GABRIEL: *Is black even technically a color? I think you're breaking rules.*
SCARLETT: *I figured you'd approve of me breaking rules.*

I cringe at my past attempt to get him to realize that I'd like to break rules with him. *So smooth, Scarlett.* But he didn't miss a beat.

. . .

GABRIEL: Leave the rule breaking to me, ladybug. I'm better at it.

My inner muscles clench with a rush of heat between my legs. *Why can't he break his own rules with me?*

I scroll down to the bottom and read the last text he ever sent me.

GABRIEL: I can't wait to see you tonight. Been looking forward to it all day.

Why couldn't he have sent that today? Stuck in midday Manhattan traffic, I let myself daydream, imagining what it would be like to get messages from Gabriel like that every day for the rest of my life.

A different kind of warmth wraps around me. The kind I felt every time my phone would buzz with a text from him, and I'd rush to see what he'd said.

We aren't that different, Gabriel. Bump said I made you smile. Why can't this work?

I've never taken *no* well, and especially not in a situation like this, where I think the other party's reasoning is completely flawed.

Why can't Gabriel Legend have me? Not a single rational reason comes to mind. What could he possibly be thinking?

I stare down at the blinking cursor in the text box on my phone screen and compose a message in my head. After a few minutes, my thumbs move, making the words appear on the screen.

SCARLETT: ~~I really hate not talking to you.~~

. . .

No. Stop, Scarlett. I tap the backspace key until it disappears. Then I try again.

Scarlett: ~~Do you need me to come to the club Friday or Saturday night? I'm free.~~

No. Definitely not that. Just as bad.

Scarlett: ~~Talk to me.~~
Scarlett: ~~I miss you.~~
Scarlett: ~~You can't give me the best sex of my life and then take it away.~~

No, definitely not that either.

Before I realize it, the cab slows at the curb in front of Curated, and I haven't sent a single message to him. I suppose that's probably a good thing, because as soon as I walk inside, I have to sprint upstairs to my bathroom before I puke my guts up all over the store.

NINE

I *feel like hell, look like hell, and I haven't showered in two days. Shout-out to all the other people who are embracing themselves despite everything going sideways. You're a queen. Just remember, there's nothing wrong with lounging in your PJs all day and eating Nutella from the jar. I support you. #LifeIs-Messy #EmbraceTheMess #LoveTheMess*

I read the caption of the photo over again before staring at the picture of Scarlett on her bed in pajama pants and a sweatshirt three sizes too big. Her hair is caught up in a messy bun and glasses perch on her nose. She doesn't look like hell, though. She looks beautiful. But why does she feel like hell?

With a quick glance, I skim over some of the comments.

Thank you for keeping it real.

You're gorgeous even when you feel like crap.

Hope you're okay!

Get well soon!

I drop the phone on my desk and grind the heels of my palms into my eyes. A person should go blind for how much time I've spent staring at my phone like an asshole the last couple of weeks. It seems like every other damn minute, I'm tapping in my password to open that stupid app to see if she's posted a new picture. Every time she does, I get a ridiculous thrill that I'm too old to admit to. But it happens all the same.

Last week, she posted a photo of her and her friends, and it almost brought me to my knees. They had to have snapped it before they came to the club that last night. Scarlett in her white dress, looking like a frigging angel who stepped out of the heavens for a moment to mingle with the mortals.

Mingle? You mean get manhandled and fucked before you tossed her ass out?

The guilt and shame from that night have been riding me so hard, I can barely get anything done. My brain doesn't work right anymore. It's always full of thoughts of her. How she's doing. Where she's going. Who she's with. If she's safe.

If she could see inside my brain, she'd slap me with a restraining order.

Even knowing that not a single bit of it is my business after I told her to leave, I can't stop wondering and worrying.

"Hey, boss. You got a minute?"

When Zoe's voice comes from the doorway, I flip my phone over on my desk like she just caught me watching porn.

"Yeah. What's up?"

Zoe's gaze flicks to the phone before landing on my face. "You text her yet? Call her?"

"Who?" It makes me a bigger idiot to even ask the question, but I have an image to uphold.

She walks forward and helps herself to a chair in front of my desk. "How long are you going to torture yourself?"

When I don't reply, she keeps going.

"Don't forget, I've known you just as long as my brother.

Just because I don't have a dick doesn't mean I don't understand what the fuck you're doing."

She pauses, as if waiting for me to add something, but I've got nothing, so I stay silent.

"I'm willing to put money on the fact that you not only want Scarlett Priest, but you had her, fucked it up, and now you've been stomping around ever since like a lion with a thorn in its paw. Anytime someone tries to talk to you, you swipe at them."

"I'm not that bad."

Zoe snorts and covers her face with her hand. "Right. Not that bad. Lie to me again, Gabe. I know you. We all know you. You have to do something about this because your *pretend-she-doesn't-exist* strategy isn't working for you or anyone else."

"Don't take this the wrong way, but you don't know shit, Zoe."

She lifts her chin and crosses her arms. "I don't know shit? Yeah, right. Because you're not moping around like a kid who lost his favorite toy and is taking it out on everyone else."

"She's not a fucking toy," I grit out.

"You're right. She's not. She's a grown-ass woman, and that means she can make her own decisions. If she decided she wanted you and then you pushed her away, whose fault is that?"

My fingers curl into claws around the arms of my chair. "You know what happened to Jorie."

"She's dead, Gabe. And you didn't kill her."

I bolt upright. "No, but I fucking got her killed. Do you know what it's like to live with that on your conscience? Knowing that you can't go after the man who ordered it because you're still waiting for the right moment? How can I bring Scarlett into my life knowing that as soon as I have enough money and power, I'm going after Moses to kill him the same fucking way his crew took out Jorie? With a bullet between the eyes. How the fuck do I start a relationship with a woman who has lived in such a sanitized world that she's probably never even touched a gun herself? She doesn't know violence. Why should I be the one to bring that shit into her life?"

Zoe doesn't flinch during my tirade. She crosses her arms in her lap and speaks softly.

"She lives in New York City. How many muggings happen here every day? Violence could easily be part of her life tomorrow, and the only thing you're doing is making sure you're *not there to protect her from it*. Pull your head out of your ass and look at the big picture. Do you really think you come along with so much evil and ugly that you're going to ruin her snow-white life? Have you ever considered that you just might add some color to it and make it worth living?"

"Unless there's something work related you need to talk about, get out of my office."

Zoe rises slowly, giving me a measured stare. "You know I'm right. I just hope you act on it before it's too late. Before you really lose her." She strides out of the office and shuts the door behind her, leaving me alone with my mess of a brain and my phone.

I grab it off the desk and open Scarlett's favorite social media app again. As I stare at the picture of her, my attention snags on the hashtags again below it.

#LifeIsMessy #EmbraceTheMess #LoveTheMess

Goddammit, Scarlett. What the fuck do you want from me? All I know is messy. I've clawed my way out of the gutter, but I'm a million light years away from your ivory tower. I'm not good enough for you. I'll never be good enough for you. But if you want messy, I got that down.

The picture and the hashtags haunt me all day. I'm not fit company for anyone, so I keep to my office, and later, watch the club from behind the two-way glass. My attention catches on every single blonde, like there's a chance in hell she would show up. But she doesn't, and none of them compare to her.

What if she's sick? What if there's something wrong with her? Who's going to take care of her? Her dad? He sounds like a dick. Her friends? The ballplayer's wife would probably give her the wrong meds and be more likely to kill her by accident.

The very thought threatens to send me into a rage. *If anything happens to her . . .*

My brain picks that moment to chime in. *Then what, Gabe? What are you going to do about it? She's not yours. You threw her away. You don't even deserve a second fucking chance. Remember the look on her face? You fucking broke her. What kind of guy does that? A shitty one who doesn't deserve a woman like that. You're doing a bang-up job, asshole.*

Hours later, I crawl into bed and palm my cell once more. I don't have to go to the app anymore, because I saved the fucking picture to my phone. That's how pathetic I am.

I may not deserve her, but no one is taking this picture from me.

But what if you just told her everything?

The thought floats into my head and gives me pause.

Could she understand why I did what I did? Could she forgive me? Is there any way we could make this work? Could I keep her safe from Moses? Figure out a different way to handle him?

The questions chase away sleep, because I know how I

want to answer them. If there's a single scenario in which Scarlett Priest could be mine, I want to find it.

I'm not giving up on us, ladybug. At least, not if you can forgive me. I'll figure this out.

And if later, I jerk off to the image of her with no makeup and bed head, looking more beautiful than any woman has a right to look, that's no one's fucking business but my own.

TEN

Scarlett

"I think we need to take you to the hospital, Scarlett. Something's wrong." Amy, my manager, looks at me with concern in her eyes.

She's right. I haven't felt like myself in days, and my doctor is out of town this week.

"I hate the hospital," I say, letting my head flop against my pillow. "My mom . . ."

I can't finish my sentence, but Amy gets it. My mom spent her last six months constantly in and out of the hospital, but there was nothing they could do to save her. Cancer is a fucking asshole, and it can fuck right off.

"I understand you don't want to go, but I think it's necessary. Let me call the car service. I'll go with you to the ER, unless you want me to call someone else?"

I'm weak, and the only thing I can think is that if Gabriel hadn't told me to leave, this wouldn't have happened. It's irrational and completely ridiculous, but I don't care. I feel like death. I haven't gotten out of bed, except to puke, all day.

"Scarlett?"

Amy says my name again, and I turn my head so I can see

her. What did she ask? Oh yeah. If I wanted her to call someone else.

"My dad. Call him. Tell him I'm probably not dying, but I'm not totally sure." I pause, licking my dry lips and hating how shitty I feel.

What if I am dying? No. I'm not delusional enough to think that.

Then another face pops into my brain. *Flynn.*

"Call Flynn. Tell her. She'll be pissed if I don't. I canceled my appointment with Kelsey, but she sounded worried. If she shows up when I'm gone, have someone tell her I'll keep her posted. She doesn't need to worry."

I want to tell her to call Gabriel because this is all his fault somehow, but I don't. My stomach is screaming in pain again, and all I can do is curl up into the fetal position.

"Fuck. Get me to the hospital. I don't care anymore. Just make it stop."

ELEVEN

"They already told me he's here, so don't even think about trying to keep me from talking to him. Unless you get some kind of sick thrill from manhandling women who are underage."

"I didn't touch you, Ms. Elliott. And I assure you, I have absolutely no interest in manhandling you, underage or otherwise."

What the fuck is going on out there?

A woman is yelling at Q in the hallway outside my office, and he sounds like he's barely keeping it together. But who the fuck is Ms. Elliott? I don't know any Elliotts.

I rise from my desk but pause when she goes off on another tangent.

"Then get the hell out of my way and point me in the direction of his office. My sister may not have much time left. She's heading into emergency fucking surgery right now. Or maybe you don't think Legend gives a shit. But he liked her well enough before she put out."

Everything in my body freezes. *No. She's not talking about*

Scarlett. That's not possible. Scarlett doesn't have a sister. They can't be talking about her.

And yet, a knock comes on my office door and Q pokes his head inside. "You have a visitor. Flynn Elliott."

"Oh, just get out of the way and let me fucking talk to him. I guarantee he's going to be pissed you didn't bring me here immediately. *Emergency surgery*, asshole!"

I don't even remember moving, but I'm yanking the door fully open to stare at a petite brunette dressed in jeans and a librarian-looking sweater, carrying a backpack.

"Who the fuck are you talking about?"

She glares at me, her eyes raking up and down my face. "Who do you think? Or have you thrown multiple women out of your office after you fucked them lately? I thought it might have just been Scarlett."

My hands clench into fists at my sides, and I quell the urge to reach out and shake the hell out of her. "She doesn't have a sister."

"Ex-stepsister. Still counts. We're connected through mutual loathing of our deadbeat, selfish parents."

"What the fuck is going on? What surgery? What emergency? What's wrong with her?" I'm asking questions faster than she can even open her mouth to answer them. My heart thunders in my chest, like I've just gone five rounds and am about to collapse.

"One of her employees called me from the ER. Said they rushed her in because she was in excruciating pain."

The thought of Scarlett in pain damn near brings me to my knees. "What is it? What's wrong? Is she going to be okay?"

Flynn's lips are pressed into an angry line. "She could still die, asshole. It's emergency surgery. But you're not supposed to care, because you don't want her in your life, right? You fucked her and tossed her out on her ass like yesterday's trash. Did you even wonder if she might've been pregnant? What if she's losing a baby right now?"

Oh my fucking God. A wave of pure terror washes over me, leaving my entire body feeling as if I've been doused in kerosene and a fireball is racing toward me.

"She isn't. Please. Fuck."

Flynn glares. "Not as far as I know, but that's just another thing you should've thought about. Asshole."

"I—"

Flynn takes two steps closer to me and crosses her arms over her chest. "You fucked up. You took the best thing that could've ever happened to you and shit all over it. Is that what you do good people? People who just want to make the world a better place?"

With every slicing statement, she flays me. I know I deserve all of it, if not worse.

"I know! I fucked up. I already figured that out. I'm going to make it right."

Flynn's shoulders hunch forward. "If you even get that chance."

Goddammit. All I wanted to do was protect her from the shit swirling around me, and I could lose her anyway.

"I was trying to do the right thing, okay?"

Her chin rises even higher. "And see where that got you? She could die, and all you've done is cheat you both out of what you wanted. Smart, Legend. Real smart."

"Hey, watch your mouth, kid," Q snaps from the doorway. "Tell us which fucking hospital so he can go. He doesn't need you ripping him a new asshole right now. You should both be there."

Thank fuck for Q, because I'm frozen in place, crumbling inside and trying to hold it together. When Bump told me about Jorie, it was too late. There was nothing I could do.

Right now, I might not be able to do anything for Scarlett, but I can sit in that fucking waiting room and pray.

"Come on. I'm driving." The girl turns, her ponytail swinging.

"No way in hell." Q glares at me. "I'll get a car. We'll follow her. I'm not riding with that fucking woman anywhere."

I only have one word for him. "Hurry."

TWELVE

T he private waiting room is silent except for the
sounds of the people in it shifting in their seats or
getting up to pee, get coffee, or pace.

Amy, Scarlett's store manager, took one look at me with
Flynn and sat back down without a word. She's been on her
phone ever since, answering messages and emails.

"Is her dad coming?" Amy asks Flynn after she looks up
again.

Flynn tilts the Styrofoam cup of burned hospital coffee in
her hand from side to side. "I couldn't get in touch with him.
His secretary said she'd make sure he got the message. He'd
better fucking show up, that's all I know." Flynn mumbles
something under her breath that sounds a lot like *that fucking
asshole*, and I can't help but agree.

Amy takes that moment to excuse herself from the
waiting room to take a call.

If my daughter were in emergency surgery, I'd be here as
fast as I could. Except I don't have a daughter. Flynn's words
from earlier come back to haunt me.

"Did you even wonder if she might've been pregnant?"

I didn't wonder, probably because I've never *not* been careful. After Jorie, I couldn't imagine having a family with anyone, couldn't imagine wanting to bring a life into this crazy, fucked-up world. But with one single sentence, Flynn unleashed a part of me I've kept locked up for years. Until Scarlett showed up in my office, wrapped in a goddamn rug.

How the fuck is this even real?

I scrub my hands over my face, wondering what the hell happened to my well-ordered life. As the owner of an underground club, I was a king in a shadowy world where good girls like Scarlett didn't exist. Maybe it was on purpose? Because I knew that none of the women who'd show up in a place where men beat the hell out of each other for entertainment—and police raids shut us down on occasion if I didn't keep the right palms greased—were a threat to my existence.

Then when I tried to step out into the light of respectability and make the promises I vowed a reality, I got my ass handed to me. The shooting and subsequent failure of my club hammered home just how out of my league I was. The things that kept people coming back to my club— violence and bragging rights—didn't exist anymore. I thought for sure we were headed into bankruptcy and I'd lose everything.

Until Scarlett.

I could have just taken the help and forgotten about her . . . if I were a different man. But I'm not. And something about her called to me at a level I didn't know existed. She tugged at parts of me that have been buried for years.

It scared the living hell out of me.

The thought of finding another woman who could be taken from me was more than I could handle.

Flynn's chair squeaks against the industrial flooring, bringing me back to the here and now.

The reality is that Scarlett could be taken from me whether I'm noble or not. If I lose her today, it'll hurt just as much, if not more, than if I'd spent these last couple of weeks surrounded by her light and laughter.

I didn't know I needed her . . . and now it might be too late.

I look over at Flynn, who hasn't spoken to me since I arrived. Q dropped me off at the front of the hospital with a nod and a "let me know what happens."

Footsteps click down the hall, and another familiar face comes into view. The black-haired one, Kelsey. Except instead of the sleek and put-together woman I've already had one run-in with, her hair is flying in all different directions and her chest is heaving. Her gaze locks on Flynn first.

"Oh my God. I came as soon as I heard. Is she okay? What do we—"

Her head jerks to the side and she goes silent when she sees me, her mouth hanging open. She finds her voice quick enough, though.

"What the fuck is he doing here? Seriously. How big are your balls to show up?" Her attention cuts back to Flynn. "And how is there not blood spatter on the walls? Why haven't you killed him already?"

"I told him to come." Flynn leans back in her chair, her arms crossed over her middle. "So far, he hasn't said anything stupid enough for me to spend life in prison, so he gets to live another day."

She's small and mighty, but the hardest fights I've ever won were against opponents who weren't as big as me. I don't doubt Flynn Elliott could hold her own.

Kelsey glares in my direction, and I wonder if life in prison is enough of a deterrent to keep her from doing the job herself. Finally, she shakes her head and cuts back to Flynn.

"Any update from the docs? How is she doing? When is she going to be out?" She asks all the questions that have been on my mind since the minute I took up vigil in this purgatory-like room, mixed in with the mental beating I've laid on myself.

"Nothing yet." Flynn lifts her arm to check her watch. "I'm really hoping we hear something soon. I don't know how long this is supposed to take. I'm afraid to google it because I'll get sucked down the rabbit hole of awful possibilities."

Kelsey crosses the room and takes a seat on the maroon vinyl cushioned bench beside Flynn. She slings an arm around the younger girl and hugs her to her side. "I'm so sorry, kid. I've been praying hard. You should've seen the shit-ass contour I did on my client after you called. She kept asking for more and more color, and I was in too much of a hurry to blend it long enough to make her look human."

A weak laugh escapes Flynn, and for the first time, she looks as underage as she claims to be. *Ex-stepsister.* I'm going to have to ask Scarlett about her.

Wait. I pause because that's a hell of an assumption. There's a good chance Scarlett may never speak to me again after what I did, and she'd be fucking justified.

Then why am I here? The question comes from the asshole in my brain, but the answer is a simple one—because I have to be. No matter what happens next, I need to know she's okay.

"I hope they got to it in time," Flynn murmurs, and Kelsey nods.

"Me too."

Got to it in time? The phrase sends bone-chilling spears of fear into every inch of my body. I can't stay quiet any longer. I have to ask.

"What the hell is she in surgery for? What do you mean—you hope they got to it in time?"

Kelsey jerks back, nearly whacking Flynn upside the head as she jerks her arm from around her shoulders. "You didn't tell him?"

Flynn's expression turns placid. "I was content to let him suffer in silence, thinking the worst. Seemed like fitting punishment for what he did to her."

"Holy shit, you're ruthless. I love it," Kelsey says before rising from the bench and walking toward me. She stops three feet away and props her hands on her hips. "Do you have any idea how many rich and famous clients I've worked on?"

Her question catches me off guard. I have absolutely no idea why she's asking, so I stay silent.

Her pointed chin lifts. "Hundreds. And you know what? I used to think they were all the same too. Oblivious and entitled. Unable to relate to reality. Assholes, basically."

She pauses again, and I know she's waiting for something from me, but I don't have anything to give her.

"Whatever point you're trying to make? Get on with it." My rough tone would make grown men question whether they should keep talking, but Kelsey doesn't miss a beat.

"My point is that I was wrong. They're not all assholes. Some of them are just normal fucking people. And you know what? Scarlett is *the best of them*. There's no one else like her. She's warm and genuine and kind and caring. She inspires everyone who crosses her path, because she's so fucking thoughtful and sweet. Has she ever had to worry about money? No, not a day in her life. She probably never will either. But that doesn't mean she's not a class act on every level, and overall, one of the best human beings I've ever known. Hell, maybe even one of the best humans walking this planet."

She's not telling me anything I don't already know, so I wait.

"I don't know how you passed the Flynn test, but I'm Scarlett's best friend, and that means right now, I can't stand the sight of you. If you make one wrong move, I will throw you out of this hospital myself."

I lean back in my chair and raise an eyebrow in response.

"I know you don't think that's possible, but my Korean father made sure I took judo and tae kwon do until I could kick every one of my brothers' asses, so don't give me that look, Legend. I've seen you fight. I know your moves. I'll take you on. I might not win, but you'll be the one getting arrested, not me."

The sad part is that even if she instigated the fight, *on camera*, she's probably right. I'm a six-two man and she's a five-foot-nothing woman. No hospital security guard or cop is going to believe that she attacked me without me doing something to provoke her that just happened to be *missed* by the camera.

"Cut him some slack, Kelsey. He came. He's obviously worried about her. He wouldn't have come otherwise."

Kelsey shoots a look at Flynn. "He's lucky you're giving him a second chance. I'm withholding judgment." Her attention swings back to me. "But know that I will fuck you up if you do anything to hurt my girl again."

"Duly noted." My words come out dry, but there's respect behind them, whether Kelsey realizes it or not.

Most men won't dare speak to me like that, not if they know who I am. Most women . . . well, let's say when I'm walking the streets alone at night or with Roux, they clutch their purses against themselves or cross to the other side of the street so they don't have to face me directly. Kelsey, however, deserves a medal for being a hell of a best friend— and Flynn too, for that matter. I can't even be upset about it.

Every word they spoke, even when it cut deep, was deserved. Actually, if I'm being honest, part of me wants to smile at Kelsey's threats to fuck me up. I know it's twisted, but I'm glad Scarlett has people like this in her corner. Every woman needs crazy friends who are willing to threaten to kill someone for them.

And if Kelsey is withholding judgment, that means I get a second chance from her too. *Now if I could only see Scarlett and know she's okay.*

Except . . . "Again, what the hell is wrong with Scarlett?" I grit out the question one more time, but Amy rushes back into the waiting room before Kelsey or Flynn can answer.

"I spotted the doctor coming down the hall. I think she's out of surgery." Amy moves back to her chair in the corner, next to the laptop balanced on a stack of magazines. As soon as she takes a seat, a tanned woman in scrubs stops in the doorway.

"Scarlett Priest's family?"

Flynn is already out of her chair. "I'm her sister. We're all here for her."

The doctor nods, and I count every beat of my heart until her lips curve into a smile. "Your sister is going to be just fine. The appendectomy was textbook. We caught it before it ruptured and were able to do it laparoscopically."

A textbook appendectomy?

I look at Flynn, and part of me wants to wrap both hands around her shoulders and shake the fuck out of her. The other part of me wants to hug the hell out of her for scaring the shit out of me by withholding that key information. Not that an emergency appendectomy isn't a big deal, because I know any surgery can have complications, but *sweet fucking Christ*, I thought it was something a million times worse.

The claws of fear that have been gripping me loosen until

I can take my first true deep breath since Flynn stormed my office.

"She's in recovery, but on her way to a room. Scarlett's very lucky, though. She really cut it close."

The doctor shakes Flynn's hand and leaves the room. I realize I missed all the other information she gave us, but I don't care. The only thing that matters is that *Scarlett is going to be fine.*

I'm getting my second chance.

One I'm not going to fuck up.

Flynn spins to smirk at me, and this time, I can see a manipulative yet victorious gleam in her eye. Before, I was too freaked out to notice.

"I had to, Legend. You'll forgive me someday."

I rise from my seat and cross the room to tower over her. "You ever do that to me again, and we'll have fucking words."

"Fair enough. Now, stop trying to intimidate me or I won't tell you which room they've assigned her."

THIRTEEN

I feel like I'm swimming through an opaque haze, and there are voices in the distance, but they're garbled. My head is stuffed with cotton batting and sawdust, like that antique pillow that disintegrated on my window seat after being exposed to the sun for too long.

Wait. Why am I thinking about sawdust and pillows?

I crack one eye open, but the bright light has me flinching and squeezing it shut again just as quickly.

"Scarlett? Can you hear me?"

"She's waking up again. Just let her come out of it."

The voices are clearer now, so I can make out the words, but confusion swamps my senses.

Where am I? How did I get here? What are those beeping noises? My toes are cold. Why are my toes cold?

I try my eyes again, and the light dims. *Thank you.* I try to murmur the words, but my throat is scratchy and they don't come out.

"Do you want some water?"

The sound of ice sloshing in a pitcher steals my attention, and I see a blue cup with a bendy straw in front of me.

It might be levitating there, but I don't care. I just want water.

I take a sip and shake my head, trying to clear the cobwebs. "What?"

"You're okay, Scarlett. Everything's good. You just had surgery, but everything's fine. Don't worry about a thing."

The voice suddenly has an identity. "Flynn?"

"I'm right here, big sister." Her hand squeezes mine, and I realize my hand is cold too.

"Why am I cold?"

"I'll get her another warm blanket. I saw where the nurse grabbed one."

I turn slightly to see the back of Amy's head as she leaves the room. "Amy?"

"She'll be right back," Flynn says with a smile. "We'll get you all nice and warm. You've got a private room too, so you don't have to worry about someone named Earl ripping ass on the other side of the curtain while you recover."

"Earl?"

"Now you're just confusing her." Kelsey's dark hair pops into view around Flynn's shoulder. "How are you feeling, babe? You scared the hell out of us. I'm so glad you have Amy. She was not fucking around with your health."

I nod because she's right, but I still feel like I'm floating through clouds rather than tucked into a hospital bed.

Behind Kelsey, in the shadows of the room, there's another person. A man? I blink twice, but my vision is still fuzzy. Or maybe I have gunk in my eyes.

"Dad?" I say the word hesitantly, hope rising inside me, and I reach up to grasp it.

He came? Oh my God, he came.

The IV tugs at my hand as Kelsey steps aside, and I see through the shadows and realize exactly how wrong I am. It's not my father.

67

It's Gabriel Legend.

"What . . ." Confusion and shock flood my system. My lungs catch, and my heart seems to twist inside my chest.

The amorphous beeping coming from inside the room speeds up, and Flynn's attention jumps to the other side of the bed, where my IV is connected to a pole.

"I can go." His deep voice rumbles through the room like thunder from a hundred miles away. He takes one step toward the door, his face still bathed in shadow.

"No. Stay." I don't know why I say it.

Maybe because in that moment, those are the only two words in my entire vocabulary. Maybe because it's so good to see him, hear him, feel his presence, that I need to hold on to this moment for a few more breaths. Maybe because even with time and space, the way I feel hasn't changed.

Then the memory of that night charges back into my brain.

You should go. And don't come back, Scarlett. This isn't happening.

The heart rate monitor beeps again and again, and everyone in the room seems to hold their breath until Flynn breaks the tension.

She grabs Kelsey's hand. "We'll give you two a few minutes alone. We'll be right outside." Flynn shoots a hard look at Gabriel before dragging Kelsey outside.

As soon as the door shuts behind them, the silence in the room turns to leaden weight.

I don't know what to say. I don't know what to do. I'm too weak to figure it out.

But, thankfully, I'm the one hooked up to the machine, so I can't go far, which cuts down on the number of decisions I can make. However, that heart rate monitor is annoying as hell, because I feel like I'm hooked up to a lie detector test.

Part of me wants to rip the leads off my chest, but I don't want to summon the nurse.

Gabriel takes a step toward me, leaving the shadows of the corner to enter the dim pool of light coming from above me.

"How do you feel?" he asks, closing the distance between us until his big hands curl around the back of the chair beside the hospital bed.

"My toes are cold."

He reaches down to grab the hem of his shirt, and before I realize what he's doing, he pulls his T-shirt off and tucks it around my feet, under the thin sheet and blanket covering me.

The beeping picks up the pace as I attempt to school my breathing.

I've never seen Gabriel in a tight white tank before, but that's all he's got on after stripping off the T-shirt. His shoulders and arms ripple with muscle, and I can't help but follow one thick vein down his forearm.

"Nurses must love you," I mumble, now remembering the three times they had to poke me to get this stupid IV in my arm.

"I don't know many nurses, but I do know one thing." His hand wipes across his mouth and chin. "I fucked up, ladybug. Real bad." He bows his head, and his dark blond hair falls forward into his face. "I shouldn't have done what I did, Scarlett. You deserved better than that. A million times better. You don't have to forgive me, but I need you to know how much I regret treating you like that."

His pulse thrums in his throat, and I have to wonder what the heart rate monitor would sound like hooked up to him right now.

When I don't reply to his apology, he glances at my face, and those vivid blue eyes spear into me. "You're probably thinking I'm only here because your stepsister told me you were dying, but I realized how bad I fucked up before all that. I had to tell you how sorry I was. I was working it out. This . . . this just happened first."

Flynn told him I was dying? Holy shit.

"I'm not dying. Well, not today, anyway."

He nods slowly. "That's what I hear, and I'm really fucking glad about that."

"Why?" I can't help but push him. Maybe it's unfair, but he's the one who threw me out of his office while I was still riding the high from the best orgasm of my life.

Without waiting for an invitation, he releases the chair and steps around to sit at my bedside. "Because I figured something out." His voice is lower and more sincere than I could ever imagine him sounding.

"What's that?"

His Adam's apple bounces in his throat. "Someone's going to get to be your man, and there's not a single guy on this planet who is good enough for you, including me."

My brows tug together in confusion. *This again.* "I don't understand your point."

"I'm not done."

I incline my chin, indicating he can continue anytime.

"If one of us unworthy assholes gets to have you, it damn well isn't going to be another guy like your ex who doesn't know what kind of woman he's got."

"You don't know that," I say, even as I try to shove thoughts of Chadwick out of my head.

Gabriel meets my gaze, and something burns in his blue eyes. "Yeah, I do, because if anyone gets to have you, it's going to be me. There's something between us. You felt it. I sure as fuck did too, even if I couldn't admit it. It goes deeper than you wanting me just as much as I want you. That's why I fucked up. Because you got to a part of me that I thought was dead and gone forever. It's not, though. It was just waiting for you."

My mouth drops open at his declaration. Static buzzes in my head, and I'm not sure I heard him correctly. But Gabriel keeps going, and I hang on his every word.

"I'm not what you need, ladybug, but I'll learn. You were right. We have to see where this goes. I want to make this real."

Tears flood my eyes, and no amount of blinking can keep them back.

"Fuck, don't cry."

"Flynn told you I was dying."

"I knew what I wanted before that."

"Like when you threw me out of your office as soon as you slid the condom off?"

He bows his head again. "I fucked up. *Bad.*"

All the emotions I felt in that moment come rushing back like a rogue wave. "No, you didn't just fuck up, Gabriel. I put myself out there. You didn't have to be on board with it. I get that I was taking a risk. But the least you could've done was treat me with an ounce of fucking respect. You'd just been inside me, and you threw me out like *trash.*"

The heart rate monitor is going crazy beside me, and Gabriel squeezes his eyes shut like he's in agony.

"I wish I could take it all back." He opens his eyes, and his blue gaze is piercing. "You probably don't believe me, and you shouldn't. Words aren't enough. I know that, but I'll show you."

There's a knock at the door, and we both turn.

Flynn pokes her head in. "Oh, good, you didn't kill each other. The doctors will be happy." She comes in with Kelsey and Amy behind her. All three of them stare at Gabriel in his ribbed tank.

"What happened to his shirt?" Kelsey asks, always the one to address the elephant in the room.

"Her feet were cold," Amy whispers, holding out the warm blanket she fetched for me.

"God, that's too fucking cute," Flynn says as a nurse also bustles in the door.

"That's enough visiting for now. She needs to rest so she can heal. The doctor is hopeful she'll be discharged tomorrow afternoon." The nurse looks around the room at Flynn, Kelsey, Amy, and Gabriel. "Who is staying with her? Just one of you, if you please."

FOURTEEN

"I'll go," I say as I rise from the chair beside her bed. I don't want to say the words, but I know I'm the odd man out here. I meet Scarlett's gray gaze. "For now. I'll be back."

Kelsey, Amy, and Flynn debate who will stay, and Flynn wins. Although, it wasn't much of a debate. Flynn is impossible to argue with since she's the only one with the smallest hint of a family connection.

Scarlett nods at me, and even though it isn't much, I'll take it. Fuck, I'll happily accept scraps for however long it takes me to earn back her trust. I deserve that.

I make my way around the women, who are saying their good-byes, but Flynn follows me out into the hallway. I'm glad for that, even if her goal is to read me the riot act again.

Before she can get a word out, I shut the door and ask the question I didn't want to voice in front of Scarlett, because I'm afraid the answer would crush her. "Is her dad coming?"

Flynn's face falls. "I doubt it. He's got a huge bash this weekend in the Hamptons, and he'd never miss it."

Anger, my old friend, ignites in my gut. "Are you fucking serious?"

"Sadly, yes." Flynn's tone is just as disgusted as mine.

"What a fucking prick. His daughter just had emergency surgery."

"Yeah, I know. And even the guy who dicked and dashed on her showed up. Makes dear old daddy look even more like the asshole we all knew he was from day one."

I let Flynn's dig slide. I deserve that too.

"So you'll stay with her. All night? I don't want her waking up alone. If there's any chance of that, I'm not fucking leaving this building."

"I have a race in Jersey. I'll only be gone for a few hours. Back by four a.m. at the latest. She won't even know I left."

"Race?" I stare at the little brunette in confusion. "What the fuck kind of race?"

"Street race. For pinks. I assume you're well aware that's a thing."

She's right, but *she* shouldn't know it's a thing. "Are you fucking kidding me? You're going to leave your sister after surgery for a walk on the wild side? You're not fucking going."

It's the wrong thing to say, because Flynn pokers up. "One, you don't get to have an opinion on my life. Two, I've been racing since high school. This is how I've paid for college. I might be a trust-fund kid, but not all of us get to cash in on that shit when we want. And just so you know, I'm damn good at it."

Not even sure what to say, I mumble, "Jesus Christ, save me from rich girls with no fear."

"Whatever. If you don't want her to wake up alone, then I'll have Kelsey or Amy come back. I just didn't think that was fair since they both have to work tomorrow morning."

"I'll come and sit with her. What time?"

"I need to leave by eleven. The race starts at midnight."

"I'll see you then. Don't fucking leave before I get here."

"Don't be late."

"Not for her."

Flynn smiles. "You just might prove all of us wrong, Legend. Your odds are improving by the second. You're still the underdog, but we'll see how you do." She winks at me, and I take that as my cue to get the fuck out of this hospital.

But as soon as I leave, I'm counting the minutes until I get to come back.

FIFTEEN

Scarlett

The door closes behind Flynn and Gabriel, and the nurse, whose name tag reads JOANNA, has no idea that I'm silently freaking out for reasons that have absolutely nothing to do with what's happening with me, and everything to do with the man who just left my hospital room. While she busies herself with checking my vital signs and entering them in my chart, I eyeball Kelsey and wait for her to explain how he ended up here. In my hospital room.

Thankfully, she doesn't take too long.

"It was all Flynn. She told him. He was here before I was. I had no idea, Scar. Seriously. I could kill that kid right now."

I give her a shaky wave. "No need. I just . . . it was a surprise, you know? I mean, who expects to come out of surgery and find the guy who kicked her out waiting to see how she's doing? Why wouldn't he be here, right?"

Amy comes toward me and smooths out the blanket over my feet. A corner of Gabriel's black T-shirt sticks out. She tugs it free and holds it up. "You want me to give him his shirt back before he goes?"

She takes one step toward the door before I struggle to lean up, but manage to quickly snatch it out of her hands.

"No, thank you. I'll keep that." I lie back on the bed, the black ball of fabric clenched in my fingers, and my entire body protests my sudden movement. "Damn, that didn't feel good."

Joanna whips around to check on me. "No jumping around, men's clothes at stake or not. You need to take it easy. It might've been laparoscopic, but your body has been through a lot, Ms. Priest. No sudden movements would be the smart choice."

The waves of pain relent as I lie still on my stack of pillows. "I'll remember that."

She rattles off more instructions and gives me a rundown about how the night will go in the hospital—sleep as much as I can, when I can, because they'll be checking on me regularly, and it's going to make resting more difficult than normal. She also removes my heart rate monitor, muttering under her breath that they could have removed it in recovery and been just fine.

That would have been great to know when I was setting it off and leaving no one in any question about how I felt when I saw Gabriel.

Finally, she mentions that the food leaves something to be desired, and I should have my friends and family bring alternative meals to save me from the hospital kitchen.

"Thank you for the warning," I say as one word of that sentence brings back a harsh reminder.

Family. As in, the only blood relative I have left can't even bother to show his face. *Thanks, Dad. Good to know you're not concerned about your daughter, even when she has emergency surgery.* Thank God for Flynn, Kelsey, and Amy.

Friends are the family you choose for yourself. I'm lucky I have the amazing people in my life that I do, and I'm thankful my relationship with Flynn is growing stronger than it was when we were stepsiblings. We're more family now than ever.

Joanna finishes her tasks and then reminds Amy and Kelsey that only one person can stay.

"All but one of us will be out of here shortly. We promise, ma'am," Amy says in her most polite, professional tone.

Once Joanna opens the door, we all crane our necks to see if Flynn is still out in the hallway talking to Gabriel. Or at least, I do.

But there's no sign of him. Flynn nods at Joanna and slips back into the room.

"She told me we have five minutes to decide, and then she's throwing us all out. Nurse Hatchett is kind of a downer."

"I'm fine, you guys. All of you can head home. I'll sleep and see you in the morning."

Kelsey looks at me with her eyebrows almost reaching her hairline. "You're clearly high on painkillers. No one is leaving you alone. Someone will be here every minute you are."

"She's right," Flynn adds with a smile. "And I'm taking the first shift, so everyone else can leave."

"You sure you got this?" Kelsey asks her.

With a pageant-style wave, Flynn says, "'Bye, ladies. See you both in the morning. I'll let you know if we get any info on when our girl is getting sprung."

Amy squeezes my hand. "I'll see you tomorrow, boss. Everything's in good hands. I promise."

"I know. I'm not worried at all."

She smiles and steps away, making room for Kelsey to lean in and hug me. "Love you, babe. Try to get some rest. I won't even judge you if you plan to cuddle that T-shirt all night."

I huff out a laugh, and it causes a pinch in my abdomen near my belly button. "Love you. No more laughing for a while. See you tomorrow," I say to both of them.

The two women file out, leaving me alone with Flynn. I give myself enough time to take one breath before I ask the question that I've been dying to get out.

"Why did you tell him? What are you trying to accomplish here, Flynn?"

"I was terrified. You'd just been taken back into surgery. I needed to tell someone, but my mom is on a flight to Australia, and your dad won't answer his fucking phone. I panicked." In that moment, she looks younger than her age.

"I'm so sorry, Flynn. You didn't need to call anyone. It's just my appendix. Not a huge deal."

She drops her hands onto her hips. "It is a huge deal. Amy told me they had to bring you in an ambulance, and she'd never seen you like that before. You may not be my blood sister, but you're the closest thing I have to a sibling, and now that I've got you back in my life, I don't want to lose you again."

Her eyes shine in the dim light of the hospital room, and I reach out to snag her fingers.

"You're not going to lose me. Thank you for coming and worrying about me."

Flynn plops into the chair that Gabriel occupied only a short time earlier. "You want to know the truth? I was scared, and I used that fear like a weapon. I wanted him to feel it too. I wanted him to know that he could lose you. I wanted him to feel that pain. Maybe that makes me a terrible person, but I don't care."

I pat the top of her hand. "You're a good sister, Flynn. The best one I could ever ask for."

She glances up at me from under her lashes. "You don't want to kill me for letting him think you were dying?"

Maybe there's a latent mean streak in me, because I'm not heartbroken over the trick she played. It was clever.

"Just don't do it again. Whatever is or isn't between me and Gabriel will be for him and me to decide."

"Oh, there's a hell of a lot of something there." Flynn leans back in the chair and crosses one ankle over her knee. "The man is gone for you. I don't think you'll be wondering how he feels much longer. If I were a betting woman, which I am," she says, tossing her hair over her shoulder, "I'd bet that you and Legend are going to be the hottest couple this town never expected to see. You're going to tame the wild beast."

I chuckle carefully this time, so as not to cause a twinge of pain. "We'll see, Flynn," I say with a yawn. "We will see."

SIXTEEN

Sitting in the dark, I listen to each even breath and watch the slow rise and fall of Scarlett's chest. In. Out. In. Out. Each movement reminds me that she's alive, and that's enough for me right now.

Alive is good. Especially when I can't shake the lingering fear that Flynn drilled into me earlier.

I can't even be mad at the kid for what she did. Hell, if anything, I owe her a massive thank-you. I may never recover the couple of years she shaved off my life, but I've never been worried about living a real long time, anyway. That's not something you expect for yourself when you grow up the way I did.

After my mom got arrested, I ended up in foster care during her trial. She couldn't make bail and couldn't afford to bond out, so they held her over, and I got acquainted with a broken system in the up-close and personal way unwanted kids do.

My first house didn't last long. Emergency placement, they called it. I was dropped on someone's doorstep, and they fed me some dinner and sent me to bed like the rest of the kids in the house.

I never went back to the trailer park. They wouldn't even let me get my stuff. I wore the same clothes for three days, before a caseworker showed up to take me away again.

I figured that's how it would be from then on, but it wasn't.

The second family I was placed with was even more chaotic than the first, but in the best way possible. Because that's where I met Bump and Jorie Billips, the two people who would become the only family I thought I'd ever need.

Jorie and I were the same age, and Bump was four years younger, but he refused to be left out of anything. Jorie took care of him like he was her kid, and I helped. Together, the three of us made life worth living. And once Jorie and I aged out of the foster care system, she and I both worked every second we could so we'd make enough money for her to get custody of Bump.

The first night the three of us spent in our shitty little one-bedroom apartment in the projects was one of the best I'd ever had up until that point. We were poor as shit, but we were happy because we were together.

Until I fucked over Moses and painted targets on all of our backs. Then I lost them both.

Bump would never grow into the man he was meant to be. Jorie would stay forever young in my memories, and would never sing at the clubs in LA the way she'd dreamed about.

I lost myself after that. I morphed into a stranger, doing things to survive that were downright criminal. There was nothing I wouldn't do to numb the pain. I punished myself by taking every fight I could. When I started stashing money away, it was to somehow prove to Jorie that it wasn't all for nothing. That I could make something of myself. That I could become a man she could be proud of again.

Two gunshots, ordered by Moses Buford Gaspard, ended life as I knew it. And ever since then, I've been going through the motions and picking up the shattered pieces. Slowly but surely, I fought my way out of the dark, but nothing has ever been the same.

Until the woman in this hospital bed beside me changed life as I knew it one more time.

Sitting here in the dark, I feel things swirling inside me. They're not things I should be thinking or feeling. I have no right after what I did, but I can't stop.

Scarlett should have thrown me out the minute she saw me. But she didn't.

I'm not so naive as to think second chances come around all that often, so I'm not fucking this one up. That is, if it's really a second chance and not a cosmic joke at my expense.

Even if I don't know how to be what she needs, I'm going to learn.

With that vow burning itself into my brain, the door opens and a nurse shuffles inside. She stops short when she sees me.

"What are you doing here? Where is her sister?"

Her hand is inches from the security button near the bed, and I slowly rise with both hands out to my sides.

"I'm Gabriel. I'm Scarlett's . . . friend. Flynn had to go and asked me to make sure Scarlett wouldn't be alone. That's all. I promise." My voice is a hushed whisper, since I'm trying not to wake Scarlett.

"You were here earlier. The other nurse mentioned you. You own that nightclub where there was a shooting."

The fact that either of them were able to identify me and connect me with the shooting after seeing me for a short

83

time tells me just how *not* under the radar my identity is anymore. If Moses remembers even a fraction of what I look like, it won't be long before he sends someone up north to finish me off. Except this time, I'm going to be ready.

I glance down at Scarlett. I have to keep her safe. That's nonnegotiable. I'll figure out the details with Q, and we'll put it all in action as soon as possible. I can't be distracted when her well-being is at stake.

"Yeah, that's me."

The nurse's gaze flicks between me and Scarlett. "And Ms. Priest was recently photographed at your club . . . I think I see what's going on."

She has no clue, but I don't mind letting her think she does.

"Thank you for understanding."

The nurse's chin goes up. "I wouldn't say I understand, but I know what a man looks like when he's falling for someone."

I freeze, unsure of what to say to her.

"Let me give you some unsolicited advice, young man. Take damn good care of her. She won't want to admit she needs help, but she will."

"That's absolutely my plan, ma'am. Thank you."

"Good. Also, if you try anything weird, I'll have security drag you out."

"I just don't want her to wake up alone," I say honestly.

"Not just falling . . . you're already in love. That's cute." She shakes her head and walks out the door before I can pick my jaw up off the floor.

What the fuck did she say? "You're already in love. That's cute?"

I stare at the door, like I expect her to walk back in and explain herself, but I'm left in the dark with new questions weighing on my mind.

Does Scarlett always have to deal with people thinking they know more about her personal life than she does? Is this something I'll have to get used to? And even more so—

What am I going to do now?

SEVENTEEN

W hen I wake up, Flynn is slumped in the chair next to my bed, wearing her leather pants, leather jacket, and her hair is back in a tight braid. Instantly, a caption for the sight pops into my head. *Innocent Badass*. I take a mental picture for my files before reaching out for the water to soothe my parched throat.

As soon as I move, her eyes flick open.

"You're awake!"

"And you look like you left, raced cars, and sneaked back in without me being the wiser . . . except your black leather look is giving you away."

Flynn tilts her head to the side with a sleepy smile. "Don't worry, you weren't alone for a single second."

I blink at her in confusion. "Did you pay a nurse to sit with me all night? You know they have other patients to deal with, so they really shouldn't do that."

Her smile turns smug. "No, of course not. Legend stayed with you. I doubt he fell asleep on the job either, unlike me."

My entire body jerks forward, and thankfully, the twinges

of yesterday aren't as intense today. "Gabriel came back? How? What? Why?"

"Hey, whoa. Chill out. No sudden movements, remember? Relax."

I scan the room, searching for traces of him. "You just told me someone watched me sleep without my knowledge, so chilling out isn't really on the agenda for this morning, Flynn. What the hell?"

She rolls her eyes, and I'm reminded that she is, indeed, twenty years old. "You didn't even know, and if I hadn't told you, you wouldn't be freaking out right now, so chill out. Be happy I told you. Be happy he was all gung ho for the job and would've stayed around the clock if I hadn't told him I had it covered."

Two weeks ago, he told me to go, and it crushed me. Now . . . I'm terrified to believe what's happening. But his words from last night are still fresh in my mind, and my heart.

I wish I could take it all back . . . You probably don't believe me and you shouldn't. Words aren't enough. I know that, but I'll show you.

"He told me he'd show me," I whisper.

Flynn leans closer to me. "What?"

"Gabriel said he wished he could take back what he did. That words weren't enough. That he'd have to show me."

Flynn slaps a hand over her chest in the vicinity of her heart. "That's so fucking sweet. Oh my God. I totally made the right call."

"I still can't believe you did that."

She shrugs. "It was a calculated risk, and I had nothing to lose. If he didn't care, I was never going to tell you, but since he did care *very, very much*, now we're in a completely different situation." She pauses and pitches forward to check the door. "By the way, the nurse said earlier that they'll check you out this morning and assess your progress. If you're doing well, there's a chance you could be going home this afternoon."

"Knock-knock . . ." Harlow's voice comes out a whisper from the hallway. "Is anyone—"

"She's awake. Come on in," Flynn calls out.

Harlow slips inside, shutting the door behind her with a giant vase of wildflowers.

"Oh, thank God! You're okay!" She drops the vase on a ledge with a thump and rushes toward me. "I was so worried about you! I'm sorry I couldn't be here last night. Jimmy had a meeting with a client in Vegas, so we hopped on a jet and swung out for dinner, and didn't get home until six a.m. I haven't even been to sleep yet." Harlow covers the yawn escaping her lips as she leans down to gently hug me.

"Thank you for coming. It means a lot to me."

"Of course I came as quick as I could. And I didn't bring roses. That's what being a best friend is all about."

I laugh, *carefully*, and lean back in my hospital bed. "As you can see, I'm fine. I'll be going home later today."

"And Legend took the night shift and watched Scarlett sleep."

Harlow's eyes go wide. "What? He was here?"

Flynn catches her up quickly, summarizing how she scared the hell out of him and got him to the hospital, and how he apologized to me and told me he'd show me he was serious.

Harlow's eyes are filled with tears when Flynn finishes. "I've never been so happy for anyone to need their appendix removed ever! He just needed the fear of God in him. Monroe is going to freak out. I have to text her. She's at an away game with Nate."

"She went to an away game?" I ask, my tone bordering on shocked. "She hates leaving the city for anything to do with the team or baseball."

Harlow's face creases into a weird mask that tells me immediately that something's wrong.

"What is it? What happened? Is Monroe okay?"

Harlow glances at Flynn and then me. "Double vault?"

"Absolutely," I say, then quickly explain the double-vault concept to Flynn.

Harlow waits for Flynn to nod her agreement before she continues. "Monroe thinks he's cheating. She's trying to catch him."

My head plops back on the pillow. "Hell."

"Shit," Flynn whispers. "Really? That's a bummer."

I turn to Flynn and Harlow. "This isn't the first time. This is also not the first time Monroe could be totally and completely wrong about Nate cheating. Remember when she barged into that restaurant where he was having a meeting with Jimmy, thinking he was with a woman?"

"God, it would've been funny if it weren't so sad. I don't know how Nate's going to take it either. He's about at the end of the line when it comes to trying to get Monroe to trust him."

We need to talk some sense into Monroe before this gets out of hand. "We'll talk to her this week. Try to get her to see reason."

A line forms between Harlow's brows. "If that'll even work. I don't know. So, what do they serve for breakfast in this joint, or are we ordering in?"

Flynn gives her a wry glance. "Oh, we're definitely ordering in, and you're paying."

All through breakfast and then lunch, I kept stamping out the tiny ray of hope that continued to grow in my chest that my dad would come walking through the hospital room door with a balloon and a teddy bear, like he did when I had my tonsils out when I was seven. The memory is hazy, but it happened. So what if he didn't stay very long, and he and my mom were arguing by the time he left? He still came.

Scraps. That's what I'm willing to take from my father, and I'm not too proud to admit it.

But he doesn't show up. He doesn't even call or text. Nothing. Not a single attempt to check on his only child after surgery. The hole in my heart gapes, but I pretend I don't care and paste a smile on my face to greet the surgeon who stops in to check on me.

And when the doctor exits the room, after pronouncing me free to leave after I'm discharged, I can't wait to get the hell out of the hospital and away from the proof that my father doesn't give a single damn about me.

"Can you go track down the nurse with the paperwork? I want to get out of here before they come up with a reason to keep me."

Amy and Kelsey, who arrived when Harlow and Flynn had to leave, both look at me strangely.

"Are we in a hurry?" Kelsey asks.

"I just want to shower, put on my clothes, climb into my own bed, and sleep for a day."

"No problem, boss," Amy says with a smile. "I'll go find the nurse right now and see where she is on the discharge paperwork. We'll be out of here before you know it."

When Amy disappears in search of the nurse, Kelsey sits on the edge of my bed.

"Is something wrong?"

I shake my head. "I don't know why I keep expecting him to care. He's proven over and over that he doesn't."

"Legend?" Her brow creases in confusion. "But he was here all night."

"No, my dad."

Realization hits. "Oh God. I'm so sorry, Scarlett. I can't believe . . ." Kelsey trails off, but she doesn't need to finish the sentence. And because of the history between my father and me, I'm certain she can, in fact, believe he doesn't care.

"It's fine. Let's talk about something else."

A thrill flares in her dark eyes. "Like Gabriel Legend? Because I can't get over the fact that he waited with us, took our very passive-aggressive verbal lashings, and wouldn't budge because he's so hung up on you."

Skeptical, I let my head fall to the side. "Or he feels guilty."

"Shut up, Scar. You know that's bullshit."

I smile ruefully. "Okay, so maybe he likes me a little." I glance down at the area where they cut me open. "Not that there's anything I can do about it right now."

"Well, you can't really bang him, that's true. But there's no reason he can't just get on his knees and apologize with his face in your pussy."

"Kelsey Pak!"

She shrugs with a laugh. "Don't you first-and-last-name me. It's a great idea, and you know it."

EIGHTEEN

Scarlett

ater that afternoon, I put down my phone after replying to the group text between me, Ryan, and Christine. They wanted to make sure I was feeling okay and got the gift basket they sent. *At least they care.*

Flynn gives me a hug and a kiss on the cheek before she has to leave. "I can skip class if you want me to."

"What? No. There's no reason for that. I'll be fine. I'm an adult, and I can get myself home without an entourage. Actually, it's probably better if we keep it low key."

"If you're sure," Flynn replies, uncertainty wrinkling her forehead. "Because it's just a night class that I need for credits. I don't actually care about the subject matter."

"Go, Flynn. Thank you for being here as much as you have been. It means a lot to me." I squeeze her hand one last time before releasing it—and her—from my hospital room.

"Good thing you've only got one appendix, because I'm in no hurry to do this again, and I'm sure you're not either."

Actually, I'm just glad the worst is over, and the pain is gone. She's right. I never want to go through that kind of torture again.

From the corner, Amy smiles at Flynn's sweet statement. "'Bye, Flynn," she says as my former stepsister slips out of the room, leaving the two of us alone.

I smile at Amy, who has been amazing in every way, but she has to leave for her niece's first birthday party by five, which I've forbidden her from missing.

And then I'll be all alone.

I silently scold myself, hating that sadness is creeping in.

It doesn't matter. It's basically like checking out of a hotel. Why would I need a whole crew of family and friends around me while I'm getting discharged from the hospital? I don't.

And yet, here I am, ragged over the fact that the only person who is still here with me is on my payroll. Kelsey had clients she couldn't reschedule on such short notice, and Harlow and Monroe both had commitments.

Stop it, Scarlett. Save the pity party for when you get home, and no one can see you fall apart because your dad couldn't manage to tear himself away from his busy schedule to see how his daughter's emergency surgery went. Your mom wouldn't have missed it. You know that.

I paste a bright smile on my face and look to Amy. "Should I ring the nurse to make sure the paperwork is coming?"

She moves toward the door. "She said it was almost done. Let me see where she's at. We'll have you out of here in no time."

Thankfully, true to her word, Amy has a young man rolling my hospital-mandated wheelchair out of the building fifteen minutes later.

"That's us," Amy says, pointing at a black SUV.

They load up the flowers and baskets and balloons from the girls in the back, and I'm champing at the bit to get out of this wheelchair, when I spot a man in a T-shirt walking up the sidewalk. His head is down and his dark blond hair hangs over his face, but I don't need to see his features to know who he is. The very tingly shivers racing down my spine tell me everything I need to know.

Amy doesn't see him, and to be honest, she fades into the background as soon as he looks up and I meet his vivid blue gaze. One corner of his mouth tugs upward in an almost-smile, and my heart stutters. I take a mental snapshot and instantly caption it *When He Sees Me.*

That half smile is everything.

Tossing away the mental trappings of the pity party I was getting ready to throw, I try not to shiver as excitement fills me instead.

Gabriel stops in front of me, and I can't look away. I'm not even sure I'm breathing.

"Hey," he says, his voice rough, like he hasn't used it since he saw me last.

"Hey," I reply, mostly because I'm held captive by those eyes, and I don't care how cheesy that sounds. It's the truth.

In the bright light of day, Gabriel Legend isn't just a man, he's a masterpiece. Sun glints off the gold in his hair, making the dark streaks shine like freshly polished teak. His skin is tanned and his jawline is covered in delicious scruff.

Damn, he is one fine specimen of a man.

"Thanks for coming to see me again," I say with a careful smile. "But I'm getting out, so you're off the hook."

His brows dip together like my statement doesn't make sense. I'm still on painkillers, so I could be the confused one. *Am I confused?*

"I know. Flynn told me you were getting sprung."

I blink at him. "So . . ." I stop speaking when I realize there's a duffel bag hanging over his shoulder.

He follows my eyes to the bag, and our gazes collide once more. "She didn't tell you." It's a statement, not a question.

"What was she supposed to tell me?" I ask, but Amy bustles toward me.

"Oh, Mr. Legend. I didn't know you were coming," she says with a smile.

"Flynn was supposed to tell you that I'm coming to help out."

"Getting Ms. Priest home?" Amy asks, tilting her head to the side.

Gabriel's attention cuts back to me. "I'm going home with you. Flynn and I worked out a schedule between us and your other friends. You won't be alone this week. Although you may want to be by the time it's Monroe Grafton's turn."

All I can do is blink. Words that I'm fairly certain I've spoken before swirl in my brain in incoherent patterns, and all I can think is—*Gabriel is coming to stay at my apartment with me to take care of me? This has to be an alternate reality.*

When neither Amy nor I reply, Gabriel's entire body goes eerily still. "Unless you don't want me to stay. I'll understand."

My chest might as well crack open and spill my heart out right on the sidewalk. The sound of him saying *"Unless you don't want me to stay. I'll understand"* almost slays me right there.

Something burns behind my eyes, but I'm not even going to think about it. Instead, I hold out a hand. "I would love to get out of this wheelchair."

"As you wish," he murmurs, and my heart flutters because I'm 99.9 percent sure he has no idea that's a line from *The Princess Bride* designed to make all Wesley and Princess Buttercup fans—including me—melt instantly.

Except I woefully underestimated what being appropriately prepared for this means, because Gabriel doesn't just slide his calloused hand across mine and squeeze. *No.* He leans down to *lift me completely out of the wheelchair and into his arms.*

The feelings of zero gravity and utter shock have me leaning close to the hard strength of his body. *God, he's solid as a rock. And warm.* I want to curl into his heat and soak it up, even though it's not remotely cold outside.

Because it's not the heat, Scar. It's the feeling of a real man. The voice in my head is two steps ahead of me, because she hits the nail on the head.

Neither Chadwick nor any of my past boyfriends would just saunter up and lift me like I weighed no more than a bag of feathers. In fact, none of them ever picked me up at all. Not even to carry me off to bed. Not once.

Wow. That's depressing.

Gabriel slides me into the back seat of the SUV while Amy and the driver watch, and once I'm carefully buckled up with my belly cushion pressed to my midsection, he steps back.

Amy has a look on her face that I can't quite decipher. It's almost like she's trying to hold back a smile but is also gathering courage. I snap my brain back into thinking mode and guess why she looks like she's prepping for an unpleasant conversation. *The birthday party.*

I don't know what time it is right this second, but I can guess. If Amy comes back to Curated with us and spends time helping me get settled, she'll be super late.

"Amy, why don't you take off and get to that party early? They'll be so shocked, they won't know what to think for once."

Her brows shoot up, and a rueful smile follows with a concerned expression. "Are you sure? I can be a little late."

Gabriel picks up on what's going on. "I've got her covered. I promise she's in good hands, whatever you might think."

Amy bites her lip. Knowing her, she has plenty to say and ask, but she doesn't want to be rude.

I smile and wave her off. "Go. I'm fine. I'll see you tomorrow. Thank you for being such a rock star. I don't know what I'd do without you." I hold out my hand, and Amy comes forward to squeeze it and give me a hug.

"Call me if you need anything. I don't care what time. I'll have my phone on, and I can be over in twenty minutes." She glances at Gabriel. "Scarlett will give you my number. If you have any questions at all or there's something you can't figure out, I'm always available."

"Thanks. Enjoy your party," Gabriel replies before stepping back and disappearing behind the SUV, presumably to climb in the other side.

Amy sees a window for privacy and goes for it. "Are you sure this is okay? I can skip the party. I don't want you doing anything that makes you feel uncomfortable, no matter what Flynn's trying to mastermind."

"I'm fine. I promise. Go have fun. Thank you for everything. I wouldn't know what to do without you." I reach out to hug her again, and she leans in against my hair.

"You know I'd do anything for you. Call me if he takes one step out of line. I'll come back with my brother-in-law. He's NYPD."

The other door opens and Gabriel slides in slowly, as if he knows Amy and I needed a minute to talk.

"Tell your family I said hi, Ames. Now go."

I wave at her through the tinted glass as the SUV pulls away from the curb with the driver, Gabriel, and me inside, and one thought slams into my brain.

Oh fuck. Did anyone clean my bathroom after the other day?

NINETEEN

I never expected in all my life to be riding in the back of a chauffeur-driven SUV with the daughter of one of America's most recognizable fashion icons.

I watch the buildings as we drive away from the hospital, and everything that is New York City washes over me as we make our way through traffic. The horns. The bustling pedestrians. The dog walkers and food carts. The don't-give-a-fuck pigeons who have more balls than most men I know. It's the city I've come to love and respect.

I remember the first time Q brought me over from Jersey, and we walked the streets of Manhattan. It was night, and there were so many sky-high buildings lit up that the kid who'd never been anywhere but Biloxi was in awe.

New York was another world. Another universe.

Men walked the sidewalks in their sleek black suits, carrying briefcases, knowing exactly where they were going and what they were about. I didn't even own a suitcase, let alone a briefcase, but I promised myself that someday, I'd walk the city and know exactly where I was going. I wouldn't stare in wonder and awe, like a boy fresh from the trailer park. I would be comfortable and confident in my new home, and everyone would know my name. *Someday.*

It's funny how your dreams change as you grow up. I do walk the city, because I love it even more than that very first day, and I know exactly where I'm going, but I don't wear suits or carry a briefcase. I don't care if anyone knows my name either. I stopped worrying about impressing people years ago . . . except I do want to impress *her.*

But I don't know how.

This woman has never once worried about money in her life, and I can't breathe easy without knowing where every penny of mine is.

And two weeks ago, before I fucked up worse than I've ever fucked up before, she told me she wanted to try things for real with me.

With me. She doesn't even know me yet.

Will she want me after she does?

That's a question I refuse to think much about, because it'll stop me where I stand. If once she sees everything I bring to the table, she decides it's not enough, then that's my penance for how I treated her. I made peace with it after I walked my ass back to the club this morning from the hospital.

Whatever happens next . . . all I can do is let fate decide.

I glance over at Scarlett, and her blond hair is pulled into a messy bun at the nape of her neck. She's staring straight ahead at the back of the black leather seat in front of her, her posture stiff as hell. Immediately, I wonder if she's in pain.

"You okay?"

She jerks her head to the side to look at me.

"Are you in pain? You look uncomfortable."

Scarlett presses both lips together and makes an awkward expression.

"What's wrong?" I lean forward in my seat, ready to jump

into action at her command.

"I puked all over the toilet in my bathroom, and I don't know if anyone cleaned it. All I can think about is how embarrassing that's going to be if you see my bathroom with a pukey toilet."

My posture relaxes as the words process in my brain. Laughter builds in my chest. "That's what you're worrying about right now? A dirty toilet?"

She nods, and I can't help it. A chuckle escapes from my lips, filling the cabin of the SUV.

"Fuck that. I've seen bathrooms and urinals a priest couldn't save. I was worried you were in excruciating pain, and you're worried about me seeing some barf you didn't flush?"

"Oh God, don't say it like that. It sounds so gross, and yet petty." A smile curls her lips, and I'm thankful the awkward expression and tension disappears.

I reach out and snag her hand, tangling her fingers with mine. "I promise I won't judge. I'll even clean it for you. Seems fair to me."

Her eyes go wide and her lower lip drops with her jaw. "What? No. Not a chance. I'll clean up my own vomit, thank you very much."

"You can argue with me, ladybug, but you won't win. I swear, I'm the most stubborn person you'll ever meet."

Her fingers grip mine just tight enough to let me know she doesn't want me to let her go, and a warm feeling spreads in my chest.

"I don't know, cowboy. I'm pretty stubborn too."

I jerk my head back. "Cowboy?"

"I was trying out a nickname. You need one too." Her cheeks flush red, and it's cute as fucking hell. "I'll scratch cowboy off the list then."

"Keep trying, ladybug. I have faith you'll find one."

TWENTY

Scarlett

owboy? Really? I called him cowboy?

It's official. I'm the biggest dork in the history of the planet. But . . . he's still holding my hand, and his thumb strokes across the back of it, giving me a thrill every few seconds.

Let's not tell him that, okay, Scarlett?

I keep my thoughts to myself for the rest of the ride, but the tension in the SUV doesn't return. Maybe it's because everything feels so . . . *right*. I don't know how that's possible, but I'm going to roll with it.

When the SUV stops at the curb, Gabriel is out and opening my door before the driver.

"I got you." He unbuckles my belt for me and lifts me into his arms before I realize what his plan is.

"I can walk. I promise."

"You can, but you're not."

His blue eyes offer no invitation to argue, so I settle against him, enjoying the novelty.

"You're pretty bossy, you know?"

He glances down at me as we make our way up the walk. "You have no idea. Which door? Front?"

"Side. I don't want anyone to see me. Go around to the right."

But he doesn't. He pauses first and calls out to the driver. "Bring the flowers and the duffel inside the front. Someone will get them where they need to go. Thanks for the ride."

"Thank you, bossy," I whisper as he starts around the side of the building and through the gate, getting me out of sight as quickly as possible.

"Still not a good nickname," he says, pausing to glance at the locks on the door. "I don't suppose you have keys?"

"In my pocket."

I wiggle in his arms, but it hurts a little to fish my keys out of my joggers that Kelsey helped me change into this morning. She's helped me in and out of enough clothes that it didn't even seem strange. Which would not be the case at all if it were this man.

A memory from a few weeks ago flashes through my brain. Gabriel snapping the elastic of my panties and then thrusting into me over and over until I lost my damned mind.

God, that was amazing. And totally not happening for a minimum of one week—from yesterday. According to my doctor, I need to heal and then let my body tell me when it's ready to undertake more strenuous "exercise." The doctor meant like working out, but my mind was in the gutter, and Flynn's comments made it nearly impossible to keep a straight face.

"So she should avoid thrusting movements? No riding? Horse-back or otherwise?"

I'm pretty sure the doctor was concerned about my blood pressure after how red my face got, but he bolted from the room as soon as I confirmed I understood the post-op instructions he'd given me.

And now here I am, being carried up four flights of stairs by Gabriel Legend, who isn't even breathing hard.

"I'm going to call you He-Man. How am I not heavy? Or, God, am I heavy but you're just really good at hiding it?"

He pauses on the landing outside the door that leads into my kitchen, and stares down at me in his arms. "I used to fight for my life. I ran stairs in a plate-loaded vest. Worked out until *I puked* every day. This is easy, ladybug. Even for He-Man. Can we get the door, though, so I can put you down where you'll be more comfortable?"

"Oh, sorry. Sure."

I fumble with the keys for longer than it should take me, because I'm not really ready for him to put me down, especially if it's no hardship for him. *We'll save that admission for the hopefully not-so-distant future, however.*

As soon as the door to my apartment opens, a fresh lemony-herb scent escapes, telling me my cleaning crew has been here. *Thank God.* No pukey toilet to scrub.

"You can set me down here," I tell Gabriel, pointing to the floor in front of us.

He shakes his head and looks around my space. "Bedroom?"

"Through there." I squeak out the reply, because what almost came out was, *"I thought you'd never ask."*

Calm down, Scarlett, before you lose it completely.

Thankfully, Gabriel doesn't notice my squeaking. In a few moments, we're in the middle of my over-the-top-feminine bedroom, where he's lowering me onto the fluffy duvet and a nest of throw pillows.

Shockingly, though, he doesn't run as soon as his arms are empty. He looks around the room, his blue eyes taking note of everything, it seems, before coming back to my face.

"It fits you."

Chadwick hated my bedroom and said it made it impossible for him to get a hard-on, but clearly Gabriel is a different kind of man. My frilly lace and serene colors don't make him look ridiculous. If anything, they make him seem even more masculine. *How is that even possible?*

"Thank you," I whisper, scooting back into the pillows. I reach forward to grab the edge of the throw blanket lying on the end of the bed, but my incision twinges and I freeze.

"Hey. Whoa." Gabriel bolts forward to grab it for me. "No sudden movements. That's why I'm here. You just lay back and chill. Tell me what you need."

When he spreads the nubby chenille throw over my legs and *tucks me in*, I can barely think straight because it's so freaking domestic and adorable and comforting.

Before he can move away, I slip my fingers into his and squeeze them. "Thank you."

"I haven't done anything yet," he says, his expression unreadable.

"Yeah, you have. And I appreciate it more than you know."

That's when he shocks the hell out of me.

With one hand braced on the bed right beside my hip and his fingers tangled in mine, he leans in until his lips are a breath away from my temple.

"*Real* starts now, ladybug. I'll show you."

His lips brush across my skin so lightly, it barely even counts as a kiss, but it's the same as everything he's giving me right now—exactly what I didn't know I needed.

Gabriel Legend, I hope you know what you're doing.

TWENTY-ONE

W hen a knock sounds at the front door, I leave
Scarlett to answer it. I don't bother to check
the peephole, given that I think it's an interior
door that leads to the store. Plus, I just gave orders for our
stuff to be brought up.

Standing in the hallway is a young woman whose
mustard-yellow one-piece outfit probably cost more than my
truck, but it doesn't stop it from being ugly as sin.

"Mr. Legend. It's a pleasure to meet you. Amy said you'd
be Scarlett's guest this evening."

"Yeah, I'll be here a while. Call me Legend or Gabe. No
mister."

She nods like her head is attached to a spring. "Got it,
Legend. Okay. Well, I have Scarlett's flowers and balloons
from the hospital right here." She grabs the handle on a cart
and pulls it into view. My duffel is on the bottom shelf, so
I nod.

"Come on in."

"My name is Liz, if you need anything this afternoon. And
just in case Scarlett is hungry, I've brought menus from all

her favorite places. If you just text me at this number," she whips a card out of her breast pocket and hands it to me, "I'll have someone bring whatever she wants immediately. Her prescriptions will be coming from the pharmacy shortly too. Amy said Scarlett has everything she needs for tonight, though, so those will be for tomorrow. Am I forgetting anything?"

From the way she wrings her hands, it's obvious she's nervous as hell, and I'm assuming that's because of me.

"Thanks. I'll text if she needs something. She appreciates your help, Liz."

The girl lights up like a Christmas tree. "Thank you. We all want to make sure she's comfortable."

"Doing a great job. I'll get her settled and let you know."

"Okay." She bobs her head and realizes that I've maneuvered her back to the door again. "I'll just go now."

"Thank you again, Liz."

I shut the door with her on the other side, and the house is silent for a beat. At least, until I hear Scarlett laughing.

I grab the menus, drift back toward the bedroom, and peek inside. *Fuck, she looks incredible.* Even fresh from the hospital and probably wanting a shower and a change of clothes, Scarlett is a goddess.

"She would've stayed all night. She might have a minor fascination with you."

Although I meant for Scarlett to sleep, I can't help but lean against the doorjamb and just stare at her. "Is she the only one who *might* have a minor fascination with me?" I don't flirt. It hasn't been part of my DNA for over fifteen years, but somehow, the words come out anyway.

Scarlett's face flushes just like I expected, but her secretive grin spears me. *Fuck, I love that little devilish smile on her face.*

She drops her gaze to the blanket before she replies. "No, she's not the only one."

Her reply shoots a bolt of adrenaline through me. All it accomplishes is sending my heart pumping faster and my mind running through the exercises of my most punishing workout to keep my dick from becoming way too fucking obvious against the zipper of my jeans. But, still, I won't leave her hanging.

"I don't have a problem with that."

The mischievous smile gives way to curiosity. "What did she give you?"

I hold up the handful of menus. "Liz brought these from all your favorites, if you want to order food."

Her gaze drops to the bed. "I don't know. I'm not sure I'm feeling it."

"No hurry on food. Just take it easy. You need anything else, or do you feel like napping?"

I glance around her bedroom as she thinks about my question. It's obviously a hundred percent Scarlett's domain, and I see no trace of male influence anywhere. I don't have a problem with that either.

Even standing in the middle of frilly, fancy lace, I'm still doing mental drop sets to save myself from a raging hard-on to rival all hard-ons. It's feminine to the max, but in a way that makes a guy well aware that the room belongs to a beautiful woman. Besides, it's not all hearts and flowers and weird shit that would send a man running. Not if he's any kind of a real man, that is.

Her ex is a fucking bitch-boy. On that count, I have no doubt at all.

That's when I see it, on the table beside the bed.

"You kept my note." I push off the doorjamb and walk toward the piece of white paper only a foot from her left elbow. It sits on a stack of books, and with the worn edges, it looks like she's handled it a few times.

As soon as my words are out, Scarlett turns as red as her name. "Oh shit. You weren't supposed to see that. I mean, I meant to throw it away. But—never mind." She shakes her head and studies the poof of a blanket draped over her lap like it holds the secrets of the universe.

I make my way to the end of the bed, and after feeling around to make certain of where her feet are, I take a seat without asking. With one hand on her shins, I study her flushed face.

"I've never met anyone who blushes like you. At least, not since I was a kid."

She shakes her head and tries to cover her cheeks with her hands, but I lean forward and tug them away. "You don't need to hide. I promise I'm not laughing at you."

"It's the Scarlett curse, or at least, that's what my mother called it."

"Your mom did it too?"

She smiles. "I know, it's hard to imagine the ultra-refined Lourdes Scarlett Priest turning beet red, but she couldn't stop it either. It's not quite a family curse, but it is a little obnoxious."

"I think it's sweet."

Scarlett rolls her gorgeous gray eyes and shakes her head.

"Yeah, it is. Because it makes it easier to know what you're thinking. If it were up to you, you'd keep everyone in the dark about how you feel, but I like having a cheat sheet. You're already intimidating enough as it is. A guy needs a few advantages here and there to keep it fair."

Her blond eyebrows shoot up to her hairline. "I'm the intimidating one? Compared to you? Not a chance."

TWENTY-TWO

Scarlett

s soon as I turn the question around on him, Gabriel's teasing laughter fades away and he stares at me with all seriousness.

"Absolutely. Guys like me are a dime a dozen. Women like you are one of a kind, Scarlett."

"How about we agree to disagree?" I offer, trying to restore the levity.

Like he knows exactly what I'm trying to accomplish, he nods. "Fair enough. But I'm still surprised you kept the note."

It takes a lot of self-control not to reach over and grab the precious paper and hold it to my chest, and even more self-control to pretend I've never actually done that before.

But I have.

I know it's just graphite on recycled cardstock, but that note felt like so much more. In this digital, fast-faster, hurry-hurry-get-it-done world, no one takes the time to handwrite a note anymore. I know there's plenty of reasons why he would, but I don't care. I'm holding on to the evidence that he was thinking about me, and I'm glad it's more tangible than a text message on the screen of my phone. If I printed those out and hugged them to my chest, then I'd have a problem.

We're not there yet, though. Thankfully.

"Call me sentimental. I liked it. It felt special."

He dips his chin, and I realize it's his way of conceding ever so slightly.

"Then you'll get more notes. Give it time, ladybug."

I don't know if it's the beginnings of the lopsided grin on his face or if it's the husky tone of his voice, but *I melt.* In that moment, there's no way to pry me off the pillows or to erase the goofy grin on my face. I'm done for. Out of commission. A casualty of Gabriel Legend and his promised incoming notes.

I don't know the last time I was so freaking excited by the prospect of something so seemingly insignificant, but Gabriel has changed everything.

Even the simple things. Or maybe not simple.

Rare. Like him.

"You want to rest for a while? Or take a shower? I don't know about you, but hospitals make me feel the need to rinse off as soon as I get out of there."

In my nest of blankets, I get what he's saying completely, but I'm also exhausted.

"Give me an hour or two? Then I'll shower and eat and be ready to crash for the night. I just need . . ." I pause, but he gets where I'm coming from before I can continue.

"You're tired. I won't push. Get some rest, ladybug. I'll be here if you need anything."

He squeezes my hand, runs it down my covered legs, and squeezes my feet. Then he rises from the bed.

Again, it shouldn't be a sexy gesture, but everything about Gabriel makes me want to curl into him, soak up his heat, and never emerge.

Soon, I promise myself. *Soon.*

Two hours later, Gabriel stands in the doorway to the bathroom as steam curls out of the walk-in shower.

"You sure you have everything you need?"

"I'll be fine."

"You'll call if you need help getting out? No trying to do it yourself if it's too slippery."

"I promise."

"Okay. Then I guess you're good. Yell if you need me. I'll be right in."

A smile lifts the edges of my lips, and I don't care if he sees it. "I swear I'll be fine. I'll call out if I need help."

Even though he looks like he desperately wants to stay because he's terrified of something happening to me, Gabriel backs away from the door frame and disappears into the bedroom. As soon as he's gone, I count to thirty and make sure he's not going to reappear. When he doesn't, I acknowledge the fact that I *wanted* him to want to stay.

As soon as I'm naked, I slip into the shower and the hot steam envelops me. I let out a moan of appreciation, and before I can even open my eyes again, I know I'm not alone.

"You okay?"

I flick a glance toward the doorway and can't help but quietly giggle. He's standing there, his eyes averted, even though he desperately wants to check on me to make sure I'm all right.

"I'm fine. The water feels amazing, though. Sorry for the false alarm."

His gaze cuts to my face, never dropping south of my chin. "Glad to hear it. Just be safe, damn it."

"I'm fine, but you're welcome to stay if you're worried about me." It's definitely Bad Scarlett who pushes those words out of my mouth, but it doesn't work.

Gabriel shakes his head. "I'll be right out here. Don't forget your robe is on the chair."

He disappears again, and my smile may as well become a permanent part of my face, because I can't wipe it off.

Gabriel is an old mother hen when it comes to worrying about people. It's freaking adorable, and I love it.

Gah. This is dangerous.

Mostly because I'm not feeling as much like an invalid as I should, and I want to torture him a little. Call it my last bit of revenge for throwing me out of his office. Then again, no matter what you call it, it's going to be fun.

TWENTY-THREE

"I'm decent, but I could use some help."

As soon as her voice comes from the bathroom, I shoot out of the chair in her bedroom and my phone tumbles to the hardwood floor, bouncing on one corner and landing on the rug. *Nice.*

But I don't care about the phone. I leave it where it is and rush to the bathroom where I learn one thing—my definition of decent and Scarlett Priest's definition of decent are very, very different.

I stop short in the doorway and look to the side, but there's a fucking mirror, so I can still see her.

A very wet, naked *her*.

"I thought you said you were decent? You need your robe? I'll grab it."

Before I can figure out how I'm going to close my eyes and walk toward her without looking like an idiot, Scarlett laughs. *Fuck me*, I'd go ten rounds in the cage just to hear that sound again.

"There's a washcloth covering everything that matters.

I'm sorry my nakedness is so terrifying." The amusement in her voice is what seals it.

I drop the polite pretense and stare right at her. "You think this is terrifying? Fuck no, this is torture."

Her smile dims a few watts, and I want to learn how to turn it up again.

"Staring at my almost naked body is torture?"

I take a step toward the glass shower enclosure, deliberately letting my gaze trail down her face, to her chin, and then farther south to the tiny white scrap of terrycloth that lies over both her perfectly rounded tits. She's shielding her lower half with her hand, and I catch sight of her Steri-Strip-covered incisions.

So back to the top half I go. Her breasts are more than a handful each, but not much more, which is fine by me. My dick twitches hard against the zipper of my jeans.

"Knowing you're here and naked, and I can't fucking touch you until you're all healed up, is what's fucking torture."

That flush of hers starts somewhere under that washcloth, and with eagle-eyed precision, I watch it spread out to her collarbone, up her neck, and to her cheeks.

"Fuck me, ladybug, but you're goddamned gorgeous."

The grin disappears from her face, only to be replaced by an expression I can't read. Slowly, her fingers flex, and it takes me a few seconds to realize what she's doing—stepping out of the shower enclosure and onto the bathroom floor, without a grip on anything to keep her upright in case she falls.

"Wait, hold on—"

Her slip comes a moment later, but I'm already across the room, my arms out, ready to catch her before she can fall onto the perfectly polished marble floor.

Water soaks my clothes, but I don't care, because I've got an armful of wet, naked, beautiful woman.

Her lungs heave with the scare as I pin her body to mine, trying to keep my mind off all the places where I'm touching her naked skin.

"You gotta be more careful, ladybug." I speak my gruff words directly into her ear, and a shiver ripples through her.

She tilts her head until that gray gaze of hers collides with mine. "Are you sure? Because I think this worked out just fine."

I can't help it. I close the distance between our mouths and steal a kiss. On her indrawn breath, she gasps.

"Be careful what you start, Scarlett, because I'm always game to finish it. I'll take a rain check on this one, though. And as soon as you're healed . . . you just let me know. I'll cash that fucker in faster than you can blush head to toe."

Her tongue darts out and swipes across her lower lip, which leads me right back in to steal another taste.

"But, *goddamn*, you're sweet."

"Only for you."

Her whispered words slay me, but I have to pump the brakes, or we're both going to be too far into something we can't even think about right now.

Yeah, tell that to my dick. It's way too on board already.

I carry her to the clear acrylic chair that has her bathrobe draped open over the back of it, and wrap the giant terrycloth sides around her, covering her up. Thankfully, it only takes her a moment before she shoves her hands through the armholes and has it tied up.

"Better?" she asks with that sassy smirk.

"Yeah. Better. Now you're going back to bed. Time to pick up some takeout so you can get some rest."

I reach down to lift her into my arms again, and this time,

she doesn't protest or squeak. She throws her arms around my neck without hesitation. Like they belong there.

Because they fucking do.

I was so stupid. What the fuck was I thinking, pushing away a gift like this? Old habits die hard, though, and when you're not used to having anything beautiful in your life, you start to think you don't deserve it. That it's not for you.

And I don't deserve her. I think we're all clear on that.

But there have to be some other forces at play here, because why else would I get a second chance?

Doesn't matter now, because I'm taking it.

Scarlett's dinner is cleared away, and she's dozing in front of Chip and Joanna Gaines. I even set a sleep timer on the remote so the TV will shut off in thirty minutes.

With one last look at Scarlett's beautiful—and worn-out—face, I slip out of her room and make my way to the kitchen where my duffel bag still waits on the bottom of the rolling cart Liz brought up.

I grab it and then force myself to find the guest room and adjoining bath to take a shower. It's been a long fucking day, and yet all I want to do is park myself outside Scarlett's door so I'm close to her if she needs anything. But that's not smart either, because the memory of the pale pink of Scarlett's nipples, barely covered by the edge of that damn washcloth, comes rushing back into my brain and sends all the blood in my head to my dick.

I pretended I didn't see them when I was flipping the edges of her robe closed, but I saw them. Jesus Christ, did I see them. The visual is burned into my brain, and I may never get it out.

Fuck. I need to take the edge off.

Closing the door carefully behind me, and leaving it open a crack so I can hear if Scarlett yells, I drop my duffel on the counter and strip in the all-white tile bathroom before reaching into the stall to flip on the hot water.

I should be jumping in a cold shower to knock the punch out of my hard-on, but I can't bring myself to do it. Not when letting the thing stay untended isn't going to do anyone any good. If nothing else, it's going to cause more trouble than it's worth. So I don't think twice about sliding the glass door shut and soaking up the heat.

And if I groan when I wrap my hand around my dick, I'll just have to pray it's not too fucking loud.

TWENTY-FOUR

C hip Gaines's laugh jolts me awake, and I look around the room, trying to figure out where the hell I am. I blink twice at the TV, and it takes that long for my brain to start working again. *I'm at home. In my bed. Watching HGTV.*

The scent of steamed rice and pot stickers hanging in the room successfully jogs my memory.

Gabriel is here. You had the blandest stuff on your favorite Chinese takeout menu for dinner because it seemed like the best choice.

Which means . . . Gabriel is still here somewhere?

"Gabriel?" I say his name quietly, expecting him to pop into my room immediately, but he doesn't.

Did he leave? Maybe he was only staying until I fell asleep? No. No, he wouldn't do that. He said he'd be here. He brought a bag.

With something akin to panic racing through my veins, I toss off the blankets and crawl out of bed. As soon as my feet hit the floor, I know I should have stayed where I was, but I have to know. *Did he leave?*

Moving slowly, I pad out into the kitchen and living room, but there's no sign of him. The Chinese food is gone too. There's not even a crumpled takeout bag on the counter to signal that it was here at all.

I take two more steps toward the sink, and that's when I hear water running in the guest bathroom.

See? He's here. He's not like your dad. He won't leave you alone.

I pretend I don't know where that thought came from, but this whole emergency surgery situation is really stirring up the abandonment issues I worked through for years with my non-sex-therapy therapist. Not to be confused with the sex therapist who my ex sent me to because he said there was something wrong with me.

That still stings, but the flare of heat that ignites low in my belly as I peek through the crack Gabriel left in the bathroom doorway tells me that there wasn't a damn thing wrong with me except I was with the wrong person. Because *ho-ly hell.*

I jerk my head back, not believing I just saw what I just saw.

No, Scarlett. Don't look again. It's rude. Horrible. Awful. You'd be mortified if he did it to you.

And yet that doesn't stop me from peering through the thin gap that may as well have been left there by God himself, because I'm witnessing a freaking miracle.

Thank you, Lord, for pushing me to choose the non-frosted glass shower doors.

Because I have a crystal-clear view of Gabriel braced with his left hand on the white subway tile of the shower, and the other . . . *sweet Jesus.* The other hand is stroking his long, hard cock over and over as his hips and ass move with the rhythm.

It's the most carnal sight I've ever seen in my entire life.

My nipples peak against my robe, and molten heat burns through me. If I were a different kind of woman, who hadn't just been in surgery barely over twenty-four hours ago, I would have dropped my robe where I stood and slipped into the shower behind him.

I can picture it so vividly as imaginary me presses her breasts to his back and reaches around to slide my hand under his, so he can use my palm instead.

Oh God. Another surge of heat hits me like someone opened a blast furnace when his head dips even lower and his movements turn rougher.

My mouth waters at the way he tugs at his cock, and I envision myself sliding around his body and dropping to my knees in front of him to take it down my throat. I've never won any major accolades for giving blow jobs, and my interest in deep-throating has always been nil, but right now, I've got the urge to sharpen those skills.

My knees go weak, and I grab the doorjamb to stop myself from falling. It must have been the movement, or maybe my tiny squeak, but something catches Gabriel's attention, and his head turns in my direction. His eyes go wide and he jerks back.

"No. God. Don't stop." It's not until he turns to face me completely, his hand still stroking his cock, that I realize I spoke those words out loud, and *he heard them.*

Oh. My. God.

Mortification rolls over me, but only for a moment. Arousal drowns it out as Gabriel keeps going, his fist gripping harder and faster. His blue eyes drill into mine.

It was dark the night we were in his office, and I didn't get to see every detail and nuance of his face when he came, but I can see them now. The steam and water can't hide the moment of surprise when he realizes he's going to come. Right then. Right there. With an audience.

His face contorts and his mouth opens, and it's the most beautiful sight I've ever seen. Splatters of white hit the glass door of the shower, and I clench the door frame to keep myself upright.

His eyes close, and his forehead presses against the glass as one word is torn from his throat.

My name.

TWENTY-FIVE

"**S**carlett." It was supposed to come out as a whisper, but my groan sounds like a roar in the small bathroom. My lungs are burning, my balls have finally stopped flexing, and my dick is slightly less hard than granite in my hand.

I can't believe I just fucking did that.

She stood frozen at the door—watching. As soon as I saw her, I should have stopped. Turned around. Done *anything* except what I did.

It hasn't even been a day since she had surgery, and here I am, yanking it like a thirteen-year-old in her shower because it was the only thing I could think of to take the edge off.

But, instead, it just made it worse. Because now I want to see her face when she's coming at the same time, and I can't have that yet. She needs to heal, and I need to regain her trust after what I did.

Judging by the red-faced woman in front of me, it's going to take a few years for the embarrassment of this moment to fade away.

I rinse as fast as possible and shut the water off. Before

the spray stops, the end of a towel flips over the top of the shower door. By the time I tug the towel to my body, Scarlett is speaking twice as fast as she normally does.

"I shouldn't have seen that, and I should probably just go get back in bed and pretend this never happened, but I can't. Still, I'm sorry. I shouldn't have intruded. Clearly, you needed . . . um . . . *personal time*, and I interrupted. I apologize."

In no time at all, I scrub my body dry and secure the towel around my hips before opening the shower door and stepping out into the small bathroom. She won't meet my eyes, and that's the one thing I can't handle.

Using my thumb, I maneuver her chin to the side and up until she meets my gaze.

"I'm not complaining, ladybug. Only downside right now is that I gotta wait for my chance to see you do the same. But you better believe me, babe. It's gonna happen."

Her face was rosy before, but now it's approaching a shade of fire-engine red.

"I . . . I . . ." She blinks twice. "I don't even know what to say to that."

"You don't have to say anything, as long as you're on board."

Those gray eyes are almost hazy when she replies. "Then I guess this conversation is over."

I do a mental fist pump of victory. "Let's get you back in bed. You need some rest before you're gonna be in fighting shape."

Together, we move out of the small guest bathroom, and wearing only the towel, I follow her to her bedroom.

Once she's tucked into bed again, her lashes flutter against her cheeks and she yawns. "I can't believe how tired I am."

"Healing takes more energy than you realize. I get the feeling that you don't hold still much, but right now, that's what your body needs. Everything will still be here when you're feeling better. It can all wait."

"Okay, Dr. Legend." A note of sarcasm enters her tone.

"'Fraid that isn't going to work as a nickname either. You'll find one. Keep going." Another yawn interrupts whatever she was going to say, and I reach out to brush her hair off her face. "Good night, ladybug."

"'Night, Gabriel."

TWENTY-SIX

"Fucking piece-of-shit motherfucker."

The curse is whispered, but the voice speaking it is deep enough that it rouses me from sleep. I blink open my eyes, but I feel like my head is swimming.

Did I get hit by the extra-tired bus?

Normally, when I first open my eyes in the morning, I'm wide awake. I don't hit snooze and usually just pop right out of bed. But today should definitely qualify for snooze-button consideration. I lean over to look at the antique brass clock beside my bed.

That is dead because I forgot to wind it. My cell phone is MIA and . . .

"Fucking piece of shit. Seriously?" The whisper comes again, and I remember why I feel like hell and why there's a man in my house.

Because he's taking care of me after my surgery. The surgery I had to have after my appendix decided it didn't want to be in my body any longer.

"Motherfucker." This whisper is so low, it might as well be a growl.

Carefully and quietly, I roll to the side and wrap the robe that I slept in around me. Getting up produces a few twinges in my abdomen, so I gingerly inch off the bed until my feet finally touch the chilly wood floor. It only takes me a half dozen steps to see the source of the hushed swearing.

Gabriel.

He's hunched over a laptop at my kitchen table, and his dark blond mane is wild and sticking up at the ends like he's jammed his hands through it a dozen times. Add in the cursing, and it's enough to tell me he's frustrated as hell about something.

"Can I help?" I ask quietly.

I didn't want to freak him out, but he jolts out of his chair and spins to look at me. He's a few motions away from being in a fighting stance, so I think it's fair to say my quiet approach didn't work.

I hold up both hands. "Just me."

"Shit. Sorry," he says as his posture relaxes immediately. His hair is still unruly, though, and I want nothing more than to close the distance between us, smooth it away from his face like he did to me last night, and press a kiss to his jaw.

The fact that I most definitely have horrific morning breath is helpful in stopping me from becoming too familiar. Next time, though . . . I might as well take advantage of having him in my space.

So what if he learns he's madly in love with me and can't stay away after seeing me up close and personal in the midst of my healing glory? I could think of worse, and more realistic, things.

"You feeling okay? You want to sit down? I saw you have a shit ton of different kinds of tea. I can make you a cup, but you're going to have to tell me which kind, because I got stuck between Lemon Berry Vanilla Swirl and Fall Pumpkin Chai Spice. And just for the record, I have a dick, so I don't know what either of those things taste like."

It's a miracle that my knees don't give way, because that statement carries such an unexpected swoon factor that I'm not even sure what to do with myself. *Tea.* That's right. I need to pick some tea.

"Lemon Berry works for me. But I'll make it. No problem." I glance at the laptop in front of him, which still has the clear plastic sticker stuck to the silver lid. "Is there something I can do to help you, though? I heard you . . . being frustrated."

His gaze darts to the bedroom door and back to the computer before landing on me again. "Shit. I didn't mean to wake you up. Although I guess this is better than you freaking out after I toss this thing out the goddamned window."

I move closer and peer down at it, but I'm only giving it part of my attention, because the heat radiating off Gabriel's body steals the rest of it.

"New computer?" I inhale that woodsy spicy scent, and I want to curl into him and just soak it up, along with his natural warmth.

"Yeah, mine took a crap and Zoe bought me this one. But it's nothing like my old one, and I can't figure out how to open the spreadsheet Q sent over. I'm about out of options except for sending it back to Zoe."

I tear my attention away from the man to look at the computer again. The little apple with a bite taken out of it tells me everything I need to know. "Did you have a Mac before?"

"No. Never."

"Did Zoe ask you if you wanted a Mac now?"

He shakes his head. "She just said she was getting me

something that wouldn't get viruses so I could—" His words cut off abruptly as he pinches his lips together.

"So you could what?" I grip the back of the chair for support as I arch my back to work out a kink between my shoulders.

"Nothing," he says, staring above my head, like there's something fascinating high on the wall behind me. "Forget I said anything."

"Okay . . . but she's right. Macs are usually easier to keep running and working right, at least from my experience." Then a thought hits me, and my lips and tongue keep moving, even though I shouldn't be talking. "Oh my God, she bought it for you to watch porn so you wouldn't get viruses!"

Gabriel looks at the floor and his hair hangs forward, obscuring much of his features, but I still see the ruddy hue on his cheeks.

I keep going. Why . . . I'll never know. "It's okay. Nothing to be embarrassed about. I watch porn too. And my Mac has never gotten a virus. She was right. It's a good choice. I've never had any issues."

By the time I finally manage to get my babbling under control, heat stains my cheeks, and Gabriel stares at me with bemusement stamped on his face.

"You are something else, ladybug."

This time, I'm the one dropping my gaze. "I'll just get some tea and go back to bed. It's the painkillers. Yes, let's blame the painkillers."

He closes the remaining distance between us and cups my hip with one of his hands. "Go back to bed. I'll bring you the tea and your breakfast menu. You're overdue for a pain pill, but I didn't want to wake you. We'll get you back on schedule, though."

"You don't have to stay," I tell him, glancing at the

computer. "You have work to do. I'll be fine. Don't worry about me."

He leans forward until he's in that position that makes me melt—with his lips a breath away from my temple. "I'm not going anywhere, Scarlett. Come on, back to bed you go."

He leads me back into the bedroom and once again helps me under the covers.

"You're a pretty good tucker-inner," I say as he arranges the throw blanket over my legs and feet. "You get a lot of practice at this?"

I want to know more about his past, to know more about him in general, but that's as much as I'm willing to pry.

"Not really. But it's easy with you. At least, if you'd stay still."

One corner of his mouth tugs up in that lazy almost-grin, and it's a good thing I'm lying down because . . . *goddamn, he is a beautiful man.* Ridiculously blue eyes. Shaggy dark blond hair mixed with brown, a few months past due for a haircut, but it looks so good against his tanned skin. Gabriel Legend practically vibrates health and vitality in comparison to my invalid status.

"Before you drift off again, I'll bring in your tea and the menu for breakfast. Pick something, and I'll wake you up when it's ready. Then you can take your pills."

"You're pretty amazing, you know?"

He brushes off my compliment. "No sleeping until I have your order."

"Okay, but only if you bring your computer too, so I can try to help you set it up."

His whole face turns into a thundercloud. "No work for you."

"But I can help."

"Later."

"Fine." I roll my eyes, and his almost-grin comes back.

That makes conceding the point a hundred times better, in my book.

It doesn't, however, prepare me for the massive mug and plate he returns with on a tray. Normally, I brew a pot of tea and pour it into one of my teacups. But not Gabriel. No, that must have been too feminine for him to contemplate.

Next to the mug is a handwritten note that obliterates my heart.

Legend's Diner
It isn't fancy, but it's honest food.
Wednesday specials:
Scrambled eggs with turkey bacon
Breakfast sandwich fried egg and turkey bacon
Pancakes – Waffles – Toast – English muffin
Yogurt
The cook is also happy to make a combination of any of the above
items as long as he doesn't have to mix yogurt with eggs and bacon.
Because that would be nasty.

Never in my life have I seen something so unbelievably touching. It's all written in that same dark scrawl of the note he sent me, and I already know that I'm keeping this menu forever. I might even frame it, if I can get away with it.

"You are . . . wow. Just . . . wow." I don't know what else to say. I'm unbelievably overwhelmed at the time and care he's taking with me.

At the hospital, Gabriel told me he'd show me he meant what he said, and *oh my word,* I had no idea what that entailed.

"I can get bagels too, but I'll have to leave. Really, I can get you whatever you want from wherever you want. Just say the word." His eyes won't quite meet mine, and I can't help but wonder if he's embarrassed.

"No, no. This is amazing. I'd love some scrambled eggs, toast, and yogurt. I should be able to handle that, right?"

"I read the doctor's instructions, and they said you can go back to eating normally whenever it feels right. Google said try bland foods first, just in case. Anyway, I think all of those count."

A blanket of warmth wraps around me. "You googled it for me?"

Gabriel nods. "I wasn't going to take the chance of fucking you up after they just got you fixed. I may not be a doctor, but I know how to take care of someone."

Bump. His name pops into my head immediately, and I can imagine Gabriel taking care of the younger man after he got shot in the head. *Jesus.* The last thing I want is for him to get dragged back down memory lane by taking care of me, but he doesn't seem upset. Just . . . slightly embarrassed about the menu.

"Thank you, Gabriel. This means a lot to me."

"Whatever you need, ladybug. I'm your guy. Be back in a few."

TWENTY-SEVEN

The toast pops out of the toaster just as I slide the eggs on the plate. *Good timing.* There's a carton of strawberry yogurt on the counter, and I've been debating whether to put it in one of those fancy miniature bowls she has.

Seriously? You want to dirty another dish just to make the tray look good?

Yeah. Yeah, I do. Because this is Scarlett we're talking about. Although I'm pretty fucking sure she won't say one word about eating directly from the carton, I want to impress her, even if I'm being ridiculous.

I grab the toast and cut it diagonally. *Shit, I didn't ask her what she wanted on it.*

So I cut a chunk of butter off the end of a stick in the fridge and put it on a saucer next to twin mountains of raspberry jam and orange marmalade, also from her fridge. The yogurt goes into a little porcelain cup with handles on both sides. I'm not entirely sure what it's for, but that could be said of damn near half the dishes in her cupboards. They're old and delicate, and they fit her perfectly.

I eye the serving bowls, because they're the only man-sized dishes in the whole place. I can't help but feel gratified about that. *Scarlett doesn't usually have men in her apartment.* Fine by me.

I pick up the tray but put it right back down. *Fuck*, I need silverware, a napkin, and salt and pepper. The first two are easy, even though the napkin is cloth and pink. I guess I can be okay with the bright, cheery look it gives the tray.

Then I turn to the wall of salt and pepper shakers. And, yes, I do mean *wall*.

Christ.

I didn't notice them before when I was checking out her space. I thought it was just a wall of knickknacks, but the holes in the top of all of them help with the identification.

Scanning the shelves they're displayed on—like a shallow set of bookshelves—I try to find the most masculine-looking ones possible. I don't give a shit that the napkin on the tray is pink. I am not serving her breakfast with kitten salt and pepper shakers. *Fuck no.* I have limits, because I have a dick and balls.

Too many fucking choices. She's got snowflakes and windmills and baby birds.

Hurry up, the eggs will get cold. I drop to the next shelf. *I will not choose two giraffes that look like they're hugging at the neck. But I don't hate them either. That one giraffe has game.*

So I grab one giraffe head and tap some of the contents into my hand. Salt. Excellent. Now I just need pepper.

That's when I spot them—a cowgirl and a cowboy on the bottom in the center. I recognize the busty cowgirl from the diner a few blocks from the club. *Dolly's.*

Huh. Did my good girl steal salt and pepper shakers from a restaurant? I don't know why that thought makes me so fucking happy, but it does.

I put the giraffe back and grab the cowgirl and her man

and pop them on the tray. The red shirts don't look all that great with the pink napkin, but I don't care. I bring the entire tray into her bedroom to find the mug of tea on the nightstand and Scarlett lying back against the pillows with a small smile on her face.

"Breakfast is served." I carry the tray to her, but pause. I need something to set it on.

"I have a stand thingy. It's under the bed. I know, not a great storage space, but that's where it fits."

I nod. "Good call. Hold on."

I set the tray on the dresser near the door and drop to a knee at the side of her bed. There's a frilly white lace skirt around the bottom that I lift up, and sure enough, there are clear tubs beneath it holding holiday decorations . . . and something wooden sits on top of them.

"Got it."

I set it up on her lap and then grab the tray to slide it in front of her. "If you want anything else for your toast, I can get it. I forgot to ask."

But there's no sound from Scarlett. I tilt my head to get a better look at her face, and her lower lip is slowly dropping.

"Oh my God."

"Is something wrong?"

She shakes her head and lifts a hand to her mouth. "This is . . . no one has ever done anything like this for me before." Scarlett looks up at me, and her gray eyes shimmer through unshed tears.

"Please don't cry. I'll never cook again. I swear. Just, please, don't fucking cry."

She presses her lips together and swallows before blinking a few times. "Dammit, Gabriel. You really do know how to surprise a girl."

The widest smile I've ever seen on another human's face,

including Bump's on the day we got Roux, appears across Scarlett's lips.

"You're so fucking beautiful. Just like this."

Her eyes lift again, and this time the tears threaten to spill over. "You picked Dolly and her cowboy. And you put my yogurt in a bouillon cup. I don't even know what to say."

"I don't know what a bouillon cup is, but I'm glad you like it." I settle on the edge of her bed. "But you gotta tell me about the salt and pepper shakers. Because I'm willing to put money on the fact that you stole them from Dolly's."

TWENTY-EIGHT

I'm in complete shock that a man who is rumored to be as brutal as Gabriel Legend would put my yogurt in a *bouillon cup* and spend time picking out my salt and pepper shakers. That's on top of the awe and wonder caused by him cooking me breakfast himself.

He's full of surprises in the absolute best way possible, and I am in serious danger. My heart can't take many more gestures like this without me falling harder and faster.

Even though he said he was going to show me, I wasn't counting on it. Not this much, this soon. It hurt a hell of a lot to put myself out there and get rejected. But *he used a bouillon cup.*

Deep breath. *Don't read into it. It's fine.*

But I'm certain of one thing—Gabriel wanted this breakfast to look pretty for me, and it means a lot. More than he'll ever know.

"You pleading the fifth?"

His question yanks my mind back to where it needs to be. The salt and pepper shakers.

"I didn't steal them."

"You bought them?" One of his eyebrows goes up, and I bite my lip to keep from laughing. *Because I'm being interrogated about salt and pepper shakers, and I freaking love this.*

"No. Not exactly."

"Then you stole them."

"Flynn stole them to cheer me up after the night at the club."

His brows dart together this time. "Because of me."

I shrug. "I needed cheering up for a few reasons." Reaching for Dolly, I then tap some pepper on the eggs. "Besides, if she hadn't stolen them, I was seriously thinking about asking the waitress if I could buy them."

Gabriel crosses his arms over his chest. "And if she'd said no?"

I bare my teeth, grimacing guiltily. "I might have encouraged Flynn to make sure they came home with us, but we'll never know, will we?"

That flirty lopsided grin comes back to his scruffy face.

"It's now my mission in life to find you every restaurant with cool salt and pepper shakers to test your willpower and haggling skills."

Oh my God! Inside, I'm squealing, because he's talking about *a future together.* And one in which we *go places so I can lust over salt and pepper shakers.*

"I'd be okay with that." *Be cool, Scarlett. This isn't junior high. Don't scare him away the first time he shows you this side of himself.* "But I have high standards when it comes to shakers. Only the coolest and most unique make the cut."

Gabriel tilts his head to the side in the sexiest way imaginable. "I saw the lovebirds you have in there. I can do better than that. Just wait."

I fork up a bite of the eggs and pop it into my mouth. "Delicious too. I guess that means it's game on, Gabriel."

"While you eat, you're going to tell me how this started.

Because I recognize an obsession when I see one." He shifts on the side of my bed, one leg propped beside me atop my plush duvet.

I take another bite of eggs and pause. "How did you make them so fluffy? Mine always turn out flat and either chewy or too runny."

"I'll teach you when you feel better. Now spill."

He leans over on his elbow and watches me eat while he waits for his answer. I'm enjoying how comfortable he appears and how well he fits here.

"I gave them to my mom as a kid, because my allowance would only stretch so far for the holidays, and she always made a big deal about them. It became an annual thing, and sometimes even more often. The lovebirds were for Mother's Day. The giraffes were from the first trip I ever took to Africa. She loved them, or at least she said she did."

Gabriel's hand wanders to the top of my feet next to him, and he gives them a squeeze. "She wasn't pretending, ladybug. She loved them. It'd be impossible not to."

The yogurt is calling to me, and I reach for the spoon to dig into it. "I like to think she did too. And when she passed away, they all came back to me, along with this building. About a year later, Curated was born. Every time I find cool salt and pepper shakers, I snag them for myself. I can't help it. And you're right—it's becoming an obsession."

"It's a good one. You can have that come right after your obsession with me."

I gape at him, but because I'm hoping he'll tell me something about himself if I'm honest with him, I confess without hesitation.

"I only watched a few videos. And stalked your social media. *A little*. You've barely made it into obsession territory." My teasing sounds weaker the more words I speak, so I trail off to find Gabriel's expression shifting into something I've never seen before.

Joy.

It's followed by booming laughter that fills my room.

The yogurt on my spoon hangs suspended in midair while I soak him in. *God, that's a good look for him.* His head thrown back, his hair swaying, the tendons of his throat flexing.

Perfection.

When Gabriel finally stops, he smiles at me, and I know there's nothing I wouldn't do to see him laugh like that again. Every. Single. Day.

"You should do that more," I whisper before eating the bite of yogurt.

He looks at me with a bemused brow cocked skyward and his jaw slack. "Do what more?"

"Laugh. It suits you. You look good happy."

He glances down at the cowboy salt shaker. "Seems like Dolly should've been the salty one."

"Nah, women like her are too happy to be salty. But they can be spicy."

"And what kind of woman are you, Scarlett Priest?"

The kind that's falling in love with you, I think.

Instead, I say with a smile, "The ordinary kind."

Gabriel shakes his head. "That's where you're wrong. There's nothing ordinary about you. You are extraordinary in every single way. Now, eat your breakfast before it gets cold, or the cook might think you don't like it."

TWENTY-NINE

E very time I wake up, it's with this feeling that every moment that has come before is part of a dream. To be more specific, every moment that involves Gabriel Legend feels like it was all a dream.

When I open my eyes, I glance around my room, looking for signs that the conversation we had about salt and pepper shakers wasn't a figment of my imagination. But there's no sign of the breakfast tray. Just a glass of water on my bedside table . . . and the menu.

He was here. It was real.

As I stretch and yawn, I ignore the twinges from my incisions and focus on the warm feeling building in my chest. Gabriel Legend is good for my recovery.

Sure, we're from two completely different worlds, but we can work. Right? Because if we can't, I need a sign now because I'm already headed into too-far-gone territory.

I wait a few seconds, but there's no sign from the universe. *Okay, then. Good talk. I'll take that to mean we're all set. Smooth sailing from here on out.*

It may sound naive, but in my experience, optimism has never been a terrible thing.

Carefully, I get out of bed, stop in the bathroom to take care of business, and then peek out into the living room and kitchen. The warm feeling grows as soon as I see his blond head bent over his laptop at my kitchen table.

"I didn't hear any swearing this time, so I'm taking that as a positive sign."

Gabriel whips his head to the side to look up at me and then pops out of the chair. "Shit. I was going to help you out of bed when you got up. I got sucked into trying to figure out this damn thing again."

"I appreciate the thought, but I can get up on my own."

I carefully tighten the belt on my robe, which is apparently my new favorite piece of clothing, and walk toward the table to pull out a chair. When I'm seated beside him, I hold out my hands and waggle my fingers at him.

"Let me try. I'm pretty good with computers."

His blue gaze cuts from me to the laptop and then back to me again. "You don't need to be working. You need to be resting."

"Trust me, this isn't work. I'm helping my . . . friend." I stumble over the last word, and the tension that seems ever present in Gabriel's face fades.

I wanted to say boyfriend, I tell him silently, but his expression is unreadable. I didn't mean to friend-zone him after everything, but I chickened out.

He swallows and clears his throat. "I'm not used to having many *friends* who are willing to help me with no strings attached. Thank you, though."

He pushes the laptop across the table so it sits open in front of me while my heart cracks.

How could this man not have friends who are willing to do him a solid without expecting something in return?

I don't know him as well as I will, but even after the last few weeks, I get the sense that he's a fiercely loyal man. Once someone is in his circle, I'd be willing to bet that there's nothing he wouldn't do for them. Maybe that's why he keeps his circle small—*because* he's ferociously devoted to them. Once someone is in, they have the power to hurt him. It makes sense now that I put the pieces together.

I stare blankly at the laptop as I complete a small corner of the puzzle that is Gabriel Legend. The fact that he has to be so guarded sends a slice of pain through me.

But aren't you the same way? It's that pesky voice in my head, and she's right.

I am guarded with people who I think are trying to get close only because they want something from me. I keep my tribe at minimum capacity because my mother taught me from a young age that I have things others want and are willing to behave unfairly to get . . . and I've been burned more than once before.

It's a harsh lesson, but one that seems he and I shared in learning.

"Scarlett?"

Gabriel's voice brings me back to the present and out of my head.

"Sorry, I was off on a tangent." I lift my eyes to his. "I get lost in my head sometimes. Not daydreaming, just . . . thinking."

Instead of nodding and moving on, he does something that surprises me. He pulls his wallet out of his pocket and peels off a stack of twenties and sets it in the middle of the table.

"What is that for?"

"I don't have a penny, which is fine, because your thoughts are worth a hell of a lot more."

After blinking at the stack, I look back at him and stare in wonder. "You want to know what I'm thinking about?"

That new ease in his features, the one that lets the corners of his mouth rise into an almost-smile, slays me. "Of course. You're the most fascinating woman I've ever met."

It's a miracle I don't liquify right there on the chair. Instead, heat starts at my chest, and I can almost pinpoint my spreading blush. With a smile stretching my mouth, I press my lips together.

Finally, I say, "No one's ever asked me about my tangents, not since my mom."

"Their loss. You gonna tell me what made you look like you wanted to punch someone and then get so sad?"

Gathering my courage, I nod. "I was thinking that it sucks that you don't have many people who will do you favors without strings attached. Then I realized I keep my inner circle small too, because my mom taught me young that people would try to take advantage of me, and I couldn't trust everyone."

"Some things shouldn't be the way they are, but that's life. Anything else?"

"I was thinking that I'd be willing to bet money that you're extremely loyal, and that's why you're guarded when it comes to getting close to new people. That kind of loyalty isn't something you can spread all over town."

He leans back in the chair and rocks his square jaw before replying. "Small circle means less exposure. It's about risk and survival."

"I hate that you have to worry about survival." The thought comes out so quickly, that I don't have a chance to reflect on how entitled and privileged it sounds until after it hangs between us.

"Not everyone grows up in an ivory tower, ladybug, but

that's life. That's the way it has to be. If it were fair, it'd be the most boring fucking experience ever."

I couldn't agree more with him. "I've never heard someone put it that way."

"Probably because I'm not a philosopher, and it's been a day or so since I've slept."

I can practically feel my eyes bug out at his statement, and guilt rushes in. "You stayed up all night for me. You should go home. Go to bed. *Sleep*."

He sits up and leans his elbows on the table. "I'm used to it. Besides, I'd rather be here making sure you've got what you need, than at home trying to sleep while Bump plays video games way too loud on the other side of the wall."

"Where do you and Bump live? I just realized I never asked. I'm such an asshole." I drop my head into my palm and face him.

Gabriel reaches out and uses his fingers to lift my chin. "You're not an asshole. Trust me. We haven't exactly done any of this the normal way. Besides, we live in Jersey. Not much to talk about." He points one long finger at the screen in front of us. "You really think you can get this laptop to work? Because I've downloaded this spreadsheet a dozen times, and it keeps trying to open some weird program I don't know anything about."

Taking the hint that he doesn't like talking about himself much, yet thankful for the glimpse into his life, I turn my attention to the laptop and crack my knuckles for effect. I've never used my computer skills to impress anyone, but I'm ready to rock it now.

"Of course I can. Give me a few minutes."

THIRTY

I shouldn't be so fascinated with watching Scarlett work, but I can't help it. Her fingers move so gracefully over the keyboard rather than the hunt-and-peck style of typing I've adopted. Hell, I'm just proud of myself for being computer literate at all.

It's not like I went to a school that had resources. None of my foster homes had computers either, so I didn't have much of a chance. It wasn't until I got it in my head that I was going to open a club that I realized I'd have to learn or I'd never reach my goals.

So I had Q hire me a tutor—his youngest sister. That's how Zoe ended up working for me. The youngest female Quinterro is a math geek and a computer nerd, which is in total contrast to his other sisters, who both snagged their husbands the old-fashioned way—beauty, food, and sex.

Zoe has always been completely uninterested in men, as far as I can tell. But, then again, she doesn't seem interested in women either. Hell if I know where her preferences lie, and I don't really care.

The only woman whose sexuality actually matters to me is the blonde I'm with.

When Scarlett turns the laptop around, I see the damn spreadsheet that's been locked down like Fort Knox is open.

"How the hell did you do that?"

"You needed a license for Microsoft Word if you didn't want to use Apple's programs, so I set you up with a thirty-day free trial. You'll have to pay for it when it expires if you still want to use Excel. It's kind of a racket, but there's really no other option, if that's what you're familiar using," she states so matter-of-factly. As if it's totally common knowledge.

"Thank you. I appreciate it," I tell her as my attention gets sucked in by the numbers.

They're better than they were, but they're not where they need to be, according to any of the projections Q and I have put together. We made this month's payments to all the investors, *barely*, but operating costs are going to eat up the rest of the cushion we thought we were going to have.

We submit monthly financial statements to the investors, and I know they're not going to be happy when they see the latest one. But more customers means more staff than the skeleton crew we were running on after the shooting and before Scarlett.

"Is everything okay at the club? Do you need me to come back and help bring more people in?" Scarlett asks.

I have two choices—lie to her or tell her the truth. Well, I guess there are really three choices. I could also sugarcoat the truth and make it sound like we're in safer territory than we really are. None of those choices are perfect, but I know saying *don't worry about it* is the absolute wrong way to go.

Pushing off the table, I rise and head for the fridge to grab her a bottle of water and one for myself. I hand hers off and crack the top on mine.

"We're heading in the right direction, but not fast enough. The lull after the shooting meant that all the cash we'd set aside for a rainy day is gone. We don't have a cushion right now, and it makes Q nervous as fuck."

Holding her palm against her stomach, she slowly eases herself against the chair back. "What are we going to do about it?"

I huff at the word *we*. Scarlett is a fixer. *Like me.* She would have to be to do what she did for me and the club. I still don't know why she didn't call the cops after Bump grabbed her, but it must have been her fixer nature that had her charging to the rescue like the cavalry back in the olden days.

"I'm not sure yet. I have a few options, but none of them are great."

Concern etches lines into her brow that I don't want to see there. "Like what?"

I'm even more tempted to shut the subject down, but I don't. If there's a chance in hell that I get to have Scarlett Priest in my life, I can't keep her locked outside. She has to know what she's getting into with me.

Well, to a point. She doesn't need to know *everything*. Especially not about the mess I left in Mississippi. Not yet.

"Go back to fighting. I can make quick cash, and that's what we need. Just enough to tide us over. A few fights. One big one, maybe."

Scarlett's lips press together, and I wait for her reaction. It's not a test, but it sure as fuck will tell me a hell of a lot about whether I'm crazy for thinking we can make this work.

"You're going to fight Bodhi, aren't you?"

I'd almost forgotten she knew about the bad blood between me and Black. And that the motherfucker is still her self-defense instructor.

"I don't know, but if the number's right, it might be the

best chance I have to dig out of this hole." As soon as I say the words, something else hits me.

The woman sitting next to me at the table probably has enough money that she could bail out my club without thinking twice or even feeling a financial pinch. *And I would never, ever let her fucking do it. It might fucking kill my pride even to hear her suggest it.*

She opens her mouth, and I hold up a hand.

"I'm not trying to be rude, but if you're going to offer anything other than your beautiful face showing up in my club to help bring customers in, please don't. I won't ever take your money, Scarlett. Not fucking ever. That's not the kind of man I am. It's not why I'm sitting in your house right now, and that is one thing that will never fucking change." I meet her gray gaze and make sure she understands. "I'm here for you. Nothing else. Get me?"

Her lips press together in a flat line as she blinks up at me. "I get you. But I would never insult you by coming in and throwing money at your problems to fix them. Still, you have to understand where I'm sitting, Gabriel."

She pauses and sucks in a breath, like she's gathering the courage to finish. I give her space, and she speaks again.

"It terrifies me to think of you stepping into a cage with a man who teaches me how to kill people. I didn't just get a second chance at having something *real* with you to lose you just as fast."

Fuck.

My chest. It feels like I'm having a goddamned heart attack.

But I'm not.

I'm falling for this woman who I have no business bringing into my life.

Then why the fuck are you sitting at her kitchen table, asshole? I thought we already made this decision. You're in this. Now stop being a fucking pussy and man up. It's that fucking conscience of mine, and it's right.

Our gazes collide and hold for long moments, and I give her the most honesty I can.

"There are no guarantees in the cage. Once a fight starts, all you can do is trust the skills you've spent years honing."

"But, Bodhi . . . he's—"

"I beat him once," I tell her with all seriousness. "And if I fight him again, I'll beat him. *Again.* I won't have a choice. That fight will be do or die."

Horror contorts her face, and I could rip my own fucking tongue out for saying it. *Jesus Christ, man, she's recovering from surgery. This is not how you handle shit. Keep it light.*

But Scarlett doesn't dissolve into tears. I should have given her more credit, just like I wish she'd give it to me.

"Whatever you decide, I'm done training with Bodhi. But you have to promise me one thing."

"What?"

"If there's anything at all I can do to help, without straight-up offering money, you will ask me. I might have been raised in an ivory tower, but I do understand the real world, and there are things I bring to the table that can be helpful."

She's right, and the promise should be easy to make, but my basic instinct is to keep her safe.

"I'll make you a deal, ladybug. If there's anything you can do to help that won't put you or your business or your reputation at risk, then I'll ask you. That's the best I can offer right now."

She holds out her hand, looking adorable with her rumpled hair and wearing a robe, but her handshake offer is official as fuck. "I'll take your deal, bossy."

A chuckle escapes my lips as I pretend to spit in my hand before I take hers to shake.

Her eyes are like saucers, but she doesn't flinch and repeats the motion into her palm. Hearing her fake spit for a good-old-boy handshake might be the cutest fucking thing I've ever seen.

But it's official now, so we shake.

"Good. But *bossy* is never going to stick."

Her smile couldn't be wider. "It might. You never know."

THIRTY-ONE

Scarlett

The next time I wake up and slip out into the kitchen and living room, I stop short in the doorway. Flynn is laid out on my sofa, her phone in her hand and headphones over her ears. I scan my apartment, but there's no sign of Gabriel.

What? Like you thought he was moving in and staying forever?

I'm not a fan of the reality check.

I call Flynn's name, but she's oblivious. I walk closer and wave both arms over my head, wincing at the stretch. *Bad plan. Don't do that again anytime soon.*

Flynn jerks off the couch, her headphones fall off her head, and her phone goes flying. "Jesus Christ, you scared the hell out of me. What was that about? Are you practicing standing on top of a building waving down a rescue helicopter or something?"

"What are you doing here? How did you get in?"

She rolls her eyes at me before she drops to her hands and knees to fish out her phone from under the couch. "Legend. Although Amy would've let me in. We bonded at the hospital.

I'm pretty sure I could rob you blind now, and she wouldn't even raise an eyebrow."

She continues rambling about something, but my brain is stuck on her first word. *Legend.* He let her in.

"He left?" I ask, interrupting her.

"Well, yeah, Scarlett. The man does have a club to run. He said something came up at work when he texted. He didn't want you waking up alone when he left for a few hours, and since I don't have class again until tomorrow at eleven, I said no problem. But, I have to say, your couch might be cute, but it's uncomfortable as fuck." She stretches her neck from side to side. "I almost crawled in bed with you, but judging by your response to finding me in your living room, I'm guessing that would've scared the piss out of you."

"Good choice," I tell her, but inside, I can't help but think the only person I want to wake up and see in my bed is the man who had to leave. The image of a tousled blond head on the pillow beside mine rises in my brain, and I'm in no hurry for it to leave. *What a way to start a day.*

Flynn, unfortunately, doesn't know that.

"Did you know that there's a scientist who is starting to think the appendix might have some kind of use? Better hope it's not true, because you'll be fucked."

"Thanks, Flynn. That's exactly what I want to hear right after they took mine out."

She shrugs. "Yeah, I know. But it's better than the alternative, which would have been it rupturing and you dying a long, painful, disgusting, agonizing—"

"I get the picture."

I release a long sigh and remind myself how grateful I am to have her back in my life. I've even written about her in my gratitude journal a few times lately, because it's so nice to feel like I have family again.

And that thought brings me back to a shitty one I don't

want to think about—my father still hasn't tried to see me. At all.

"What's wrong? Are you thinking about your bunk appendix?"

I glance up at her and hit her with full honesty. "I'm thinking about how it sucks that my dad doesn't give a damn about the fact I just had surgery."

Flynn's face lights up. "But he does! He did. He called!"

"What? When?"

"While you were asleep. Your phone was out here. I saw his name come up on the screen, so . . . I kind of answered it."

Oh Lord. I send up a silent prayer as I ask her, "What did he say? What did you say?"

Flynn's lips pinch together, and I know guilt when I see it. "Flynn . . ."

"Look, I just told him the truth—that he was a garbage human for not coming to the hospital when you were having surgery. I also might've mentioned that he was a super piece of shit for not sending flowers or calling to check on you sooner."

"What did he say?" I brace, because my father doesn't like being reminded of his shortcomings.

"That he was busy, and you would understand because, unlike his ungrateful former stepdaughter, you are an adult who gets that there are sometimes *business matters* that must be handled before personal ones. He also said, and I quote, '*Scarlett can handle herself. She doesn't need her father holding her hand anymore.*'"

"He never held my hand," I say quietly, before turning around so she can't see the pain on my face.

"Oh shit, Scarlett. I'm sorry. He's a fucking asshole and a shit dad, and I wish I could change that for you. At least he's around sometimes, though. I haven't seen my dad in fourteen years. I don't even bother to Facebook stalk him anymore because he looks so happy not having me in his life. I fucking hate him for that." By the time Flynn finishes her statement, she's standing in the kitchen with her arms wrapped around my shoulders in a hug. "We can make voodoo dolls and stab them, if it'll make you feel better. I may or may not know where to get the scary shit that makes it work for real."

I lean against Flynn for a moment, soaking up the sisterly affection. It's something I'd wanted for years, until my first stepsister, Martina, turned out to be a manipulative monster who my mother wanted to strangle on my behalf. I stopped going to my father's house during the days he was supposed to have custody, but he never complained or really even seemed to notice.

I got the message loud and clear, Dad. Reinforced over and over again until there's no chance of me misunderstanding. I don't matter to you at all.

"Let's put the brakes on this pity party and get you some food, okay?" Flynn says, releasing her grip on me and meeting my eyes.

"Sounds like a plan. What are you making?"

Flynn chokes out a laugh. "Like I know how to cook? I grew up a rich kid in Manhattan. Takeout is my life. But I can find some home cookin' and pretend I made it, if that makes you feel better."

I can almost smell it. "Mashed potatoes do sound really good right about now."

"I know exactly the right place. I drowned myself in their fried chicken after this stupid frat boy tried to humiliate me in class because I wouldn't give him head in the library."

My mama bear instincts rise to the surface with a vengeance. "What's his name? I will ruin his life."

Flynn stares at me, blinking over and over for a few beats. "You . . . you'd do that for me?"

She sounds so young and surprised, that my heart hurts

for her. She didn't have a good mom, and I should know, because her mom was my stepmother too.

I wrap an arm around Flynn's shoulders. "We're family, Flynn. Nothing changes that. I'll always have your back."

Her smile could light up the entire city. "I'm really fucking glad that limp dick of an ex-boyfriend sent you to my therapist's office."

"Me too, kid. Me too."

THIRTY-TWO

As much as I'd rather be at Scarlett's place instead of the club, I don't have a choice. Q called and said Rolo showed up and wanted to see me. When Q told him I wasn't around, Rolo made a scene, accusing me of dodging him and generally being a bitch.

Not in my house.

So here I am, walking into the club wearing ripped jeans and a black hoodie, something that wouldn't meet our dress code, but I don't give a damn. If Rolo wants to call me out, he can do it to my face, and I don't have to worry about fucking up one of my very few suits when I beat the shit out of him.

Except I should have known better. I should have known Rolo wouldn't dare step up to me in person. Instead, he's all smiles when I walk into the VIP section where Q put him to shut him up until I could get there.

"Man, it's been weeks, and you haven't answered my texts. I've been working my ass off to put together some action for you, but if you're going to keep blowing me off, I'll work my ass off for someone else."

"I didn't ask you to do anything, Rolo."

He leans back against the leather bench seat and gives me a chin jerk. "I know you, Legend. Better than most of the assholes in this town. You need cash, and I'm your man. So, why not get rich together?"

He's sold me before using the same speech, but I'm not the same man I was back then. Something Rolo doesn't know and will probably never realize. But . . . I still need money. Once the investors review the most recent financial statements, phone calls are going to start coming in, and I'll have to answer for the disappointing numbers. But Rolo doesn't know that, and I'm not going to let him see me sweat. Not a chance in hell.

"I'm out of the game, Rolo. No more underground fights. I'm not living that life anymore."

Rolo leans back, and he fucking *laughs.* "Guys like you don't get out of the game, Legend. They live it until the end when they die in it. You may think you're better than me now, but I've heard the rumors. Your club is struggling. You need help."

Rage burns through my veins.

"You don't know shit about my club, and if you're the one spreading those rumors, you and I can step into the cage *together* and sort it out."

Rolo holds up one hand and backpedals. "Damn, man. Must be worse than I heard. I didn't mean to poke a sore spot. I'm just here to help. I didn't start any rumors, but that doesn't mean they ain't out there. Like the one about Black wanting his rematch bad enough that he's willing to fuck up your life to get it."

The fury I'm feeling turns ice cold as I reach out and grab Rolo by the collar of his shirt. "What the fuck are you talking about?"

All remaining traces of humor disappear from the man's face. "Hey. Chill out. Don't shoot the messenger."

My molars grind together as I'm filled with the urge to shake the answers loose, but I don't release my grip. "Tell me what the fuck you meant."

"Rumor has it Black could've had something to do with the shit that went down at the club. I didn't hear much. Just a whisper."

I let go of Rolo's shirt, and he slumps against the seat. "Where the fuck did the whisper come from?"

"I ran into Black's buddy, his cutman, on the subway coming back from Brooklyn. He didn't say much. Just that he wanted the fight, bad. You can make a fuck ton more from a grudge match because of the hype. You know it. I know it. Let's make it real and cash the fuck in."

I don't answer him. There's nothing left to say. I get up and walk the fuck away.

"Legend. What the fuck?" Rolo yells after me, but I keep going. "Gabriel! Wha—"

He finally goes silent when I disappear through the hidden glass door. I don't turn around to see his face, but I can picture him gaping after me.

I don't give a shit.

If Bodhi Black did anything to fuck with my club, he's going to answer for it. I've let the need for revenge against Moses Buford Gaspard eat at me for fifteen years, and I'm not doing that again.

It's time to handle shit.

THIRTY-THREE

Scarlett

I'm stuffed after the pint of mashed potatoes I managed to devour, and now Flynn and I are laid out on my bed, flipping through our phones and comparing social media feeds.

Hers is all cars, exotic locations, and dark-haired men with tattoos, while mine is light, fun pictures of families, design, decor, flea markets, auction houses, secondhand stores, fashion, and fitness. We couldn't be any more different if we tried.

"You really follow these families, people don't know, like they're celebrities?" Flynn still can't get over my obsession with my favorite hashtag, *#LifeIsMessy*.

"Why should I care more about what celebrities are doing than real people, living real lives?"

Flynn gapes at me like I'm nuts. "Uh, I don't know. Maybe because first, you are a celebrity, and second, they're your biggest clients."

"Which is exactly why I follow all the stuff they don't know about so I can show them what they want."

"That seems unbelievably backward."

My phone buzzes with a text, and I'm surprised to see it's Christine, my financial advisor. Then I remember the time difference—she's in California.

CHRISTINE: *You up for a call tomorrow? Ryan and I have been trying to hold off. He really wanted to bring the gift basket to the hospital personally, but I wasn't sure you'd want even more company than you already had.*

SCARLETT: *You know I love you both, and having it delivered was more than enough. My schedule is wide open. Amy has banned me from working until next week.*
CHRISTINE: *Good, then you'll have time to catch us up on what the hell is going on with you. Ryan's worried.*
SCARLETT: *You mean you're worried and passing it off on Ryan because you don't want me to know you have feelings?*
CHRISTINE: *My heart is black. I'll text with a time in the morning. Take care and heal fast, Scarlett.*

I send one last reply with a dozen heart and kissy faces, which will make her throw her phone down in disgust. Christine doesn't do emotion. She lives for the numbers and hard facts.

The sound of a car engine revving from Flynn's phone steals my attention. "What are you watching?"

"Race videos. Want to see me kick some ass?"

My head jerks back and I stare at her in surprise. "You post videos of your races online? They're illegal, Flynn! That is the *dumbest thing* you could possibly do. It's like robbing a bank and posting a picture of the money!"

The side-eye I get from my former stepsister borders on legendary.

"Do you really think I'd take a risk like that? I'm not stupid. Ever since boarding school, I've worn a black helmet with a bandana over my mouth and nose under it, so I'm totally anonymous, even when I flip the visor up. No one knows who I am in real life. They only know me as the Black Widow."

I drop my phone on the bed and dip my forehead to rest against my raised fingers. "You didn't just say that."

"Sure did. And no, I didn't give myself the nickname. I'm not that arrogant. Some asshole did after he lost his GT-R to me. It had a stage three Cobb tune and everything. He was *pissed*."

I don't know much about cars or what a stage three anything is, but I know a Nissan GT-R isn't an inexpensive model to start with.

"What did you do with it?"

Flynn smiles. "Sold it. I told you, that's what I do with almost all of them. It's not like I could afford to keep them all in Manhattan, but I am thinking about renting some space over in Jersey. It's been heartbreaking to sell some of these beauties. At least my broker gets me good deals."

I pinch the bridge of my nose under my glasses. "I don't know what to do with you."

She leans over and rests her head on my shoulder. "Just love me for the awesome badass I am."

I slide my arm around her to squeeze her against me. "You know I do."

"I know. So, tell me about Legend. Is he really hung like a stallion?"

THIRTY-FOUR

I find myself walking the streets of Manhattan again with Roux at my side. Sometimes, it's the only thing that can calm me down.

The wrath I felt as I was leaving the club carried me all the way to the building where Bodhi Black trains his celebrity clients. *Including Scarlett.*

I know she said she wouldn't go back, and that's a damn good thing, because there's no way I'd let that shit fly now. Before, it was just bad blood. But now, if there's a chance he risked the lives of innocents just to ruin my club and push me into a fight, she will never breathe his air again.

If she wants to keep training, she can train with me or someone I handpick.

But since it's after eleven when I arrive, the building is completely dark. I look down at Roux. "What the fuck do we do now?"

Not surprisingly, she doesn't have an answer for me, just tugs at the leash, so we keep walking. I don't have any particular destination in mind, but somehow we end up at the gym near the club.

Like anything else open twenty-four hours in Manhattan, it's never empty. Through the windows, I see two guys in one of the rings and a half dozen more punching bags or jumping ropes.

I have two choices—turn around and spend all night trying to walk off the anger that's riding me, or get it out a hell of a lot faster by hitting the bag until I can't lift my arms.

Roux nuzzles my leg, and I pat her head. "You choose, baby. What do you want to do?"

Like she can understand, she licks my hand and tugs at the leash as she takes a few steps toward the door.

"All right. I hear you. You're telling me I've been slacking and missing workouts, and I need to get my shit together."

Her tail wags, and I swear to God, my dog is more intelligent than most people I've met.

Together, she and I walk into the gym and make our way to the lockers, where I keep extra gear in the locker I rent. I tape my wrists and wrap my hands before tugging on my gloves. I'm halfway to the heavy bag when a familiar voice calls my name.

"Yo, Legend. Haven't see you in a while. Been waiting for that chance to spar."

I turn my head to see Silas Bohannon slowing his jump rope until it stops. The last thing I want to do is make small talk right now, but I give him a nod anyway. "Been busy."

"Yeah, I saw you got a few important people stopping at your club these days. Shit doing better?"

"Doing all right."

From my short answers, there's no way he can miss that I'm not here to chat, and his next sentence acknowledges it.

"You wanna spar rather than talk? Because I'm getting the sense that you're fucking pissed off right now, man."

"Now isn't the time to get in the ring with me," I tell him, by way of warning.

A slow smile spreads over his face. "You agree to pads, and I'm in. I just might learn something you'll see show up in a movie."

"You got a death wish?"

He laughs this time, and I can't figure this fucking guy out. "No. But I'm a hell of a lot better than you think. Let's do it."

I pound my gloves together. "Fine, but it's your funeral."

Bohannon walks to his locker and starts pulling out pads. "Just try not to fuck up my pretty face too bad. My shooting schedule is packed."

Even though I know it's a terrible idea, I go back to my locker, give Roux a few scratches where she lies in the corner, and grab the rest of my gear. Once I've got my pads strapped on, I adjust my chin strap and glance at Bohannon.

"Last chance to back out."

He shakes out his arms and bounces on the toes of his bare feet. "Let's do this."

"Fucking crazy bastard."

I lift the ropes and slip between them, then do some stretching and shadowboxing. I know I shouldn't spar without warming up properly, but my blood's already pumping from Rolo and the miles I walked with Roux. Besides, our skill levels are wildly different. There's no way Bohannon will beat me, which I'm pretty fucking sure he knows too. Guess we'll find out for sure in the next few minutes.

We meet in the middle of the ring and touch gloves.

"Clean fight. No low blows, eye pokes, or other bullshit," Bohannon says.

"Afraid to fight dirty?"

"Against you? Fuck yes. I'm not stupid, and my manager would fucking kill me for stepping into the ring with you."

I narrow my eyes at him. "Then why the fuck do I have pads on in this ring right now?"

Bohannon grins. "Because I'm a grown fucking man, and I do what I want. Let's go."

He bumps my gloves again, and we bounce away from each other.

As soon as he throws the first punch, I'm transported to a different place. A different headspace. All the bullshit with Rolo and Bodhi Black falls away. It's only me, Bohannon, and the four rope sides of the ring. A ring I'm not leaving without a submission from him, because that's the only way I can end this session and not feel bad about fucking up a movie star. But, first, I'll soften him up.

Bohannon catches me in the pad at my cheek, and it lights the fire in me.

God, I've fucking missed this feeling.

My hands move of their own accord, popping out combinations.

Jab, jab, cross.

Bohannon's head flies back when I connect.

Jab, jab, hook.

Bohannon bobs and weaves out of the way, and I go right to the body, landing two strikes before he can throw a kick that slaps against my thigh.

After two minutes, I have a new respect for the man across from me, but I also know there's no fucking way he can win. He telegraphs his moves, making himself predictable. This session will last until I end it. I throw a few more combinations, then a low kick.

We go on for another minute, trading punches and kicks, and my head clears.

God, this feels fucking good.

I've spent so much time this last year getting the club up and running, trying to keep my promise to Jorie and become the man she wanted me to be, that I've forgotten parts of the man I *am*.

I might be able to walk in both worlds, but this is what I know. This is what I'm good at. When everything else is going to hell, I can always step into a ring or a cage and find my footing.

Scarlett said she watched those videos of me fighting. It scares her, but she likes it.

As soon as the thought of her enters my brain, Bohannon catches me with an uppercut that sends spit flying out of my mouth.

He grunts in victory, and I throw myself back into the fight.

It's ending on my terms. I unleash a flurry before shooting for a takedown.

Bohannon isn't ready for it, and he lands hard on the mat while I overtake his guard with little effort. I could rain down elbows to ground and pound the fuck out of him, but I remember what he said about his face, and I'm not a dick. Instead, I do something completely unorthodox. I spin around, grab his leg, and lock it up until he taps.

As soon as I release the submission hold, Bohannon's head flops on the mat.

"Damn, man. I didn't see that shit coming. You gave up mount to get me to tap on a leg bar? Seriously?"

I shrug, breathing harder than I was while we were fighting. "You have to be ready for anything in the cage."

Bohannon sits up and I rise to my feet, offering him a hand. He takes it and stands. "I guess I should just be happy you didn't get me in a heel hook like you did Bodhi Black. I heard it took a year for him to get back in fighting shape after you tore up his knee."

The mention of Bodhi Black's name again, right fucking now, is the last thing I want to hear.

"He didn't tap. He should've tapped if he wanted to save his knee."

Bohannon shakes his head. "You're right. I'm not saying it was a dirty move, I'm just saying it was fucking ruthless." He pauses to wipe sweat out of his eyes. "You going to fight again one of these days?"

All I can do is shrug. "Don't know."

"Well, even if you don't, I heard about something that might be a hell of an opportunity for you, if you're interested."

"A fight?"

"No, although I'm sure you can get those, no problem. This is a whole card of fights. Supposed to be happening next month at a club uptown, but the Feds just raided the place, and fight organizers won't hold it there anymore. They're looking for a venue that's high-end and exclusive. Your club would fit the bill, and I could put you in touch with the right people to throw your hat in the ring."

I put together what he's saying. "I'm not in that business anymore. My club is legit. No underground fights."

"That's the best part. It's not underground. It's fully sanctioned. Totally legal. You could easily charge a couple grand a head, if not more."

A couple grand a head or more?

Fuck. If I could fill the club for a fight at that price—or a little more—I could pay off a chunk of what I owe my investors. The club would be a hell of a lot closer to being mine, free and clear.

But that's not what Jorie would want.

As soon as the thought enters my head, I pause. *I loved her, and I've honored her wishes, but she's not here. She would want me to do what's best for me and my life, as long as I wasn't putting myself at risk.*

"A couple grand a head? Really?"

Bohannon nods. "People love watching fights, and a club like yours would be a badass location. All those pillars and shit would make it look like something out of ancient Rome."

"You've seen my club?"

"Not personally, but I've seen a ton of pictures on social media lately. Been meaning to get over there."

I lift my head to meet his gaze. "Who'd you hear from about the fight card that needs a home? Reliable source?"

"My trainer for this movie is one of the best pro MMA coaches—"

"Fucking tell me it's not Bodhi Black."

Bohannon's shoulders shake as he laughs. "No, it's not Black. He's not fighting on the card either . . . although, I bet if the two of you wanted to settle your score, in a sanctioned fight, people would lose their fucking minds. Damn, I'd pay serious money to see that."

The wheels in my brain are turning. A sanctioned fight would mean no dirty shit. While we could do significant damage to each other, the odds of either of us leaving the cage in a body bag would be slim to none.

"Let me know if you want me to pull some strings and get your club on the list of possible venues. I know people."

I can't give Bohannon an answer right now. I need to talk it over with Q, and I've learned my lesson from being way too impulsive in the past. I'm a businessman now, not a kid fighting for survival on the streets. But, still, this opportunity is too good to let slip by without letting them know we could be interested for the right price.

"Why don't you bring your people to the club later this week? Have a look around. See what they think, and we can talk it over."

"I can make that happen," Bohannon says with a nod. "I'll text you when I've got more."

I hold out my hand, and he bumps his glove against it. "Thanks, Bohannon. I appreciate that."

"Bo. And I like you, Legend. I don't know why, but I do."

I shoot him a wry look. "That's because I don't give a shit that you're a fancy movie star, and I can kick your ass in the ring."

THIRTY-FIVE

I wake up the next morning to the smell of coffee. Flynn pops her head in the bedroom, holding a steaming demitasse cup on a saucer. As happy as I am to see her, I can't help but wonder if Gabriel decided he was done playing nursemaid and went back to his normally scheduled life.

"Hey. I gotta get home before I head to class. Kelsey will be by to hang out in a little bit, but she just messaged to let me know she's running late and won't be here for an hour or so. Her client has changed her mind four times on her hair, and she's going to run way over on the makeup too."

"That's fine. I'll be okay alone. I promise I'm not going to accidentally drown myself in the bathtub or something, especially since I have to wait to be able to take an actual bath *bath*."

"You sure? Because I can easily be talked into skipping class, even though it is my favorite." She walks toward me and sets the coffee on my side table.

"Go, Flynn. I'll be fine."

"Breakfast menus are on the counter. Amy said she'll

order whatever you want. You also have a call with Ryan and Christine in a half hour, which is really why I'm waking you up. That and I didn't want you to think you'd been abandoned."

I give her a small smile, because we both know I have issues. "Thank you. I hope you got some sleep."

"Not really, but I'm used to it. I've got a date with my bed after class, unless you need me."

"I appreciate the offer, but if today is anything like yesterday, I'm going to have a date with my bed all day too. Enjoy class and your nap. Thank you again for everything." I reach for the cup and saucer and take a sip of the bitter, delicious espresso.

"You got it."

She leans down to give me a hug and then steps away. "I'm impressed you haven't asked if Legend was coming back. I mean, after you refused to spill the dirty details, I would have expected more from you."

"What do you know?"

"He'll be back. He had work stuff to handle. I put money on him showing up in a few hours, at most."

"I'm not betting against you. You'll take all my money, *Black Widow*."

She smirks. "That's only when it comes to cars, and you don't even own one."

"Then I guess I'm safe."

"Safe from me. But Legend . . . he sounded annoyed that he couldn't make it back sooner. He said he'd text you after you were awake. He didn't want to bother you while you were resting."

Warmth that has nothing to do with the coffee fills me.

"I like him, Flynn."

"I know you do, sister. Just be careful. He might seem tame, but his reputation can't be all talk."

"I'm always careful."

"Until you're not." Flynn winks. "I'll see you later."

I wave to her, lie back in my bed, sip on the espresso, and think about Gabriel. Tame or not, I'm ready because I'm finally *living*.

Unfortunately, the one thing I'm not ready for is the inquisition I get from Christine and Ryan a half hour later.

"You know I'm always on your team, Scarlett, but I'm a little concerned about Gabriel Legend," Ryan says in his trademark soothing tone. "When I asked if we needed to hire assistance for you post-surgery, Amy mentioned that Legend was spending time with you."

"Agreed," Christine says. "I didn't like you going to his club to begin with. Men like that are always looking for their next mark. It may be smart to start distancing yourself from him."

For the first time since Ryan and Christine began working for me in a professional capacity, I'm 100 percent offended by their comments.

"Excuse me?" My voice is quiet, but my tone carries a warning.

"We're not trying to tell you how to live," Ryan quickly adds because he can read me better than almost anyone. "We're just concerned about this new development in your life."

Christine doubles down on Ryan's statement to go for the kill, as per usual. "Look, Scarlett, you're a target. You know it. We all know it. I've been digging into Legend, and he is *not* a good guy. By all accounts, he's looking for a cash influx, and you're not going to be that for him."

I don't answer. The silence stretches, growing more and more awkward with every second that passes.

"Scarlett?" Ryan says my name in a gentle tone, but it

doesn't mollify my sense of being attacked. I'm not a child, and last I checked, my money was mine to use as I see fit.

"I'm trying to decide how to respond to you right now, because you're both crossing lines you've never crossed before."

"We get that it's your personal life, but—"

I interrupt Christine. "Yes, it's my personal life. And while I've been friends with both of you forever, there are certain areas of my life that I'm not discussing with you."

"Please tell me you didn't already give him money," Christine says.

"No, but I'm seriously contemplating hanging up the phone right now, so we can start this conversation over in a fashion that doesn't involve you treating me like I'm an idiot or a child."

"That's not what we're doing. We're just concerned. You've been through a lot lately, and we want to make sure that you're okay." Ryan's statements are intended to settle me down, but right now, I don't feel settled.

Christine starts again, but I tune her out for a beat as a question pops in my head.

Why am I being so defensive about this? Because they're treading into territory that's none of their business . . . or because I did think about how I could help Gabriel financially?

". . . so that's all I'm saying on the subject. We'll leave it alone if you want."

"Yes, we're leaving it alone for now. If or when I have something to report about my relationship with Gabriel Legend that would be relevant to you, I will let you know."

"Whoa. You've *never* shown balls like that before. Where is Scarlett, and what have you done with her?" Christine asks, and if it weren't for the hint of pride in her tone, it would have pissed me off.

"Next topic?"

"Have you made any progress with Meryl Fosse? I know she's on your list of goal clients, but I haven't heard you mention her in a while."

Damn, they're pulling no punches this morning.

"I saw her a few weeks ago, but no, I've made zero progress on getting her to come into Curated. After I'm back to work like normal, I'll work on setting up a meeting with her."

"She's hosting a charity gala in two weeks. They're raising funds for an addition to the youth center they've already outgrown. It's going to be a who's who event. You need to be there," Ryan tells me.

"I don't even know if I got an invite. I'll check with Amy. If I did, I'll definitely go. If I haven't, I'll stop at the charity offices and finagle one." I pick a piece of lint off the belly pillow I have pressed against my stomach as I sit up in bed.

"Good plan."

There's another moment of silence, and I know they want to mention Gabriel again, so I go there first.

"I get that you're worried about me. I do, and I appreciate it. But, please, just let me handle some things on my own. If or when I need your advice or opinions on something personal, I'll ask for them."

"She just told us where to go," Christine mumbles dryly to her brother.

"We respect you and know that you're a capable, intelligent adult," Ryan says. "But you're also like a sister to us, and I'm just telling you what I'd tell Christine."

"Aw," Christine says with blatant sarcasm. "Now I know why Scarlett is telling us to fuck off, because I'd do the same to you if you tried to interfere in my personal life. Thanks, big brother, that was very educational."

"I love you both and thank you for the goodies you sent. I

really appreciate the thought." Their get-well basket is still on the cart Liz rolled up when Gabriel was here.

"I'm just sorry we weren't there in person," Ryan replies.

"Well, my dad couldn't make it to the hospital in person or even via phone call, so you're doing better than him."

As soon as I say the words, my phone buzzes with a text, and I pull it away from my ear to check the screen.

I have a moment of panic when I see Chadwick's name on the display. *Why did I unblock him?* Oh, that's right, if something happened to my dad when they were together, I wanted to make sure he could reach me. I obviously should have waited a few more months, though.

"I'm so sorry, Scarlett. You know how we feel about Lawrence. You deserve better," Ryan says, trying to console me over my daddy issues, but I'm too sidetracked by the box on my screen and the message taunting me to click on it.

"Thank you, guys. Talk later."

They say their good-byes, but I'm barely listening as I disconnect the call and toss my phone beside me on the bed.

"What would he possibly have to say to me that I would want to hear?" I ask the empty room, but unlike moments ago, there's only my question and no voices of reason to answer.

I don't have to read it. I'm allowed to ignore it. I don't have to entertain whatever he has to say.

I remind myself of all these things, but I can't help myself. When I tap the stupid text message, the window opens.

Immediately, I wish I hadn't.

It's a photo of Chadwick and my dad. *Together.* Laughing with fishing poles in their hands.

What. The. Fuck.

. . .

CHADWICK: Sorry your dad couldn't make it to the hospital. We were having too much fun fishing in the Hamptons.

My dad didn't come to the hospital while I was having emergency surgery because he was fishing with my asshole ex-boyfriend? Tears burn the back of my eyes, and I can't hold them in. They spill down my cheeks in hot streams.

How can fishing with your daughter's ex-boyfriend be more important than your daughter?

Gut-wrenching grief for the relationship I never had with my father tears through me, doubling me over.

And that's how Gabriel finds me.

THIRTY-SIX

"Fuck, are you okay? Do you need to go back to the hospital?"

I charge into the room and drop to my knees next to the bed, terrified that something's horribly wrong with Scarlett. I have my phone in my hand, and I tap the 9 key before she looks up. It's the worst expression I've seen on her face, other than the one I put there when I told her to leave my club and never come back.

Needless to say, I never want to see it again.

"I'm calling 911. We'll get you an ambulance."

She shakes her head.

"Stop trying to power through the pain. If you're hurting—"

"It's not that," she says, interrupting me with a sniffle. "I'm fine. It's not from the surgery."

Everything in me stills. "What did I do?" It's the only other thing I can think of that would make her so fucking unhappy. *Me.*

Again, she shakes her head, but tears keep streaming down her face.

I reach out, trying to catch them on my thumbs, and I'd put them back in her eyes if I could, but they won't stop falling. I rise to slide onto the bed next to her and wrap my arm around her shoulders.

"Who do I need to kill? You give me a name, and it'll be done."

Scarlett chokes out a laugh.

"I'm serious. Whatever you need me to do. I'll do it."

She looks up at me from beneath wet, clumping eyelashes and half snuffles, half laughs. "That might be the best offer I've gotten to get me to stop crying, but you don't need to kill anyone. I'm just being a baby about the fact that my father couldn't come to the hospital because he was *fishing with Chadwick the fucking douchebag.*"

Her tone turns hysterical at the end of the sentence, and now I really want to kill the bastard. Fuck, I'd take out both of them.

Instead, I curl my other arm around her front and carefully hug her. Comfort isn't something I know how to give or receive, but I'm going on instinct here. "Your father doesn't deserve to have a daughter as amazing as you, if he's going to fish with that fucking cocksucker when you're in the hospital."

She lets out another snuffle-laugh and leans into me. "I don't get it. I don't get how your own daughter could be so unimportant in your life. It doesn't make sense."

I think of how my mother left me and walked into Charlie's Liquor and never looked back. "There are a fuck ton of parents who don't deserve the title. Trust me, my mom was a piece of work. I ended up in foster care because she didn't give a shit about me either."

I've never shared that bit of information with anyone but Bump, Jorie, and Q, but it's so fucking easy to share it with

Scarlett. The shame that always comes with it is still there, though.

Her head jerks up immediately, and her teary eyes are big and wide. "Oh my God, Gabriel. That breaks my heart. She didn't deserve you either."

She burrows into me like she belongs at my side, and I fucking love the feel of her there. Together, we lie on her bed, no doubt thinking about our respective shitty parents and feeling sorry for ourselves. But for the first time since my mother picked looting a liquor store over me, I feel less shame about her choice. Her demons were stronger than both of us.

I still want to strangle Scarlett's father, though. Even if I'd been a crappy son, there's no way in hell Scarlett is a bad daughter. She's . . . a goddamned miracle. She could have grown up to be an entitled trust-fund kid with a drug problem, blowing through her family's money before she was even twenty-five. But she's the complete opposite.

She works her ass off, cares deeply about her staff, and is fiercely loyal to her friends.

Her dad is a giant fucking asshole.

That's when I see the photo on her phone screen—two men holding up fish on a dock, both wearing sunglasses and tans that say they play more than they work.

I've already met her ex, but I memorize the image of her father. If I see either of them on the street, they're going to feel my wrath for making my girl cry.

My girl.

My gaze cuts from the picture back to the woman curled up next to me.

Yeah. That's what she is. Whether I deserve her or not, I'm not going to be another man in her life who shits all over her. It may take me years to make up for how things started, but I won't stop until I do—or however long she lets me stay in her life.

Scarlett is a gift, and even though I don't have a lot of experience with those, I'm going to treat her the way she should have been treated all along.

With respect and like a fucking queen.

THIRTY-SEVEN

I wipe the tears from my eyes and take a few deep breaths as I soak up Gabriel's strength. Despite our wildly different backgrounds, we share this harsh common ground of not being enough for our respective parents.

He brushes the strands of hair that have fallen out of my messy bun away from my face, and his blue eyes are full of compassion.

I rarely let people see me fall apart. It's another thing my mother schooled me on relentlessly. *"If you let them see you cry, they'll know how to hurt you."*

I may as well have a master's degree in burying my emotions and putting on a good front. But this time, it feels really good to feel what I feel and not try to cover it up for the sake of appearances.

"I brought you something," Gabriel whispers against my temple.

A swirl of curiosity breaks through the grief. "You didn't have to bring me anything," I reply, tilting my head to see his face.

"I didn't *have* to. I *wanted* to. Nothing fancy, so keep your expectations low."

Minutes ago, I wouldn't have believed it would be so easy to pull myself out of this crying jag, but Gabriel managed to do it anyway.

I catch a hint of excitement in his blue eyes before I lose his heat as he climbs off the bed. He disappears into the living room and returns with a paper bag in his hand.

"What is it?" I ask, my anticipation rising. I'm a gift giver by nature, so being on the receiving end is new for me.

His expression is serious when he replies. "You have to promise not to get too excited."

Too late, I think, but I excitedly nod as I try to school my features into a sober mask. From the shake of his head, I can tell I'm not pulling it off.

"Please, the suspense is killing me."

He mumbles something under his breath before holding out the sack. I grip the brown paper and peek inside.

From the top, I can see a book. But not a novel. A thinner book with dark edges. I reach inside to pull it out and blink at the cover.

Oh. My. God.

My head jerks up, and I meet his blue gaze. "You got me a coloring book?" I look back down at the cover. "Of ladybugs?"

His expression morphs into one that's almost sheepish. "I thought you might get bored. I know you've got a phone to keep you busy, but I thought you might like to take a break from that and just . . . color. Shit. It sounds stupid now that I'm saying it. I'm sorry. I can take—"

My heart is in danger of bursting from joy as I hug the coloring book to my chest. "No. Not stupid. Perfect. I love it. Thank you."

"You sure?" He sits on the edge of the bed and reaches for the bag.

I'm tempted to snatch it back in case he tries to take it, but I watch as he lifts it and spills the remaining contents onto the duvet.

Markers. Colored Pencils. Crayons.

Excited laughter bubbles up in my chest. "You have no idea how deep my love of office supplies goes. This is *amazing.*"

"Yeah?"

I reach out to tangle my fingers with his. "Yeah. Thank you so much. I don't remember the last time someone gave me a gift that was so thoughtful." I kiss his massive knuckles.

He shrugs and drops his gaze to the duvet. "It's not much. Plus, you're the girl who has everything."

I squeeze to get his attention and wait until his blue gaze lifts to meet mine. "It's perfect. Thank you, Gabriel. You have no idea how much this means to me."

"You're not crying anymore, so I believe you."

The pang of loss that hits me isn't as sharp this time, and I'm taking that as a win. "Definitely believe me, because it's true."

As we sit there, my call with Ryan and Christine pops into my head. Well, the part of it about the charity event for Meryl Fosse.

Before I can second-guess myself, I blurt out, "And I'm not the girl who has everything, because I don't have a date to this charity event, and I would really like for you to go with me."

Gabriel's head jerks back. He stares at me like he's still processing what I just said, so I barrel forward, spilling out the information.

"It's in a couple of weeks. It's hosted by this woman named Meryl Fosse. I've been trying to get her as a client for

Curated because she needs what I can offer, but she thinks I'm fake and she only does real. It eats at me because I'm terrified there's some truth to her opinion, so I need to prove her wrong."

Those vivid sapphire eyes turn to flashing thunderclouds. "You can't let her have that power over you. You don't need to prove shit to anyone."

In theory, he's right, but Meryl's words cut deep and revealed one of my biggest insecurities—does what I'm doing even matter?

"I know, but I still want to go. I want her to see that with you, I'm as real as it gets."

"I don't like her." Gabriel practically growls the words, which make me chuckle.

"Thank you for being Team Scarlett, but . . . does that mean you don't want to go?"

He's silent for almost a minute. "Are you sure you want to do this? I don't have the best reputation, and I sure as hell don't want to tarnish yours."

My heart hurts for the young boy whose mother didn't care about him the way she should have. If he'd had a mother like mine, he wouldn't wonder if a woman would be proud to stand next to him in public.

"When I said I wanted to make this real, I meant it. You and me. Out in the open. In front of God and all of Manhattan."

Gabriel takes a long, slow breath and releases it. "Okay. We'll do it, but if that bitch says one more fucked-up thing to you, I'm taking you the hell out of there."

A smile stretches my cheeks so wide that they almost hurt. "Deal. Now, let's color some awesome ladybugs."

THIRTY-EIGHT

By the time Saturday afternoon rolls around, I'm tired of being cooped up in my apartment. Gabriel watches me with an eyebrow raised.

"You're going to reorganize your nightstand again, aren't you?"

I glance over to the left at the ruthlessly organized side table and back to him. "I've got cabin fever. Time for a jail break."

"And where exactly are we going?"

I love how he says *we* like it's a foregone conclusion that he's coming with me.

Rain beats against the windows, so going outside doesn't appeal. "How about downstairs? They should've finished switching over a few rooms, and I always do a walk-through."

"Twenty bucks says you can't do it without reorganizing something." He says it with one of those almost-smiles that tugs at the corner of his mouth. I can't get enough of them.

I shoot him a wink. "That's literally my job, and I'm damn good at it."

"I think that's pretty obvious. And I wasn't making fun of your . . . quirk. It's cute as fuck. I can't imagine what you'd make of my place. You'd never leave because you'd be so busy moving everything around. Then again, I don't have much in the way of knickknacks."

All he's told me about his place is that it's in Jersey and nothing special, but I desperately want to see it. I want to understand more about this man who has spent so much of his time with me while I've been recovering.

"I wouldn't touch a thing . . . unless you asked me to." I make the promise solemnly, but the half smile almost makes it to a full smile, and it's hard not to cheer silently. In the last few days, I've gotten them out of him more and more often, and every single one is a genuine reward.

I want to kiss him while he's smiling.

I slide out of my bed, and his gaze follows me every step to the closet.

After seeing him take care of business in the shower, I haven't been able to get the mental image out of my brain. *I want him.* I swear, I've spent half of my recovery trying to figure out how to get enough alone time to relieve all the urges I suddenly have—and failed, because I'm never alone.

I'm ready to shred the doctor's orders and climb him where he stands. But the nagging twinge in my belly when I pull off my robe tells me that while most of me might be willing, another day—or hell, another few hours—worth of waiting would be wise.

I've never wanted to ignore my better judgment more.

Aside from brushing his lips over my temple or pressing them to my forehead, he hasn't even kissed me.

That ends today.

I throw on some cute lounge pants, a lace-edged cami, and a nearly sheer cashmere cardigan. It's not the sexiest outfit in my closet by a long, long stretch, but it's by far the most fashionable thing I've worn since my hospital stay.

Today is the day. I'm getting some make-out action, at the very least.

When I emerge from the closet, Gabriel is there waiting for me. Approval glints in his eyes, and I have to wonder if his head is where mine's at—getting more of each other. I'm not brave enough to say it out loud again yet, but I'm working on it.

When we reach the door in my apartment that leads to the fourth-floor office space, he pauses with his hand on the knob.

"Promise me you're not going to attempt to lift anything heavy or overdo it."

His concern feels good instead of stifling.

"I promise. If there's any heavy lifting to do, I'll make sure to call in the muscle." I use finger guns to point at the biceps stretching the short sleeves of his black T-shirt.

His lips twitch and he opens the door, stepping aside to let me pass through first. Gabriel may not have been raised by a mother who gave a damn, but somewhere along the line, he learned his manners well.

The offices are quiet, as they usually are on Saturdays. As we make our way downstairs, there's no noise or movement, and I peer into each room looking for employees.

"They must have gone to the storage units to get more inventory," I murmur as we walk into the front room that houses my favorite living room setup and leads into the kitchen.

"I'm surprised you don't have a warehouse at this point," Gabriel replies.

"It's on my list of things to do, but I didn't want to split up my employees and have some isolated in a warehouse. You're right, though—it's time. Ryan has been working on finding us space so we can expand, because we don't have any more room here."

"Who's Ryan?" Gabriel asks.

"My business advisor. His sister is my financial advisor. They're the closest thing I have to siblings—besides Flynn—and you can definitely tell by the way we bicker sometimes." I give him a quick rundown of how their dad worked with my mom, and we basically followed family traditions on both sides by continuing to work together. That, and they're damn good at what they do.

"I'm glad you have them," he says when I finish explaining our long and colorful history.

"Me too. You'll meet them eventually. Ryan doesn't come into the city as often as he used to because he's got little kids, and Christine rarely leaves LA anymore. She's become one of *those* people."

He laughs, and I start doing my thing in the front room. Tweaking setups and rearranging items to better display them on the tables and shelves. When I reach for a heavy brass lamp, he's right there, picking it up for me.

"I'm the muscle, remember?"

"Duly noted." I point to the sideboard where I want it to go. "Muscle it over there then, He-Man."

"That nickname isn't going to stick either."

Scrunching my face, I shake my head. "That's not how nicknames work. You can't just say it won't stick."

"Keep trying, ladybug."

An hour later, I'm happy with the front room, and Gabriel points to the sofa. "Break time. I'm going to get your water and pills. You're overdue."

"Bossy."

"Already told you that one was out."

"I disagree. It's a strong contender."

I stick my tongue out at his back as he heads up the stairs

to my apartment to retrieve my next dose of antibiotics, and I take a seat on the sofa in the front bay window. As soon as I lean my head on the edge and stare outside at the still-drizzling Manhattan day, I catch sight of a large hooded figure coming up the walk.

"Who the hell is that?" I ask the empty room.

The gray sweatshirt hood obscures the face, but as he comes closer, he lifts his head. *Bodhi.*

Shit. Crap. Damn.

I totally forgot to cancel my self-defense classes, and now he's *here*.

Faster than I've moved in days, I pop off the couch and rush to the door to whip it open. I have to get Bodhi out of here before Gabriel comes back down. I remember what he said—that Bodhi wants him dead—and I'm not letting that happen.

Bodhi's head jerks back when he sees me at the door. "So you are alive. I was starting to wonder. You no-show twice, and I don't even have a number to call you and find out if I'm wasting my time waiting for you to show up. Did you lose interest, or did I piss you off over protein shakes?"

Before I can reply, big hands pick me up and move me out of the doorway.

"What the fuck are you doing here?" Gabriel's voice drops to a growl as he blocks me from the entryway.

From my position at the side, I crane my neck to see Bodhi's face. Shock and rage flash across it.

"What the fuck are *you* doing here?" Bodhi seems to stand straighter, making himself inches taller than Gabriel.

"This is my woman's place, not yours. I'm asking the questions."

Bodhi's face, normally stoic, twists with contempt. "You afraid I'm going to steal her from you? Did you make her stop coming to training? You that afraid of me, Legend?

Because word on the street is you're a giant fucking pussy these days. Won't take a fight because you're afraid of getting your ass beat."

Gabriel's hands clench into fists at his sides. "We're not doing this here. No fucking way. The only thing you need to know right now is that Scarlett doesn't exist for you. Not anymore. You forget her name. Forget you ever fucking saw her face."

Bodhi's laugh comes out cruel and cold. "Keeping your bitch on a tight leash, huh?"

Gabriel's entire body tenses, and I can almost picture invisible ropes holding him back from launching himself at Bodhi for that horribly offensive asshole comment. "Watch your fucking mouth, or I'll close it with my fists."

"Hey, guys, seriously—" I try to get their attention, but the two are facing off toe-to-toe on my freaking doorstep, and neither of them is listening to me.

Bodhi glares at Gabriel. "You want to close my mouth, then take the fucking fight. We'll see who's still talking at the end. Your jaw will be wired shut, so it won't be you."

The words produce such a visceral, terrifying image in my brain that I can't stand back and let him taunt Gabriel into agreeing.

"Stop it. Both of you."

Bodhi laughs again, and I hate the sound. "She doesn't listen to you as well as she does me."

Gabriel's so still, he looks like a gargoyle. "Not one more fucking word out of your goddamned mouth. I will end you. You want a fight that bad?"

"Yeah, I want it so fucking bad I can taste it," Bodhi says, his nostrils flaring. "You took everything from me. My wife, my kid, my fucking life. I lost it all because of you."

Chills streak down my spine. I have no idea what Bodhi's talking about, but I recognize hate when I see it.

I reach out to touch Gabriel's arm. "Please, close the door. This conversation is over."

He ignores me. "Get the fuck off this street, Black. Don't come back. You'll never see Scarlett again. Go fuck yourself."

I already told Gabriel that I wasn't going back to self-defense with Bodhi, but I'm independent enough to dislike him stepping in and handling the situation for me. I've never come across this breed of man in my life, and I'm not sure how I feel about it.

"Fuck off, Legend. You're just trash who snagged a hot piece of ass for a minute. Don't get used to it. She'll drop you soon enough. Next time she wants to go slumming, she knows where to find me."

Gabriel lunges, but my hand clamps down on his arm. Like a switch is flipped, he steps back and reaches for the door handle and slams the door in Bodhi's face. Breathing heavily, Gabriel stands there, his shoulders tense, jaw clenched, and every muscle in his body poised to attack.

I dash over to the window and watch as Bodhi jogs down the walk and across the street until he disappears.

Gabriel and I stand in silence until he finally steps away from the door and faces me.

"You never see him again. Ever."

I don't know if it's the ire that started with Chadwick and his orders, amped up by Christine and Ryan telling me I shouldn't see Gabriel, but something inside me snaps.

"You are standing in *my* house, Gabriel. I'm an adult, not a child or an invalid. Whenever decisions need to be made that affect my life, *I* am the one who makes them. No one else makes them for me."

His brows dive together, and his mouth hardens. "Are you saying you want to keep training with that fucking asshole?"

"Hell no. I'm saying that I already made that decision and told you, and you didn't need to communicate it for me. I could've handled Bodhi myself. I was handling him myself, until you picked me up and moved me out of the way."

Gabriel takes a few long, hard breaths before shaking his head. "No, you don't deal with him. I'll apologize for hurting your feelings and stepping on your toes, but I'm not taking back what I did or said. Bodhi doesn't come near you. You don't exist for him. That's the way it has to be."

THIRTY-NINE

Shit. *I'm fucking up, and I can't stop because this is too goddamned important.*

Scarlett holds up her hand with one finger raised. "Let me see if I got this straight. *I'm not allowed to speak to him?* Did you not hear me tell you I'm not a child?"

I don't know how to tell her in words that will make sense and not be a total asshole about it. *Fuck.* This is harder than I thought.

"You're too important to me, Scarlett." I take a step toward her, but she shakes her head.

"No. I'm not a piece of crystal or fine china to be put up on a shelf where nothing can touch me. I'm not breakable."

But she is, my brain argues. *She's so fucking precious and delicate, and I can't fucking let someone like Bodhi get near her again.*

Something clenches in my chest, and I'm pretty sure it's my heart. I've watched her while she sleeps, and checked to make sure she's still breathing more times than I care to admit. I want to protect her from the world and everything bad in it. Is that so fucking wrong?

Looking into her blazing steely eyes, it's clear her answer is *yes*.

What the fuck am I supposed to do now?

Her chin lifts and her eyes glisten. "If you can't see me for what I am—a strong, capable, smart woman—then I don't know if this can work, Gabriel."

Fuck. Jesus Christ. No.

My jaw clamps down, and the urge to reach out and drag her to me is so goddamn compelling, I can barely stop myself. But I stand there, my arms aching to hold her, and try to reconcile my instincts with her ultimatum.

"I can't . . ." I pause to suck in a breath. "I can't hear him say those things about you without wanting to fucking kill him. It's how I'm wired. I *need* to protect you. I don't give a shit what he says about me, but I'm not the kind of man who will sit idly by while someone takes swipes at you. Those insults can't go unpunished."

Her face changes slowly as she processes my words, and I would bet she's repeating them in her head right now, so I keep going.

"You are smarter and more fucking capable than any woman I've ever met. I respect the hell out of you, Scarlett, but there are things I can't and won't let slide. It would go against everything I fucking am, and I can't cut out that part of me. It's the heart of me. You deserve respect, and if I didn't give it to you a few minutes ago, then I'm fucking sorry. I was out of line on that. But I will always demand respect on your behalf, and I will never let anyone take shots at you without answering back. That goes for him, your shit-for-brains ex, or your motherfucking dad."

She swallows, and I watch as her head dips. My stomach plummets to the floor, and everything in me goes cold and still.

This is it.

This is where she shows me the door.

Because I'm not the kind of man she needs.

When she lifts her head, tears are streaming down her face.

Fuck. This is going to hurt.

I brace myself for the pain, even though it won't help. My entire body tenses even more than it did with Bodhi at the door as she opens her mouth.

"I—"

I can't even let her get another word out. No matter how fucking rude it is, I interrupt her to beat her to the punch. "I'll go. You don't have to tell me to leave."

Her eyes widen, and a stricken expression crushes her features. "What? No!"

She rushes toward me and wraps her arms around my middle like she's planning on physically holding me in place with only her brute strength. But she doesn't need brute strength to level me. Her words do that all by themselves.

"I don't want you to leave. Jesus Christ, Gabriel. Give me a goddamned second to process this, okay? I've always fought all my own battles. No man has ever been willing to go to the mat for me, so I don't know how to handle this."

Her tears soak into my shirt, and I wrap my arms around her.

How has no man ever been willing to fight for her? She's the kind of woman who could cause a fucking riot without even trying. It's one more blindingly bright fact to show that her father was a complete and total failure at protecting his little girl, and I fucking hate that for her.

"I won't go."

She looks up at me. "You'd better fucking not. I'll just track you down and make you promise that when we're in my house or on my doorstep, I get to have a say, and you will not run roughshod over me and pretend like I'm not even here. I don't care who is at the door."

"I can't make that promise," I tell her and watch as her face crumples.

"Why?"

"Because if someone with bad intentions comes and wants to make trouble, I'm your shield, Scarlett. I stand between you and the bad shit outside that door. It doesn't touch you. I'll give you all the respect you deserve and more, but I can't lock that protective instinct away. I won't. There's too much ugliness in the world, and if it comes looking for you, it'll find me instead."

FORTY

Scarlett

"**W**ell, hell," I whisper with a shake of my head. "How am I supposed to argue with that?"

I meet Gabriel's eyes and stare into them for long enough to drown in the deep blue pools of swirling emotion.

He's giving me the truth, not just the answer that will shut me up, and that alone tells me he's different from every other man who has played a role in my personal life.

It's not easy to hear that what you think you want isn't what you're going to get. But the longer I stand here in silence, the more my respect for Gabriel Legend grows.

He is who he is, unapologetically, and while I've been getting to know him better each day, there's still so much more I want to understand.

What kind of hellfire does it take to forge a man who would throw himself in front of any danger so that it doesn't touch what he cares about? My heart aches for what he's been through, but I can't help but marvel at the man he is.

Honorable. Forthright. Unflinching in his convictions.

Shit. Now I really want to climb him.

"You can argue all you want, ladybug, but—"

I move forward and press a finger to his lips to stop him. "I need you to kiss me. Right now. And hard."

His brows dive together for a beat before that half smile tugs at the corner of his mouth. He doesn't say another word as he reaches out to wrap both arms around me and pull me against his body.

His lips crash against mine, and it takes no time at all for his tongue to demand entrance. Like the emotions running high between us, the kiss is *electric.* My nails bite into the skin at the back of his neck, and he responds by lifting me and carrying me to the sofa. Spinning around, he lands first, cradling me against his body as he frees a hand to spear into my hair.

We devour each other, lips melding to lips, tongues dueling, teeth nipping and scraping.

Before I lose myself completely to the kiss, one thought echoes through my brain—*I don't have to be strong every minute of the day with him. I can finally let go.*

It's a heady feeling, and I pour every ounce of it into the kiss, tugging his T-shirt up and scraping my nails across his bare skin. I want him so fucking badly that if I don't touch him, I feel like I might lose my mind.

"Baby, someone's coming in."

I jerk my head up to look over at the door as the knob turns. For a split second, I consider not moving, because I don't want to lose this feeling.

But I also don't want my employees walking in on me making out on our display couch.

"Shit." I jump up and twist around before Gabriel can help me, and wince in pain at the movement.

The door opens and Amy comes to a halt, with Liz bumping into her due to the abrupt stop.

"Whoa. I didn't expect you to be down here. Is everything

okay?" Amy's gaze shifts from my disheveled appearance to Gabriel.

Calmly, I smooth my sweater down but stop myself from touching my hair. I'll just look even guiltier.

Thankfully, Gabriel comes to the rescue.

"I asked for a tour. You guys do a great job with this place. It's really fucking cool. I might even have to buy that banker's lamp for my manager's desk. She'll freak out knowing it's from Curated."

Amy beams with pride. "We would be happy to box it up for you, Mr. Legend." Her gaze finds me, and from the heat burning my cheeks, there's no way she misses my blush. "And it's good to see you feeling better, Scar. If you give us another couple of hours, the whole third floor will be ready for you to play with."

She's giving me an out of this awkward situation, and I grab onto it with both hands. Well, actually, I grab onto Gabriel's with one.

"We were just going to order some food. We'll get out of your way. Just let me know when you're ready for me, Ames."

"Deal, boss."

As I tug Gabriel behind me toward the stairs, I hear Liz whisper, "Oh my God, they were totally making out on the couch, weren't they?"

"We're never talking about this ever again, but *yes, yes they were*," Amy replies in a hushed tone. "Go, Scarlett, go."

FORTY-ONE

As much as I want to continue what was happening downstairs, I saw the flash of pain across Scarlett's face when she jumped off me.

"You're still hurting, aren't you?"

She shuts the door to her apartment behind us and leans against it. The red staining her cheeks makes it that much harder to stay six feet away from her. I want to go to her, but right now, I'm afraid that if I touch her, we'll both end up naked, and she'll push herself further than her body is ready for.

"Not that much." She moves toward me, her hips swaying ever so slightly, and I know what she wants.

I don't want to tell her no, but no matter how amazing it would feel to sink my dick inside her right now, it's not worth it if she feels even a second of discomfort.

She pauses in front of me and wets her lips.

Fuck. Me. I reach out to wrap a hand around her hip and gently bring her against me. With my lips ghosting over her temple, I break the bad news.

"You could tempt the devil himself, ladybug. But I don't want to hurt you. It's still too soon."

A frustrated sound escapes her throat, and I grip her tighter to keep her from pulling away.

"I told you, I'm not an invalid."

"And I'm not going anywhere. We got plenty of time to fit in every single thing that's on your mind, and about a hundred forty-nine more things on mine. No need to rush."

Scarlett shifts her head to look me in the eye. "A hundred forty-nine?"

"Ballpark."

"Okay." She releases a long sigh, and I tuck her hair behind her ear. "I just want to be back to normal already."

"I know, and you will be soon. Give your body a couple more days, and then you'll be your regular unstoppable self."

She flicks a coy glance up at me. "And where will you be?"

"Inside you every fucking chance I get."

The rest of the weekend passes so fast, I wish I could slow down time.

The club numbers are climbing steadily, but our financials still look like shit for the time being. When Monday morning rolls around, the only thing I wish I had to worry about was giving Scarlett the last dose of her pills, but the emails waiting in my inbox can't be ignored.

Two of the investors have called for a meeting this week to discuss the viability of the club.

When I read the word *viability*, my gut sinks. No fucking way are they going to force me into pulling the plug on it already. Not a fucking chance.

But that's the problem with using other people's money and getting it the way I did. I wasn't in a position of power, and they knew it. Their lawyers added protective language to the agreements to make sure that I couldn't operate without taking into account their opinions and wishes. Almost like a board of directors.

If I wanted the money, I didn't have a choice. So I took their deal.

"Everything okay?" Scarlett asks from the kitchen table where she sips a double shot of espresso with her laptop open in front of her. "You're really quiet."

I close the email and shove my phone in my pocket. "Club stuff. It's fine."

"Anything I can help with?"

I shake my head. "I've gotta meet with my investors this week. They don't like the numbers they're seeing, but I'll handle it."

Scarlett's lips press together. "We can get more people in the doors. I can keep making appearances. Whatever you need."

I take the seat next to her and pick up her hand to play with her fingers. "You've done plenty."

"Gabriel, please. I want to help."

Her fingers are so different from mine. No scarred and busted knuckles. No calluses or rough skin.

I lift them to my lips and press a kiss to the back of them. "If you want to come to the club this weekend, I'd appreciate it."

Her smile illuminates her whole face. "Of course I want to come. And since Amy has finally lifted her ban on me leaving the building, I'm getting back to normal today, if you know what I mean."

I do know what she means, and I can't fucking wait.

"Take it easy today. Don't go running all over town. If there's anything I can get for you—"

She silences me with a shake of her head. "I promise I'm

not going to overdo it. I just have one really important errand to run, and after that, I'll be here all day." She leans over and presses her lips to mine. "Now, go do all the things you've let slide while you've been taking such good care of me. I know you have a ton on your plate. I appreciate every second you've spent with me, but it's time for both of us to get back to work."

She's right. I have let a ton of shit go, or pushed it off on Q and Zoe, because I didn't want to leave Scarlett's side.

I haven't trained since I sparred with Bohannon, and after our run-in with Bodhi Black, I know I need to get back in the gym. Whatever happens next, I need to be ready. Time to give my old trainer a call and get back to work.

Plus, Bump has been texting me damn near every hour, asking when I'll be home because Roux misses me. I definitely miss the hell out of both of them.

"All right. You do you, and I'll do me today. I'll bring dinner by tonight, though."

"Deal, boss."

I can't help but laugh. "That ain't gonna stick either. Keep trying, ladybug."

FORTY-TWO

"I owe you so freaking much. Thank you, Kels." I lean in to air-kiss my best friend so I don't mess up the hair and makeup that she came over to apply with only fifteen minutes' notice.

"You know I'd only do this for you." Kelsey shoots me a wink as she cleans her brushes and slides them back into her pouch, one by one.

"I know, and I'm so lucky to have you. I finally feel normal again for the first time since the surgery . . . and now I need to go beard the lion in her den."

"Meryl Fosse is a lioness if I've ever seen one. But I also think she'd be crazy not to give you an invite to her event, so I don't think you're going to have to beg too much."

Kelsey didn't see the way Meryl looked at me that time she told me I was too fake. The memory still cuts deep. Along with the fact that my father has zero intentions of leaving the Hamptons to see how I'm doing. *Not thinking about that.*

I push away the hurt as I disappear into my closet to produce my outfit of choice for the day. A vintage burnt-orange House of Scarlett skirt that hits right below the knees, a cream silk blouse with gold braid edging the collar, and brown-and-cream Italian suede booties.

Kelsey finishes cleaning up as I slip it on, and then she helps me with the final touches and rearranges my hair for the final time.

"You look amazing. Class personified. If Meryl won't give you an invite, you walk away with your head held high."

I nod, but in my mind, that's not even a possible outcome.

It's hard to explain why I'm so determined to get Meryl Fosse as a client, but I feel the need right down to my bones. It's not just because she's the founder and president of a charity or that she comes from money and has plenty to spend. It's more. She's practically the embodiment of all the good things I could possibly imagine. Great taste, kind heart, hardworking, and wields massive influence over the more conservative social set.

Also, for some reason, I can't abide the fact that she called what I do *fake*.

Maybe I'm out to prove a point. Maybe it's my ego calling the shots. Either way, when I make my way across town to her charity's offices, I'm on a mission.

"Ms. Fosse will be out of her meeting shortly, Ms. Priest. I'm so sorry for the wait. I didn't realize you were coming this morning." The receptionist at the front desk frowns with concern, but I smile.

"I didn't have an appointment. Totally my fault. I don't mind waiting."

I take a seat in the lobby area and fish out my phone to keep myself entertained. There's a message on the screen waiting for me.

GABRIEL: Take it easy today, killer. Don't overdo it.

SCARLETT: I took a town car, and I've only walked about fifty feet. I promise I'm okay.

GABRIEL: Good, because I have plans for you later.

A shiver of excitement ripples through me, ending between my legs. I type out a message before I lose my nerve.

SCARLETT: I want you to take me like you did in your office. Hard. Hot. Fast. Dirty.

My nipples peak against my bra, and I know this is a bad idea because my cream silk blouse will provide very little cover.

GABRIEL: Fuck. You tempt me. You'll get what you want. I'll be lucky if I can make it through the day with any blood left in my brain.

I'm staring down at my phone, trying to come up with a reply, when Meryl Fosse clears her throat. My head jerks up, and there she is, standing three feet away from me, with a slight smile on her face that says this isn't the first time she's tried to get my attention.

Well, that's just great.

Like a guilty kid, I shove the phone in my pocket as I rise. "Ms. Fosse, such a pleasure to see you again." I reach out and shake her hand.

"I'm sorry to keep you waiting. I didn't realize I'd have the pleasure of your company today, Ms. Priest. To what do I owe the honor?"

"I'd like to speak to you about your upcoming event."

She lifts her chin and then waves a hand toward the glass door in front of us. "Come with me. We can chat in my office for a few minutes. I have a call in a half hour, so I'm afraid I don't have much time to give you."

"That's totally fine. I shouldn't have dropped by without an appointment, but I suppose I let my excitement get the better of me."

Meryl says nothing until we reach her office. Instead of it being a meticulously appointed space with floor-to-ceiling windows and thousands of dollars in furnishings, I'm surprised to see a fairly basic large black desk, bookshelves with photos, and a dozen piles of books and files scattered on every flat surface.

"I know you're expecting something that looks more photo-worthy, but this is how work really gets done around here."

"I'm not judging, I swear."

"Good, then you can sit. Here, let me clear off this chair." Meryl scoops up a pile of files from the guest chair and moves it to a side table. "I'm sure your office is perfectly neat and tidy at all times, ready to snap and post a photo whenever it suits you."

"To be totally honest, Meryl, I actually do most of my work at my kitchen table or in bed. I rarely sit at my desk, and that's the only reason it's always neat and tidy."

A little of the standoffishness fades from her gaze. "Ah, so you just don't show the world that piece of your life."

I smile. "My store is called *Curated* rather than *Reality* for a reason, but that's not why I'm here."

"Then why are you here, Ms. Priest?"

"Please, call me Scarlett. Ms. Priest feels too formal. And

I'm here because I want to come to your event, but my invitation got lost in the mail."

Meryl tilts her head to one side. "Can I be frank, Scarlett?"

"Of course."

"Your invitation didn't so much get lost in the mail as never mailed because I didn't think you'd care to attend. This event isn't about photo ops and publicity. It's about raising money to assist kids who might not otherwise get any support."

Her words sting and help me realize that her opinion of me is even lower than I thought.

"I care about causes too. Just because I make my living in a way you consider frivolous doesn't mean I'm heartless."

"I never figured you for heartless. Just self-absorbed."

Her quick comeback stings even more, and the chances of me getting an invite, let alone securing her as a client, are sitting at slim-to-none right now.

I straighten my shoulders in my seat and decide that I'm done beating around the bush. "And because I'm so self-absorbed, my money isn't good enough for your cause?"

That gives her pause. "I never said that."

I brace my elbows on my knees and lean forward. "Then what's your problem with me?"

She narrows her gaze on me. "You really expect me to believe that you don't know your mother practically slammed her door in my face when I was starting this place, and told me not to ask her for money ever again?"

My mouth drops open. "No . . . she didn't." A hot wave of shame washes over me at the thought of my mother, whose pedestal seems to get taller with every year that passes since she died, saying something like that to Meryl.

"She did."

I lift my hand to my face and drop my forehead into it. "I am so sorry. I had no idea."

Meryl's expression softens a bit. "I know you and your mother were very close, and I hate to speak ill of the dead. But she left a lasting impression on me, and I'm afraid I've transferred that to you rather unfairly."

"I had no idea. Truly. My mother . . . she was passionate about charity too. I'm not sure why she would've done that. She . . ."

For the first time, I realize what a lost cause pursuing Meryl as a client has been, and wonder how many other ways I've canonized my mother since she passed away. Once someone is gone, it's so easy to think of them as being more saintly than human, but I know she had her flaws too. Still, it hurts to be confronted with them in Meryl Fosse's office.

I shake my head, horrified as tears burn behind my eyes once more. *I can't cry in front of her. Not now. Jesus, Scarlett, pull yourself together.*

I pop out of my chair, intent on running out of her office, but Meryl's hushed words stop me.

"Please, don't go. I'm afraid your mother and I had our differences, but since I can't apologize to her for holding on to them, I can apologize to you. She believed your father had an interest in me before any of us were married, and I didn't think it was important to address, given that I was already in love with someone else. But I let her think she was right. I . . . it was a petty thing. I should've let it go many years ago. It never should have even started, to be honest."

I couldn't fathom why Meryl would object so strongly to Curated, but now I get it. Old grudges die hard. "Thank you for telling me that. I suppose I've done a good job of making my mother seem like she was perfect in life now that she's gone. It's so much easier to focus on the good, you know?"

"Absolutely. Although it's easier to do with some parents than with others."

I nod slowly. "It would've been a hell of a lot harder if it were my father," I murmur. "Not that anyone ever accused him of being a saint."

"Trust me, I understand that well," she says with empathy underscoring her words. "My father was no sterling example of a parent."

Slowly, I lower myself back into the chair, my hands gripping the arms. "Really?"

Her chin dips. "He left when I was six, twelve, *and* seventeen. I saw him for the last time when I was twenty-four. He vomited on a table during my wedding reception. It was humiliating, and I never forgave him. He's been gone for many years, and I wish with all my heart that it could've been different. Now I have to live with the knowledge that I'll never have a chance to have any kind of relationship with him."

In that moment, we're not Scarlett Priest and Meryl Fosse, two women who have it all. Instead, we're two little girls who only ever wanted fathers who gave a damn, and it breaks my heart.

"My father has never cared that he had a daughter. I know there's no ranking for suffering, but I can relate. I wish you hadn't had to live through that, Meryl. I wish . . ." I trail off because I don't know what else to say. Then something occurs to me. "This is why your charity is so important, isn't it? Because you're giving kids a place to go and people who care about them, no matter what's happening at home."

A radiant smile beams from her face. "Exactly."

"I would really be honored if you'd let me attend. And if you would prefer that I don't, I will understand completely, and I'll still be donating. I really mean that. I'm not just saying it to get an invitation."

"I know you're not," Meryl says as a dimple appears in one of her cheeks. "I have an excellent bullshit detector. Daughter of an alcoholic, so I come by it naturally. But I'd love for you to attend, Scarlett. That is . . . if you'll donate something to the silent auction to help us raise money on top of the ticket prices."

A smile ghosts over my lips because I respect the hell out of her negotiating ability. "I would love to. Thank you so much."

"It'll be my pleasure. Have the auction item sent over by Thursday. I'll see you Saturday night."

I freeze at her words. I thought the event was *next week*, but I keep my smile intact.

Well, we'll just have to make it work.

I'll go to the club Friday and then after the charity event Saturday, and Gabriel's investors will see that everything's moving in the right direction and there's no need for alarm. *It'll all be fine.*

Still, a feeling of disquiet follows me out of the charity offices and chases me all the way home.

FORTY-THREE

"That isn't a sight I see regularly anymore," Q says as he steps into my office at the club. The attitude I'm feeling rolling off my best friend isn't my imagination. He's fucking pissed.

"You got something to say to me? Then say it," I tell him, rising from where I was sitting behind my desk.

Q struts inside and shuts the door. "Investor meeting is Thursday at two. You think you can tear yourself away from Scarlett Priest to make it? Or is that meeting not important to you either?"

I prowl around my desk and meet him in the middle of the room, standing on the rug that started it all. "You questioning my commitment? Now? After everything I've fucking done?"

"You've been MIA damn near all fucking week while the rest of us held down the fort, so you could go play prince running to the rescue like you belong in the castle with the princess."

"She needed me."

Q lunges forward. "We need you. We need your head in

212

the fucking game or this is all over. They could pull the plug on us Thursday. You know that, right, Gabe? We're in breach of contract. They could call in the loans. And then what are you going to do? Go back to fighting at the docks and open another illegal club? Because I don't think your new girl is the type to walk through those doors."

Anger rises in my chest like the blush that sometimes stains Scarlett's cheeks. "You, of all people, know how fucking committed I am to this. I'm the one who has sacrificed everything and put every penny on the line. You think that's changed?"

"Fuck yes." Q's gaze sharpens on me. "You're rarely here. We're scraping by, barely making it into the black every night, and you're *not here*."

"Is that your problem, Q, or are you just pissed that I finally took your advice and am moving forward with my life?"

Q recoils like I slapped him. "This is you moving forward? Really?"

"Yeah, I fucking am. I'm sorry you don't like how I'm doing it, but I don't remember there being a requirement that I could only move forward using Marcus Quinterro-approved steps."

Instead of decking me like Q looks like he wants to, he turns and paces to the door. I assume he's going to rip it open and march out, slamming it behind him, but he doesn't. He spins around and leans back against the frame before jamming his hands in his jet-black hair.

"I'm not trying to tell you how to live your life, man. I'm really not." He finally meets my gaze again. "I'm just fucking worried about you. As long as I've known you, you've had tunnel vision. You never once took your eye off the fucking prize. And now . . . shit, man. I feel like I don't know who you are anymore, and that scares the hell out of me."

Having a best friend who knows you almost better than you know yourself can be a blessing and a curse at times. I could tell Q to fuck off and mind his own business because I know what I'm doing, but I owe him more than that. Not just because of our years of friendship, but also because he has some of his and his family's money tied up in the club too. His reaction is partly motivated by his fear that I'm going to let them all down.

"I'm here, Q. I'm working on a plan. One so fucking good that if it pans out, we might be able to wipe away every penny of debt and live free and clear."

Q drops his hands and cranes his neck like he's trying to see inside my brain. "What the fuck are you talking about? That fight night? That's not going to bring us enough to pay off all our debt. I've been ballparking numbers since you raised the idea, but there's just no fucking way, even if they let us keep the entire gate, which will never happen."

Emotions play out across his face as he tries to figure out what I'm thinking. I haven't said it out loud yet, so there's no way for him to know what's in my head right now.

"We negotiate for fifty percent of the gate, double the drink prices, and I fight Bodhi Black as the main event of the night and bet every cent I can on myself."

In Q's defense, his jaw only drops an inch as his face pales. He opens his mouth to speak, and then closes it again before shaking his head.

"No. No fucking way, Gabe. You aren't fighting Black. That's a fucking death wish if I've ever heard one. Besides, you've barely even been training. They want to hold this thing in like thirty days or something. You're not ready for that kind of battle, and I'm sure as hell not losing my best friend while you try to play hero and save us all. Not fucking happening."

"Black's knee will never be a hundred percent after that

last fight. I can get in shape. I know his moves. I've spent plenty of time studying the tape of our last fight. I can beat him again."

Q shakes his head like he's staring at a lost cause. "This is a terrible fucking idea, Gabe. Not to mention that you'd have to get the promotion company on board and bump the main event down to take its place. There's no way in hell they'd let it happen."

"That's where you underestimate the power of greed, my friend. A street-fight grudge match brought under the umbrella of respectability would draw a fuck ton of fans and eyes. The promoters will buy into it. My only question now is whether you'll be in my corner for it." Q knows I'm not only asking about him working with my cornerman and cutman, but whether or not I can count on his support for the whole damn thing. "You've been with me every step of the way in this city, man. I need you with me for this. I need to know you'll still bet on me too."

Q rubs at his forehead with his index finger and thumb before looking up at me. "Why do you always have to put it all on the line? Why can't we just do shit halfway sometimes?"

"Because that's not how legends are born."

He huffs out a chuckle, but there's little humor in it. Still shaking his head, he stares at me. "You're fucking crazy. You know that, right?"

"I know."

He pushes off the doorjamb, and I meet him in the middle of the rug. "I'd still bet on you over anyone else, any day of the year. If you think you can do this, then may God have mercy on all of us."

I lean in and give him a hard, back-slapping hug. "One more fight, and then I'm hanging up my gloves forever."

Q pulls back. "I sure as hell hope you know what you're doing."

I want to tell him I definitely don't have all of it figured out, but I'm going to get there, because this is the fight of my life. Instead, I tell him, "Call Bodhi's manager and let them know there'll be a call coming in, and the answer they need to give is *fuck yes*."

"You mean after the meeting with the promotion company."

I jerk my chin to the side. "No, I mean right now. Because I'm making this happen."

There's a knock on the door, and I call out, "Come in."

I see Zoe for a split second before Bump darts around her to slam against me in the form of a tackle-hug. Roux zips right alongside him, jumping up to put her paws on our arms as Bump presses his fresh buzz cut to my chest.

"I missed you, Gabe! It feels like it's been so long. Roux has been keeping me company, though, and I'm taking good care of her. Aren't I, girl?"

Roux pushes off of us and lands with all four paws on the floor once more. She nuzzles into my leg, and I reach down to stroke her soft head.

"You've been doing a great job, Bump. I really appreciate it, bud."

Bump finally releases me and steps back. "You look the same, but you smell different. Prettier."

Zoe and Q choke on laughter, and I think of where I showered last and the scented soap. With a wry smile, I say to Bump, "But you're saying I smell good?"

His head bobs. "Way better. You look good too. Are you coming home tonight? I'm going to the bar with Big Mike to watch *Monday Night Football*, but you can come with us if you want."

It's a generous invitation, even more generous than

anyone else but the people in this room would realize. Going to the bar alone with Big Mike is pretty much Bump's favorite thing in the entire world. Q's old man lets Bump order a shot glass of every single beer on tap and line them all up on the table while he pigs out on all-you-can-eat bar popcorn.

"Go with Big Mike tonight, bud. We'll hang out tomorrow night. You pick the place."

His eyes go huge. "Can we bring Scarlett? She's nice. I want to see her again."

I should ask her before saying yes, because of how seriously Bump takes promises, but I know it's important to cement this right now.

"Yeah. Scarlett will come. Text me your choice tomorrow, and I'll be by to pick you up at six."

"In the morning?" Bump sounds disgusted at the thought.

"At night, bud. We'll eat dinner and have some fun."

Bump's smile is back and beaming brighter than before. "Okay. It's a date." He looks at Zoe. "Will you take me to get a new shirt? I want to look nice for the ladies."

"Yeah, Bump. We'll get you one tomorrow on the way to work."

He holds out his hand to me, and then we both spit and shake on it. "I've missed you, Gabe, but it's worth it if she makes you happy."

A dart of appreciation for this little non-blood brother of mine hits me hard in the chest. "She does, Bump. She really does." I say it loud enough for Q to overhear, and a giant smile erupts on Zoe's face before she glances down at her watch.

"It's time, gentlemen. I'll let them in, and you schmooze them until there's nowhere else they'd rather hold their fights."

FORTY-FOUR

"I'm surprised to see you again, Ms. Priest," Dr. Grand says from the chair opposite the couch where I'm sitting.

The couch in her office, where I learned she was a sex therapist and my relationship with Chadwick was completely over. The memories still pack on the weight of shame, but I'm working through it. After all, I did come back.

"Well, you invited me to make another appointment, so here I am."

She settles her tablet on her knee and reaches for a steaming cup of tea. "What would you like to talk about today?"

Her tone and manner are so mellow that they instantly settle a blanket of calm over me that wipes away my unease.

"You said before that I wasn't broken, and I just wanted to let you know that you're right. I'm not."

"That's excellent news. I'm glad you agree." She smiles politely, but there's a hint of question to it, like she's still not sure why I'm here.

I gather my courage and blurt it out. "I'm going to have sex tonight."

To her credit, Dr. Grand barely blinks. "Okay . . ."

"Not with the guy who made the appointment for me here. Someone else. Someone I'm seeing. I told you about him. The guy who made me feel . . . not broken."

Her inquisitive look morphs into something close to a smile. "And you've scheduled sex for tonight?"

"Well, I had a surprise appendectomy last week, so that kind of put a damper on the physical side of our relationship, but I think it might have been a good thing."

"Why do you say that?" Dr. Grand has her stylus poised to write on the tablet, but she doesn't move it.

"Because it gave me time to get used to seeing him in my space. To get used to him being close. I . . . It's almost like I crave being close to him. I want him around all the time. I love seeing his face in my kitchen or my living room. And now . . . now, I want more. I want it all. The sex and intimacy and everything."

Her lips form a subtle approving grin. "That's a big step in any relationship."

"We've already had sex, so it's not like it's the first time, but . . . it kind of feels like it." I explain to her what happened the first time at the club, and her smile disappears.

"What will you do if that happens again?" Dr. Grand asks, balancing her stylus between her finger and thumb.

"It won't."

"But can you be sure?" she asks with a tilt of her head. "People don't often change overnight, Scarlett. It's a long, slow process that involves a lot of work on oneself."

I think of how Gabriel told me I didn't have to believe his words because he was going to show me. And he has. Every single day since I was in the hospital, he's been there for me, and I don't think it has a damn thing to do with the fact that he wants more sex. I think he just wants me.

"I wouldn't be with him if I wasn't sure."

"I hope you're right, but please be careful. You've been through a lot lately, and this is a big deal."

We finish our session, and as I'm walking to the door with Dr. Grand on my heels, I pause and look over my shoulder at her.

"How do you know if a relationship is working?"

Her face softens. "I think it's different for everyone, but in general, I'd look for trust, respect, kindness, mutual attraction, and a healthy dose of humor."

I love her list, because it's all the things I've experienced with Gabriel and no one else.

"Thank you, Dr. Grand. I'll see you again."

"Good luck, Scarlett."

My session with the sex therapist gives me plenty to think about but doesn't reduce my excitement by even a fraction of a degree. It's happening today, no doubt about it, and I can't freaking wait.

It's a revelation to be walking down the streets of New York, thinking about the deliciously hot sex I'm going to be having tonight. I try to school my expression just before I make it to the swanky bistro that Monroe and Harlow love to meet at for lunch.

I spot them at a table in the gated area on the sidewalk.

"Damn, who is that hottie?" Monroe catcalls and then whistles at me. "I wouldn't kick her out of my bed for eating crackers."

Harlow laughs and shakes her head. "You're a nut job."

"I'm starving," I say, slipping through the small gate built into the hip-height fence to take the third seat at the round table.

"Starving for a giant piece of man meat, most likely," Monroe adds with a wink. "You've got the look."

Clearly, I failed at hiding my thoughts. I bounce my gaze between my two friends, trying to appear innocent. "What look?"

"The *I'm thinking about getting laid tonight* look," Harlow says before taking a sip from her water. "And I agree. You do have it. Are you feeling better? Up to taking a *ride* on the wild side again?"

I think of the last time Gabriel and I had sex, and how explosive and amazing it was. We're not going for a second spin on his desk at the club tonight, but it'll be just as hot in my bed. Then I remember Chadwick scoffing at my bedroom.

"You expect me to be able to get hard for you in the middle of all those ruffles and clutter? Not happening, Scarlett. You can come to my place."

I shove down the ugly voice because it's the last thing I want to hear.

"What's wrong?" This comes from Harlow.

"Chadwick said he couldn't get hard in my bedroom," I say, my gaze fixed firmly on the snowy white tablecloth.

"Oh, for Christ's sake," Monroe says, nearly knocking over her water glass with her flying hand. "That pissant probably couldn't get hard anywhere. No amount of shabby chic decor is going to stop Gabriel Legend from pounding you into your pillowtop tonight. That man would probably fuck you in the middle of that doll store in Midtown—if the damn thing were ever empty of children and employees. Not even all those tiny doll eyes could stop him from wanting you so fucking bad that he's ready to blow his load at the first sight of skin."

I look up at her face and smile. "Despite that *beyond* creepy example, I hear what you're saying. I'm putting every single thing that ever had to do with a Chadwick sex hang-up out of my head."

"Oh, good," Harlow whispers. "But don't look now, because he's walking down the street with a tart on his arm."

"No," I whisper, gripping the edge of the tablecloth as I fight the urge to turn around and look.

"Fuck, he spotted us," Monroe whispers back. "Shoulders back. Tits out. Chin up."

I do exactly what she says, even though I don't give a single damn what Chadwick thinks of me now.

His smarmy voice comes over my right shoulder and makes my skin crawl. "Well, well. Some things never change. The Three Cuntkateers are still ladies who lunch."

That motherfucker.

I pop out of my chair and whip around to face him, with my shoulders back, tits out, and chin up, of course. I survey the young twenty-something blonde on his arm with a polite smile.

"Hello, Chadwick. It's good to see you getting back in the saddle again."

His gaze narrows on me, and the intense hatred I read there almost takes me by surprise. "I've been in the saddle the whole damn time, Scarlett. You're the only one who wasn't getting laid."

That. Fucking. Prick.

I'm really fucking glad I had my annual exam and STD tests shortly after the last time we had sex, because now I have no idea how many New Yorkers I was sleeping with by proxy. And *thank God* I always made him wear a condom.

The scrape of metal against concrete sounds as Harlow and Monroe jump out of their chairs.

"You literally just admitted to cheating in front of your new hookup? Bad form, don't you think, Chad?"

"It's Chad*wick*," he says with a sneer at Harlow.

"*Chadwick who can't get a hard dick*," Monroe sings like a nursery rhyme. "*Too bad he can't get laid, since that would take a bitch getting paid*. Damn, I really need another line here. I'm going to have to work on my poetry skills for moments like these."

Chadwick's face turns dangerously red like he's cruising toward a heart attack. The blonde beside him giggles, and he whips around to glare at her. "Shut your mouth. Don't listen to them."

"Oh, honey," I say to the girl with sympathy in my tone. "Run the other way as fast and far as you can. I promise there's nothing good down the road you're walking."

Chadwick lunges at me, but I jump back, and the fence stops him from getting closer. "You're a cunt, Scarlett. A rich bitch who thinks she has everything but can't get the one thing she wants most—for her daddy to give a single fuck about her."

I inhale sharply, sucking back oxygen with the pain of his cruel words.

"Oh no, you didn't—" Monroe bolts toward the fence, but I stop her with a hand on her arm.

"He's not worth it, Monroe. He's not worth another second of our time." Coldness settles over me, and I stare into Chadwick's mud-brown eyes. "You were the biggest mistake I've ever made. Thank God I realized it before it was too late."

The blonde's eyes are wide as she clutches her purse to her side and steps back on her towering heels. "I just remembered I have an appointment. I better go." She's gone in seconds, power walking away as fast as her stilettos can carry her.

Chadwick's expression turns even more evil. "You'll pay for this, Scarlett. I promise." And then he huffs off down the sidewalk, knocking into people with every step.

"I hate that man," Harlow says, ice coating every word.

"I wouldn't call 9-1-1 if he was on fire," Monroe adds with a shake of her head. "And I wouldn't even feel guilty about it."

They each reach out to grasp one of my hands after we take our seats at the table, and I squeeze back.

"I'm just glad he's out of my life."

"But what about your dad?" Monroe asks. "How doesn't he see that fuckwad's true colors?"

I shrug and shake my head. "I don't know, but I think it's time for me to let it go. I can't carry that shit with me anymore. I'm done with him. Let's order. I'm starving."

FORTY-FIVE

"Nice club. Really fucking nice. And it sure as hell looks like you designed it perfectly to fit a cage in the middle." Gerard Poirier, the CEO of the fight promotion company, gives me an approving nod as we walk toward the door.

"I didn't think we'd find anything to wow us like the one that the Feds raided. I'm damn glad I was wrong," Bruce Liggett, Gerard's second in command, adds.

"I'm glad you approve, gentlemen. We'd be happy to host your fight card for the right terms."

Gerard latches onto my words like he's been waiting for me to bring up the subject. "Standard contract. You get fifteen percent of the gate, all the money from the booze, and I'm sure it'll put you on the map to get more events in here."

From where he stands off to my left, Q shifts when he hears the 15 percent figure.

"I'm afraid you're not in a standard situation, gentlemen. You need a venue that wows people, or you don't have an event worth having."

"What are you saying, Legend?" Bruce asks.

"I'm saying that fifteen percent doesn't even get you past the front door. You need what I've got, and I know what it's worth."

Gerard crosses his arms, testing the strength of the thread holding the button on his suit coat. "How much do you want?"

"Seventy percent of the gate."

"No fucking way," Bruce fires back. "You're out of your goddamned mind. We've never paid more than thirty percent."

"And you lowball me with fifteen when you're desperate?"

Bruce shuffles his feet. "We hear you're desperate too."

I lift my head to scan the interior of the club, with its massive columns and soaring ceilings. "Does it look like I'm desperate? This is my kingdom, and I set the terms."

Gerard's jaw rocks from side to side. "You want fifty-fifty."

"Damn right. And if the fight isn't already sold out, you should jack up the prices of the remaining tickets, because they'll sell as soon as you announce the new location."

Gerard's gaze goes to the balcony that houses the VIP section. "We didn't have a second level at the last place. View was damn good from up there. How many seats you think we can fit?"

I glance at Q, who's already figuring.

"At least two hundred," he tells the men.

Gerard nods. "We sell them at two grand a piece, split the gate fifty-fifty, and we both make what we need and no one gets greedy."

"I can live with that," I tell them.

Gerard's mouth curves up. "Then I think we've got ourselves a deal—"

"One more thing," I say, and both men stiffen.

"What?" Bruce asks.

"Your main event is weak. You think that'll fill the seats?"

Bruce rocks from side to side. "The original matchup was better, but a fighter got hurt. We had to fill the spot with the best we could get on short notice."

Gerard appraises me with interest sparkling in his eyes. "You got a better option for us, Legend? Because I hear Bodhi Black would like nothing more than to get his revenge in the cage."

Bruce whips around to look at him. "It's a sanctioned fight, not an underground match."

"If I fight Black again, it's going to be legit. Not underground. If you can make that happen, straight up, he'll take this fight tomorrow, and we'll put on the best show this city has ever seen."

Gerard's smile couldn't get any bigger. "I'll take care of the athletic commission. Those upper-level tickets are going to go for a hell of a lot more than two grand." He holds out his hand. "It's a pleasure doing business with you, Legend. I look forward to seeing you in the cage."

I reach out and shake hands with him, praying to God that I know what the fuck I'm doing. "Get me the contract. We'll sign it and make it happen."

FORTY-SIX

I take my time in the shower, shaving every single inch of my skin below my shoulders that has ever grown hair. Tonight is the night. Our next step forward. And I feel freaking great about it instead of apprehensive.

See? This is what a healthy relationship feels like.

Bad Scarlett chimes in right after that thought. *Psh, I just need to know what his dick feels like again because it's been too long. We're getting laid tonight! Three cheers for getting what we need!*

With Bad Scarlett still in my head after I dry off and lotion up, I walk to my lingerie chest and open the second drawer. Inside, it's an explosion of lacy underthings, most of which have only ever been seen by me. But that's about to change.

Every time I purchased sexy lingerie, I felt like I was an imposter, because I wasn't the kind of woman who would wear it for her man and watch it bring him to his knees. But tonight, as I pick out a sheer pale peach bra and panty set with strategically placed lacy flowers, I feel more like *me* than I have in years . . . or maybe ever.

It's with a seductive and self-satisfied smile that I slip into the panties and adjust them on my hips before sliding on the bra and hooking it behind my back with the gold clasp.

I stand in front of the mirror, and instead of looking with a critical eye to pick out all of my flaws, I take a deep breath and appreciate what I see—a woman regaining her own power and self-confidence. It's a beautiful sight that no amount of self-consciousness about cellulite or extra pounds can overshadow.

Besides, Gabriel Legend likes me for *me.* There's something eminently satisfying, knowing that if he wanted a different kind of woman, he could have her. But he doesn't, and that's a hell of a confidence booster when I imagine him seeing every single inch of me in a few hours.

I'm getting laid! While angels don't rejoice and sing the "Hallelujah Chorus," they should, because that's exactly how I feel.

I could have called Kelsey to do my hair and makeup, but I wanted to do them myself tonight. After I slip a short silky robe over my shoulders and tie it, I brush out my curls from yesterday, softening them around my face, and get started on my makeup. I keep it light and subtle, skipping eye makeup altogether, except for touching up my brows. After applying a tinted lip stain and some non-sticky gloss, I give myself a nod of approval.

Even Kelsey would give me a high five.

Plus, I finished with a solid forty-five minutes to spare.

I could work, but I indulge myself instead by picking up my phone and tapping the icon of my favorite social media app. I haven't been keeping up with my favorite accounts as much lately, and I'm jonesing to see what the Winston triplets have been up to. It only takes a few minutes to find the page, and my face splits with a smile.

They're playing with bubbles outside in a tiny yard, but the joy on their faces is absolutely pure. The caption reads:

The tenacious triplets filled the dishwasher with liquid hand soap yesterday, so now we're obsessed with bubbles. Thankfully these ones aren't flooding the kitchen. Sorry to our downstairs neighbor, Blanche. We really didn't mean for that to happen. I promise I'm making cookies tomorrow as an apology! #LifeIsMessy #Embrace-TheMess #TheTripletEffect #BubblesEverywhere #ItWasSoHard-NotToLaugh #TheirEyesWereSoBig

My giggles grow in volume as I read her hashtags. I don't know how she still has her sanity, let alone her sense of humor, but you can feel the love shining from the photo and her words.

I'm going to post pictures and captions like that someday.

A vision of a tiny blue-eyed boy with messy hair and sticky fingers enters my brain, and I pause and imagine what it would be like to be his mom.

God, I want that so damn bad, I can feel it all the way down to the marrow of my bones.

Kids may not be for everyone, but they're definitely for me. Although, I really don't need three at once like Mrs. Winston.

Then another thought sneaks in. *Does Gabriel want kids?* That's something I'll need to find out. But not tonight. Tonight is about us and only us.

I lose track of time, and nearly drop my phone when the buzzer sounds at my back door.

I glance down at the robe I'm still wearing and consider throwing on something else. But . . . *no. No, I don't think I will.* Might as well let him see exactly where my head's at.

With a devilish smile on my face, I pad into the kitchen on bare feet and press the button on the buzzer.

"Can I help you?" I wanted to say something more risqué, but I chicken out when I consider the fact that it could be someone else at my door . . . which means I'll have to run and change in a hot second, because Gabriel is the only person who gets to see me dressed like this.

"You help me more than you know, ladybug. I hope you're hungry."

Excitement buzzes through my body like electricity. "Come on up. I'm starving." *For you,* I add silently as I hit the button to unlock the door.

I reorganize the flower arrangement on the center of the kitchen table for the few dozen seconds it takes for him to climb the three flights of stairs, and spin around to face the door when he knocks. With one more glimpse down at my robe, I smooth the lapels and step forward to open the door.

As soon as he sees me, his gaze turns hungry. Instantly, it's clear I made the right decision.

"Jesus Christ. Holy shit." He swallows, and the paper of the takeout bags crumples in his hands as his eyes devour me. "Fuck me. I sure as hell didn't need to bring dinner, because you're all I want."

The heat of my blush tingles across my skin, but the smile tugging at my lips is the stronger sensation.

I casually adjust the knot before meeting his gaze once more. "I almost changed."

He shakes his head as he steps forward, letting the door shut behind him. "Missing out on this sight would've been a tragedy. You are fucking beautiful." He leans down to steal a kiss. "Goddamn, you make me want to skip dinner and spend all night devouring you."

I bite down on my lip as he pulls away. "That sounds like a good plan to me."

As soon as I finish speaking, my stomach growls, and Gabriel's brows dive together.

"When's the last time you ate?"

"Earlier. I'm fine."

His lips twitch like he wants to smile, but he shakes his head. "You're still healing. Burning through a lot of calories. You need to eat." His blue eyes flare, equally full of concern and desire. "Trust me, you're still going to get all you can handle tonight. That's a promise."

He lifts the bag between us and deposits it on the table. I want to protest, but my stomach growls again, this time even louder.

"Okay, fine. We fuel up, and then it's game on."

Instead of a lip twitch from Gabriel, I get a full-on grin and belly laugh that fill my heart with joy.

"Attagirl. Let's eat, and you can tell me about your day. Did you get the tickets to the dinner you wanted to go to?"

FORTY-SEVEN

Eating dinner across from Scarlett, while she wears a tiny cream-colored robe that covers everything I can't wait to get my hands and lips on, is a new form of torture I would sign up to participate in every damn day of the week. *Fuck*, how is she so goddamn beautiful and funny and sweet?

She asks about Bump, and I take it as my opening to let her know about the promise I made him earlier today.

"He's doing fine. You can see for yourself tomorrow for dinner, if you're not busy."

Her gray eyes light up. "I'm pretty sure I'm not busy, and if I am, I'll take care of it. Where are we going for dinner?"

Her easy agreement and willingness to cancel anything on her schedule to fit in dinner with Bump does something to my chest. It squeezes tight and then releases, leaving a feeling of warmth behind.

I'm not used to having a smile on my face this much, but I can't help it when I'm around her. She makes my life better just by being near. It's something I've never experienced before, and I'll fight to keep that feeling—and her—in my life.

Fight . . .

Fuck. I have to tell her about that too. *But not until the contracts are signed and it's a done deal.* There's no point in getting her concerned before there's something to be concerned about. Besides, it's not like I'll keep it from her.

I need to start hitting the gym like it's my second fucking job if I want a chance in hell of beating Black again. It's our best path to being free and clear with the club.

I can do it. I have to do it.

"Gabriel?"

She says my name, which always sounds so fucking sweet on her lips, and I realize she's still waiting for an answer.

"Sorry, the robe is distracting," I reply with a wink. "I told Bump he could choose, so expect an arcade or something along those lines. He's also obsessed with anchovy pizza, so don't be surprised if that's what he wants to eat."

Her grin grows. "You had the honor of liberating me from go-kart virginity, so I'm up for whatever he picks."

As soon as she says *virginity*, my mind goes straight back into the gutter. I wish the steak in front of me would disappear in the next five seconds so I could grab her off that chair and carry her into the bedroom.

Fuck me. When is the last time I wanted a woman this bad? Never.

Scarlett is in a league of her own, and it feels like everyone who came before her was preparing me for this moment. It's weird to think in terms of fate, but I can't help it. This feels so damn right, no matter what the rest of the world thinks.

"I appreciate you keeping an open mind. Bump has a good heart, and he really likes you."

"I'm excited. Will Roux come with us too? You know, you could've brought her with you. She was really well behaved when she came up before."

"What are you talking about? When was Roux here?" Confusion clouds my thoughts as I try to think of any time when Roux would have had the chance.

Scarlett bites down on the middle of her lower lip, and I want to tug it free of her teeth. "You know, that night . . . the night after the club when . . ."

Her halting explanation cuts at me, because of how much I hurt her that night. I don't know if I'll ever be able to forgive myself for what I did, but in that moment, I didn't know what else to do.

"Anyway, Bump and Roux came here looking for you. Zoe called a car to come pick them up."

"Ah. Got it." I bow my head, my appetite gone. "I'm so fucking sorry for what I did that night, Scarlett. You'll never know how much I wish I could take that back."

When I lift my gaze to hers, she's staring at me with no judgment or anger on her face. She reaches across the table, around the flowers in the center, and covers my hand with hers.

"You already apologized. Leave it in the past. I have."

And with those simple words, I can't wait any longer.

I need my woman.

Now.

FORTY-EIGHT

G abriel rises from his chair, sending it sliding across the marble floor of the kitchen. "You get enough to eat?"

Oh. My. God. The expression on his face is the most potent combination of need and desire I've ever seen. I take a mental snapshot, captioning it *Gabriel Wants.*

The anticipation that's been riding me all day bursts back to the forefront, and my nipples harden into points. There's no way he can miss them through my silky robe.

As I nod, my fork falls from my fingers, clattering on the table.

"Thank fuck."

His words come out low and husky, but I don't have time to think about them because Gabriel's already moving my chair back and bending to pick me up. I'm weightless as he lifts me off the cushion. I wrap my arms around his neck, soaking up the heat of his hard body as need and want thrum in my veins. My heart rate skyrockets as he dips his head to breathe in the scent of my hair.

"I told myself we'd go slow this time."

I turn my head to press a kiss to his jaw. "And I don't care whether it's fast or slow, so long as you're inside me."

He groans as if in pain and charges toward my bedroom. "Say stuff like that, and I won't be able to make this last as long as you deserve."

I thread my fingers into his hair and tug so that he'll meet my gaze again. "I deserve you, Gabriel. That's all. So stop worrying about slow or fast and all that, and just give me *you.*"

He closes his eyes for a beat before opening them to reveal that piercing blue gaze, and this time, it cuts straight to the core of me. "You have me. No one else."

I attack his mouth. There's really no other description that fits. As I taste him and nip at his lips, I unleash the full power of Gabriel Legend.

He lowers me onto my bed and reaches for the tie of my robe. When he sees the lingerie beneath it, he sucks in a sharp breath.

"Jesus fucking Christ. You were eating dinner across from me wearing that? Fuck me."

I bite down on my lip. "You like it?"

His gaze darts to my face for a second before returning to my nipples. "God, yes. Anytime you want to wear something like this, just put it on, and I'll be right over to show you my appreciation. Sweet fucking hell. You're a goddamned vision."

His hands coast over my skin, lighting me up like he carries electricity in the very palms of his hands. My nipples strain against the lacy flowers, and Gabriel circles one, then the other, with his fingertip.

"I don't know what's sweeter, the way you look or the way you taste. Gotta find out."

His mouth goes to my right nipple, his tongue tracing the same path his finger just did. I arch my back, lifting it higher, forcing more pressure. But he doesn't hurry. If anything, he slows down and tortures me through the lace until there's no doubt that I've soaked my panties.

"Please," I whisper as I rock my hips against his hard thigh. The denim of his jeans provides friction that lights up my clit too.

When Gabriel lifts his head, there's a gleam in his eyes I've never seen before. "You're a greedy girl, aren't you, Scarlett? You want more so you're trying to take it, rubbing on my leg, like I don't know what you're doing." His words carry a drawl that he normally hides, and it's hot as fuck.

"You gonna stop me? Because I know what I want, and I always go after it . . . *hard*." I don't know where that taunt came from, but Gabriel's nostrils flare.

His teeth scrape over his lip, and suddenly I would do *anything* to have him give my nipple the same treatment.

"You're a naughty fucking girl, and *goddamn*, do I love it. But you'll get it when I give it to you. Don't worry, I won't make you beg . . . too much."

The heat of a wild blush streaks up from my chest, but I feel zero embarrassment. Maybe I checked my inhibitions at the door? Either way, I decide to embrace Bad Scarlett for all she's worth.

I grind against his thigh, making sure to rock hard against my clit, and let out a moan. "Then you'd better hurry, because I'm about to leave a mark on your jeans."

A devastating grin changes his expression to one I'd have to name *Deliciously Dangerous*. "Then I better lick that pretty pussy clean."

"*Oh yes*. Yes, you should," I whisper as he moves down the bed, reaching for the elastic bands hugging my hips.

But instead of yanking them down my legs, he drops his face to the center and nuzzles my clit before nipping at it with his teeth through the lace.

"Oh my God." I moan as I arch toward his face, but he brackets a hand around my hip and holds me down while he pushes the material of my panties aside and takes a swipe between my lips.

The growl of pleasure from his throat unleashes shivers that race up my skin. I plow my hand into his hair and pull his face closer, and he *feasts.*

Oh my God. Did I really just jam his face into my pussy?

I don't have a chance to answer myself because I'm already crying out in ecstasy. And Gabriel? He's all for it.

His tongue, teeth, and lips work magic, and I can't keep quiet. The noises being ripped from my throat grow louder and louder until I scream as an orgasm breaks over me.

My head flops back on my pillow as my body goes limp. He lifts his head and licks his lips, and I'm pretty sure I spontaneously come again just from the intensity of the moment.

And now, I desperately want to return the favor.

I start to wiggle out from beneath him, but he grasps me around the waist. "Where do you think you're going?"

"Wherever I have to go to get your dick in my mouth."

That drop-dead sexy smile from before returns, and he nods. "Fuck. Yes. But you stay right there. I don't want you bending too much and hurting yourself."

"I'm fine. I promise. Nothing hurts. And trust me, if it were going to hurt, it would already."

He surveys me for a long moment, and I reach out to cup the massive bulge testing the strength of his zipper.

"I swear I'm fine, Gabriel. Now put your dick in my mouth so I can make your eyes roll back in your head."

His expression turns contemplative, but I think I see pride shining in his eyes. "I should've known a CEO would be bossy in bed."

My shoulders shake as I giggle. "I like to be on top too."

"Fuck yeah. And you will be at least once tonight, but not yet."

I'm already undoing the button of his jeans and tugging at the zipper. "But, first . . ."

I trail off as his thick shaft springs forth out of his jeans. As soon as I wrap my palm around it and squeeze, he releases another deep groan before moving up my body, with his knees on either side of me until that beautiful penis is only inches from my mouth.

"Let me fuck your face."

A gush of moisture between my legs accompanies my nodding head. *Go, Bad Scarlett. You're a sex kitten.* "Yes. Now. Give it to me."

And he does. Inch by inch, he feeds that cock between my lips until it hits the back of my throat, and then pulls it free.

"Goddamn. I can't. I'll blow my load down your throat."

My inner muscles clench in protest. I desperately want him inside me, pounding away and taking me exactly where I need to go to come apart again.

"Just a little more, then I'm mounting up. Fuck, ladybug . . . I don't know what I did to deserve you, but I will do it over and over again."

I smile as he tunnels into my mouth, and suck hard with my lips until he pulls back. I can't shake the urge to almost laugh because I'm so happy. It's a first for me—being so joyful while I'm giving a blow job that I just can't contain it.

Is this what sex is supposed to be like? I sure as hell hope so, because this is fun, *and* I get to come.

A few strokes later, Gabriel pulls out and flops onto his back next to me. "You gotta give me a minute. I'm hanging on by a thread, and I want this to last."

I reach down to grip his cock in my palm and stroke it. "You can last next time."

When I release it, I shimmy off my panties and climb on

top, like I was born to ride this man. I shake my hair out over my shoulders as I center myself over his dick and rub my clit up and down it.

His groans of pleasure tell me everything I need to know. When his hands wrap around my hips, it's time to quit teasing and give us both exactly what we want.

"You sure you want to do this?"

I stare down at him like he's crazy. "Of course."

"We can try missionary. Might be easier on you. I don't want you to hurt yourself. Nothing's worth that, no matter how fucking good it feels."

My heart melts into a puddle right then and there. "Let me try, and I'll tell you. Okay?"

He nods, and I use my fingertips to lift the head of his cock to my entrance. We both freeze at the delicious contact.

Even though his hands are on my hips, and he could bury himself balls deep inside me in an instant, he lets me control the pace and depth. I sink onto his cock inch by inch, torturing us both with the pleasure.

His dark blond hair is splayed out on my pillow as his hooded eyes watch my every move.

"Your pace, ladybug. Your pace." He sounds hoarse with need, and it ignites the short fuse I've been ready to detonate all day.

I lift up and drop down fast, taking it all.

FORTY-NINE

Legend

H*oly. Fucking. Shit.*

She's a goddamned temptress sent from heaven to prove to mortal men that they don't know shit about shit. She levels me with her innocent movements that give me more pleasure than the most experienced woman alive could.

Scarlett Priest's pussy should be labeled a deadly weapon, because it just might fucking kill me. Her muscles clamp down on me as she rides, and with each stroke, I'm even closer to blowing my load.

Fuck. No condom.

I open my mouth to tell her, but she throws her head back and screams my name as her pussy flutters against my cock. She stills, and I can't hold back. I grip her hips carefully and lift my hips to thrust into her from below.

Her screams grow louder as her hair whips back and forth with her head. "I can't stop . . . coming!"

My roar fills the room as my orgasm rips from my balls and shoots me straight to the fucking moon. I ride it out as she rocks back and forth, stealing every last bit of my cum and my self-control.

When she falls forward onto my chest, I wrap my arms around her and hold her there, listening to her hammering heart.

Holy fucking shit.

It's the only rational thought in my brain, because I don't know what the fuck just happened.

We're explosive together. I thought I was making it up last time. That there was no way sex could be that insanely fucking good.

But I was wrong.

Together, we're un-fucking-believable.

Long minutes pass as the sweat cools on my skin, and our heartbeats slow to normal levels. I inhale the scent of Scarlett, mixed with hot sex, and it becomes my new favorite smell.

She shifts her hips, and I help her as she rolls off me and onto the bed beside me, flat on her back.

Her chest rises and falls, and I realize I never took off her bra. Total oversight. I didn't have the time or the brain cells still functioning well enough to do that. *Next time.*

I need a whole fuck ton of next times with her. Nothing else will ever compare to this—because I'm in love with Scarlett Priest.

Holy fucking shit.

FIFTY

Scarlett

Every muscle in my body is languid, and I'm not sure if I ever need to move again. *Oh my God. This is what great sex feels like.*

My chest shakes with a giggle, and the man beside me, with his dark blond hair spilling across my silk pillowcase, angles his head toward me.

"I hope that's a good laugh."

I don't know what my face looks like right this second, but I'll bet I'm beaming. "It's a really good laugh. And in no way is meant to make you question how freaking amazing that was." A renewed energy rises within me, and I roll onto my side to face him. "I didn't know it could be like that."

The smile that curls his lips is pure joy—and masculine pride. "We are pretty fucking amazing together. You're a miracle, ladybug. Watching you let go and soak up every fucking drop of pleasure is the most incredible thing I've ever seen."

Instead of feeling embarrassed, talking about a subject that has been so difficult for me for years, I feel *free.*

This is how it's supposed to be. Who knew you could talk

about sex and how amazing it is while you're lying there, basking in the afterglow?

At least until I realize Gabriel is leaking out of me . . . *because we didn't use a condom.* His face changes as mine does.

"I know. No condom. I promise I'm clean. I don't ever take chances. This . . . this is a first for me."

I nod, my temporary freak-out subsiding as quickly as it rose. "I am too. I got tested with my annual, and I was never with Chadwick after that again. We should be fine." I move to roll off the bed, but Gabriel reaches out and threads his fingers through mine.

His blue eyes are full of warmth and sincerity. "We will be fine. No matter what."

My thoughts from earlier about that blond-haired, blue-eyed boy come back. "Do you want kids? I mean, not right now, obviously, but . . . someday?"

I expect his expression to shutter, but he doesn't close down. In fact, for the first time since I met this intensely private man, I feel like I can see every emotion travel across his expression. *Hesitation. Hope. Yearning.*

"I never let myself think about stuff like that, or at least, I didn't." His lids lower, and I lose his eyes, but he keeps going. "Jorie and I were planning on having a couple, after she made it and got a record deal. She would talk about them like they were real. When I lost her, I lost all of that, and never thought I'd get it back."

He lifts his chin, and that blue gaze burns with feeling. "I probably shouldn't want kids. I don't come from good stock. I shouldn't want to pass along my genes to another generation, but I know I'd be a damn good dad. My kids would want for nothing. There's nothing I wouldn't do to protect them. They'd never wonder if they were loved."

Tears burn in my eyes, obscuring my vision as I blink

them back. The waves of emotion rolling off Gabriel are some of the most beautiful I've ever witnessed.

"I agree. You'd make a great dad."

He grins at me. "And you'd make a hell of a mom. The best kind."

I suck in a breath to steady myself so I don't lose my control as those tears are desperate to fall. "I hope you're right, because it's really important to me. My mom was amazing. The best. I couldn't have asked for more. I always wanted to be part of a big family, but there were no little brothers or sisters for me when I was young. And, well, you know about my dad . . ."

"You'll get what you want, Scarlett. You deserve everything."

It's on the tip of my tongue to say, *I want it with you, so please tell me we're on the same page here.*

But, instead, I go with, "I should clean up. Want to shower with me?"

He jackknifes up in bed. "I'd be a fucking idiot to turn down the chance to have you wet, naked, and slippery."

"Oh *fuck.*"

The shower started innocently enough, but somehow my palm found its way to Gabriel's dick, and those blue eyes of his heated with lust.

I couldn't keep my words to myself. "I loved watching you jack off in the shower. It was so fucking hot."

That led to him turning the handheld sprayer on a low, pulsing setting, and using it to drive me wild. Which brings us to now, and my hands pressed against the tile as he powers into me from behind.

"Jesus fucking Christ. You're going to strangle my cock. Fucking beautiful."

He fucks into me until I come one more time and my knees go weak.

"I got you. Lean back on me. I won't let you fall."

The words are so simple, but to me, they mean everything. I've never had someone who I could trust to always be there for me and hold me together when I'm falling apart.

I loop an arm backward to cup the back of his neck as he finishes us both off. "Oh my God! Gabriel!"

His harsh indrawn breath fills the shower before he roars and spills inside me. He pulls out, letting the spray wash me clean.

We both stumble back a few steps until he braces on the wall of the shower, holding us both up with his muscled forearms. "Goddamn. I feel like I'm eighteen again and can't get enough of you. You tell me to hold off if it gets to be too much, okay?"

With the water from the other showerhead beating down on us, I belly laugh until my chuckles fill the shower. "I've got years to make up for, but yeah, I'll make sure to tell you."

He presses a kiss to my cheek. "You make me really fucking happy, Scarlett. Thank you for that."

I turn in a slippery circle to press my breasts to his naked chest. "You do the exact same thing for me." I soak up his heat for a beat, and my stomach growls again.

"Time for dessert," Gabriel says.

I smile mischievously at him. "You mean fuel up for another round? Sounds like a great plan."

FIFTY-ONE

Legend

When we walk into the restaurant on Tuesday night, Bump is bouncing like his normal insanely excited self.

"She's meeting us here? Right? And she's going to play games with us? Do you think she'll let me keep her tickets so I can get a bigger prize? You always let me keep your tickets, Gabe."

We're meeting Scarlett at what might be Bump's favorite place in the city—a restaurant that's more about the arcade games than the food.

"She'll be here. You'll have to ask her about the tickets. I don't know; maybe she'll want a prize for herself."

Bump claps his hands. "Maybe I could give her *my* tickets and then *she* could get a really big one. You think she'd like that?"

"I bet she'd be thrilled, bud. Look, there she is. Right on time."

Scarlett walks through the doors with her straight blond hair shining under the lights. She's wearing jeans, which is a first that I've seen, and a silky navy-blue-and-white plaid shirt tucked in at the front. She looks fucking edible.

"She's here!" Bump rushes over to see her, and it makes me just as fucking happy to see the smile stretch her cheeks as she hugs him. The dude kidnapped her, and here she is excited to have dinner with him.

Like I said before, Scarlett's a miracle. I can't imagine any other woman who wouldn't at least try to keep him at a distance.

Bump brings her over to me, and I lean in to steal a kiss from her lush pink lips. Makeup be damned.

"You look beautiful. Thanks for meeting us."

"Thank you for inviting me. I've never been here, but I'm ready to play." She looks to Bump. "Which is your favorite game? Which ones do I have to try?"

Bump launches into a serious debate centered around Skee-Ball and motorcycle racing as I give a sign to the hostess that we're ready to be seated.

The three of us head to the table, but Bump never misses a beat. "We can race motorcycles first and then we can play Skee-Ball, and you can tell me which is your favorite, because I like old school and new school, and I'm good at both."

"Don't let him talk you into betting on it. Bump is a total shark when it comes to Skee-Ball."

The pride on Bump's face warms my heart, and helps take away some of the concern I've been carrying all day, since we haven't heard from Bruce or Gerard about the contract for the fights to happen at Legend.

I know it takes longer than a day to draft the contracts that'll make it a done deal, but I'm more worried about them not being able to get approval from whoever they might have to run it by. Q reached out to Black, but we haven't heard back from him either.

I need all these pieces to fall into place if my plan is going to work, but so far, nothing's moving. I have a meeting with some of my investors in less than forty-eight hours, and I need this plan to be sorted out beforehand. If I can tell them I have it all handled at the meeting, they'll back off with their questions and let me run my business the way I need to. But considering the current state of affairs and who my investors are, they're going to have a fuck load of questions that I'm not ready to answer yet.

Dinner goes quickly, with Bump carrying the weight of the conversation with Scarlett, at least until the food comes. Then he turns into a Hoover, and the food is gone in minutes without a single word from him until his head pops up.

"Can we play now?"

I pull out my wallet and peel off a couple of twenties. "You get started. We're going to finish up and pay the tab, and then we'll come find you."

Bump stares at Scarlett. I know he desperately wants her to come with him, but he's being patient, which is new for him. "Okay, but come find me. I'll warm up on hoops, and meet you at the motorcycles, okay?"

"That sounds great, Bump," Scarlett says, and he scampers off.

"I'm sorry about that. He's always at level ten when we're here. He has no chill when it comes to arcade games."

Scarlett's gaze follows him as he goes to change the cash for the swipe card that will unlock the hours of fun that will come next. "He's a special guy. His enthusiasm is contagious. I haven't been this excited to play Skee-Ball since second grade."

"Bump'll do that to you. You should see him at the go-kart track. He's a speed demon. Half the time, he gets black-flagged and thrown off the track because he gets too into rubbing and bumping cars driven by little kids."

"Well, I guess I'd be concerned, but considering he'd probably lap me within minutes, I think it'd be safe." She takes a long drink of her water.

"Thank you for coming tonight. I know this isn't your normal scene, but it means a lot to me and to him."

She reaches across the table to cover my hand with hers. "If this is going where I want it to go, then I plan on Bump being a big part of my life too. And it doesn't matter whether it's my scene or not, Gabriel. I like new experiences. I want to *live*, not stay locked away at Curated and never know what real life is like."

I think about all the shit that's still up in the air about the club, and all the ways things could go wrong. I won't take Scarlett down with me, but there's no chance in hell I can give her up again. I have to find a way to make this work for both of us . . . and I really need those fights to happen at the club—with me and Bodhi Black headlining the event.

I need to tell her. But not until I'm sure it's actually happening.

"You want to live, ladybug? Then I'm your guy. Because that's all I know how to do. Let me grab this check, and then I'm going to stare at your ass while you race motorcycles with Bump."

FIFTY-TWO

Scarlett

Gabriel's tense all night. I know there's something going on that he's not telling me, but with Bump grabbing me by the hand and pulling me all over the arcade, there's not a good time to ask what's on his mind.

I'm midway through kicking Bump's ass in Skee-Ball, much to my surprise, when I hear a familiar voice.

"I certainly never expected to see you here, Scarlett."

I release the ball before I'm ready, and it hits the backboard with a hard *thunk* as I turn toward the sound. "Meryl. What are you doing here?"

She's dressed like me, in jeans and a blouse, and she has a handful of tickets. "Playing games with some of the kids from the center. They won tonight through their good behavior." Her gaze lands on Bump, who is playing next to me. "And who is this?"

Gabriel returns with Bump's refilled popcorn to stand at my side as she asks the question.

"Meryl, this is Gabriel Legend, of the club Legend, and his little brother, Bump."

Meryl's eyes widen with the introduction, and it's evident

I've shocked her. "Mr. Legend. Your reputation precedes you."

Oxygen freezes in my lungs as Gabriel shifts the popcorn to his other arm and holds his free hand out to her. "It's a pleasure, Ms. Fosse. I hear you've done some great things for kids in the city. We're looking forward to your event."

I didn't think Meryl's eyes could get any bigger, but they do when Gabriel mentions the charity fundraiser.

"Ah, you'll be Scarlett's date. That's delightful. Hopefully, you won't find it too subdued for your taste. Although, the silent auction bidding can get quite heated." Meryl's words sound sincere rather than catty, but I can tell she's not sure what to make of our pairing. Her attention shifts to me. "You're full of surprises, aren't you?"

"I won!" Bump throws his hands into the air and does a victory dance that breaks the rising tension. As he's attempting to moonwalk toward us, Gabriel holds out the popcorn.

"Here's your victory popcorn, bud. Don't spill it."

Meryl's eyes narrow on the missing strip of hair on the side of Bump's head, and she looks at me. I give her a little nod, and she glances back to Bump as he starts telling Gabriel about his strategy for the game and how if he can just play *one more time*, then he'll have enough tickets to win his prize, when he adds the tickets I gave him.

"You're pretty good at Skee-Ball," Meryl says, and Bump's head jerks around to look at her.

"Who are you?"

"I'm Meryl Fosse," she says, holding out her hand. "I run a center for kids in the city who need extra love."

Bump's face lights up. "I love kids. And I love love. Did you know that Scarlett gave me her tickets so I can get a prize from the *top shelf*? I almost have enough. One more game. Right, Gabe?" Bump stares pleadingly at Gabriel, and the man behind me nods.

"One more game. Then we're going to cash out and take Scarlett home. She's gotta work in the morning."

"I promise I won't take long, Scarlett. We have to get home to Roux, anyway. She misses me."

Bump, having already forgotten about Meryl, returns to his game. Her expression is curious, and I can tell she has questions but is much too polite to ask them.

Gabriel sees it too. "Traumatic brain injury. Fifteen years ago."

"Oh my. I'm so sorry." She takes another long look at Bump. "Does he have a job?"

"He works for me," Gabriel replies. "Why?"

Meryl purses her lips. "I'm always looking for good, kind-hearted volunteers at the center. You should bring him by sometime to see it."

"You want Bump to volunteer at some fancy charity place?" Gabriel sounds shocked.

Meryl shrugs. "I don't know enough about him or his background to say whether or not I'd want him to volunteer yet, but I like his energy and his enthusiasm. You may keep him plenty busy with your work, Mr. Legend, but I find that sometimes people like Bump have much more to offer the world than we realize."

Gabriel's expression is skeptical as hell, but I want to hug Meryl Fosse. *This* is why I've been so desperate to get her as a client. Because she's real and smart, and she sees the good in people.

"I'll think about it," Gabriel says with a lift of his chin.

Meryl nods at him and then shifts her attention back to me. "I'll see you both Saturday night, Scarlett. I'm truly looking forward to it." There's a shriek from behind her, and she glances over her shoulder. "I'd better get back to my kids before they overrun the adults. Have a good night."

As she walks away, Gabriel looks down at me. "Saturday night? I thought it was next week?"

I grimace. "Sorry. I meant to tell you."

"It's no big thing. We can make it work, anyway. I just need to tell Q." He glances toward Meryl's group one more time. "You think she's serious about wanting Bump to volunteer, or was that some weird rich-bitch posturing that I don't understand?"

I slip my hand into his. "She was serious. She's good people, Gabriel. That's why I've been so anxious to get her business. She's not fake like a lot of the other ones. Meryl Fosse's organization does important work."

He turns to watch Bump throw another Skee-Ball. "Huh. Maybe she's right. Maybe that'd be good for him."

My phone buzzes in my purse, and I pull it out, more from habit than concern about it being an emergency. But when I see Amy's name on the screen, I pause.

"I need to answer this."

He waves a hand at the tickets flowing out of the machine Bump's playing. "Go for it. I'll be right here."

"Ames?" I say as I tap the screen.

"Hey, sorry to bother you tonight, but I need to ask you a question." The tone of her voice immediately puts me on edge.

"What?"

"What are you wearing?"

I jerk my head back at the question. "Why?"

"Just humor me, Scarlett. I swear I have a point."

I look down at my jeans and plaid blouse and describe them to her.

"What about earlier today?"

"Why, Amy? You're freaking me out." My voice grows

louder, and Gabriel's attention zeroes in on my face. He leaves Bump and comes to my side.

"The troll is back, and this time, he said something about you wearing a pink dress. I was gone all day, so I don't remember a pink dress. When did you wear one last?"

"Earlier today. When I went to pick up doughnuts for the girls, I was wearing a pink dress." My stomach twists, and I move back a few steps to lean against the side of a video game.

Gabriel moves beside me. "What's going on?" he asks, his gaze cutting from me to the phone. "What's happening?"

Amy keeps going. "*Shit.* He's here, Scarlett. That sick fuck is *here* in the city, and he saw you today."

"Send me the screenshots. I'll call the detective."

Harsh lines etch into Gabriel's face. I can tell he wants to rip the phone from my hand and demand answers, but he doesn't. As soon as I hang up the phone, we'll be having a conversation that I didn't want to have tonight, but now there's no other alternative.

"Sending them now. This guy is sick, Scarlett. We need to stop him."

"I know, Amy. Trust me, I know."

Once I end the call, Gabriel corners me next to the arcade games. "What's going on? Your face is white as a fucking sheet. What happened?"

"I have a troll on social media. Well, I have a lot of them, but there's one who . . . well, he's more of a stalker. And, apparently, he knew what I was wearing earlier today." My voice shakes, and I can't pretend I'm not terrified of what this could mean.

"*Fuck.*" Gabriel bites out the word as he wraps his arms around me, then pulls me against his chest and squeezes hard. "No one touches you. I fucking promise. No one touches you *ever*. We'll find this fucker, and we'll take care of him."

I want to believe him. I want to soak up his heat and strength and let him take my problems so I don't have to carry them, but that's not how I'm built.

"I have to call the detective and email the screenshots over. I don't know what else to do."

Gabriel loosens his grip on me and presses his forehead to mine. "Don't lose one minute of sleep over this. I'll handle it. Give me everything you have, and I'll put out feelers. Q has a whole fucking network of people in the city that we use for information. I don't care how many favors we have to call in, we'll find him, and we'll make it stop."

I inhale a shaky breath. "I would really, really like that. And I should probably find a new self-defense instructor. Just in case."

His blue eyes have never been more serious than they are in this moment. "I'll teach you everything you need to know. No sick fuck is going to hurt a goddamned hair on your head. Not while I'm breathing."

FIFTY-THREE

I t takes every ounce of willpower I have to wait for Bump to finish and pick out his prize—a giant stuffed elephant—and then get the three of us the hell out of the restaurant.

We take a cab back to the club, because I'm not walking the streets, even at this time of night, with Scarlett beside me. She called the detective while Bump was finishing his game, and filled him in on everything.

My guts are twisted into knots at the fucking filth this prick is saying to her. Killing people may not be part of my repertoire these days, but I sure as fuck can find a bullet with this prick's name on it.

After we hurry back to the club and get Roux, we all load up in my Bronco, and I back out of the parking spot in the alley.

"Are you coming home with us, Scarlett? It's so cool. You can see my other prizes too. They're in my apartment."

I look across to her pale features, and even though it wasn't the plan, I'm definitely bringing her home with us. "It

258

ain't fancy, but if you want to see where I live . . ." I trail off to let her decide.

"I'd love to come home with you both."

"Sweet!" Bump pumps his fist in the air, and I give her a nod.

"You need anything from your place?"

She shakes her head. "I'm good. Let's just get out of the city."

I hate that she's getting chased out of her own town because of fear, and I vow right then that it won't last. Whoever the fuck this gutless asshole is, we're going to find out, and I'm going to take care of him.

That's a promise.

FIFTY-FOUR

I t's funny that the last two times I've left the city have been with Gabriel. Or maybe not funny so much as telling. He pushes me outside my comfort zone without even trying.

Despite the pall the troll cast over tonight, I'm excited to see where Gabriel lives. I want to know everything about this enigmatic man, but I suspect it's going to take years to peel back all of his layers.

Years. The prospect of spending a minute more with Chadwick terrified me, but with Gabriel, no amount of time I can think of feels like enough.

Because you've fallen hard, Good Scarlett reminds me. *And that's not a bad thing. Enjoy it.*

And I will, because it's impossible to slow my racing heart when he's around. My breath still catches when he smiles at me. My skin tingles when he touches it. If this is what being in love is supposed to feel like, then it's a whole new experience for me.

Thankfully, Bump keeps the conversation going without needing much input from me or Gabriel. When we pull down a side street and make a left, Roux sits up and pokes her head between my seat and the window off to my right.

"She knows she's almost home," Bump says from the back. "She likes to see it, though, just to make sure."

I sit up straighter, peering through the fading sun and the orange glow of the streetlights coming to life. It's an industrial area dotted with storefronts and a few houses that seem to be the last holdouts to all-out commercialization.

Gabriel slows in front of a blue-and-white painted concrete building with four large overhead doors labeled ALIGNMENTS, BRAKES, MUFFLERS, and OIL CHANGES. Above the doors is a sign with QUINTERRO'S in big blue letters.

Gabriel parks in front of the MUFFLERS door and shuts off the Bronco. Bump opens the back and Roux is the first one out, trotting to a patch of grass nearby to take care of her business. As she's nosing around, I hop out of the truck and meet Gabriel in front of it.

"Home sweet home. Even if it doesn't look like much." He points left with a raised arm. "Q's parents live on the other side of the scrapyard. His pop still runs it with the help of one of his sisters. That's what's behind the big fence between here and the white house down the street."

"The scrapyard is fun, but dangerous. I don't go there by myself. Only with Big Mike," Bump says with pride in his voice.

"I've never been to a scrapyard, but it sounds like a great place to find cool stuff."

"So much cool stuff. Like you wouldn't believe."

"All right, Bump," Gabriel says. "You take Roux up to your place. Make sure you check her water and food."

Bump salutes him. "Got it, Gabe. I'm going to brush her too. She'll like that."

Gabriel leads us all to a side door and unlocks it. "Good deal, bud. See you in the morning."

Bump dashes up the stairs, trying to keep pace with Roux. From the top, he yells down with a snicker. "I'll keep my TV on too. Just in case you need to be loud."

I cover my own giggle as it tumbles involuntarily out of my mouth.

Gabriel shakes his head as Bump disappears. "That kid . . ."

"He's awesome," I say, slipping my hand into his. "And he's really lucky to have you."

Gabriel's gaze drops to our joined hands before cutting to my face. "I got him shot in the head. I'm the reason he's like this. I don't know if he's lucky to have me, but I wish every fucking day that I hadn't gotten him hurt."

My stomach plummets to the cracked gray concrete beneath my feet. "Oh God. Gabriel."

"I'm not a good guy, Scarlett. One day, I'm going to get my revenge for what happened to Bump. I don't have a choice."

I drop his hand and wrap my arms around him instead. "You may not think you're a good guy, but I believe you're a good man with strong principles and loyalty that runs deep."

His chin dips for a beat before he lifts that blue gaze to mine. "I guess we'll find out who's right. Come on up. It's not much, but it works."

He leads me up the stairs covered with ancient-looking brown-and-orange carpet to a wood-paneled hallway. Noise from a TV show comes from behind the first door, and Gabriel walks past it to the last one. When he opens it, I'm expecting more of the same—old carpet and wood paneling —but I'm totally wrong.

Inside, the floors are wide planks of dark laminate wood, and the walls are slate blue. The furniture is simple—black leather sofa, dark wood coffee table. As Gabriel hangs his keys on a hook next to the door, I take in a kitchen with stainless appliances, dark wooden cabinets, and gray granite countertops.

"I was going to move out a few years back, but Bump didn't want to be that far away from Big Mike. I wasn't going to leave without him, so I gutted both apartments, and Q and I refinished them so they didn't look like the hallway."

Warmth blooms in my chest at the thought of him staying here, even when he had the money to leave, because Bump liked being close to Q's family.

"Like I said, you're a good man."

Gabriel shakes his head again and takes a breath. A serious expression settles itself onto his face. "Enough about me and what I am or aren't. We gotta talk about you."

The warmth I've been feeling cools a few degrees. "What about me?"

"This troll. Your safety. Security. I'm going to call in a favor from a friend. He's a retired boxer. Golden Gloves champ back in the day. He drives and provides security, and he's discreet. You're going to let him be your shadow."

"Thank you, but you don't need to do anything like that. This isn't the first time that asshole has shit all over my page, and it won't be the last. I'm not going to let him throw my life into chaos. Then he'd be winning."

Gabriel stops a foot away from me. "Are we together?"

I blink at him. "Yeah . . . I mean, I assume we are."

"You're right. We are together. And that makes your safety my job and a top priority. Your last guy wasn't a real man, so I don't expect you to get how this works. But keeping you safe matters a hell of a lot to me, and I wouldn't be a man—good, bad, or otherwise—if I didn't take steps to make it happen."

FIFTY-FIVE

Scarlett's face goes pale, and I automatically wonder if I'm coming on too strong for her. I know she's not used to a guy like me, but that's too bad. She'll get used to it.

"What?"

Scarlett swallows, and what looks like fear streaks across her face. "Chadwick," she whispers. "What if he's the troll?"

The blood charging through my veins slows with ice-cold determination. "Then I take care of him and the problem goes away." I don't mean to sound like an old mob movie, but if the shoe fits . . .

Her wide eyes lift to mine. "We have to tell the detective. They'll question him. Dig into his phone and computer."

The thought of tipping off the guy to our suspicions seems like a mistake to me, but when tears well in Scarlett's eyes, I forget about anything else but making them go away.

"Okay. We'll play this your way for now. Bring it in, ladybug. You need a fucking hug, and I need to hold you."

A tear tips over her lids as I open my arms. "How did you know?"

"I'm learning you. Now come here."

She steps into the circle of my arms, and I wrap them around her, pressing her flush against my chest. We stand like that, in silence, until our breathing matches and I swear we're in sync.

She takes a step back, and I loosen my grip, but not much.

"What?"

"Thank you."

"For what?"

"Being you." She rises on her toes to ghost her mouth across mine, but I need more from her. I need it all.

I reposition my arms to cup the back of her head and tilt it so I can taste her better, and *sweet fuck*, she is perfect. When her hands go to the hem of my shirt and tug it upward, I'm more than on board with whatever she wants and needs from me right now.

We break apart so she can lose the shirt, and my fingers find the buttons of her blouse. One by one, I free them, revealing her lacy bra and rounded tits.

Without another word, I lift her into my arms and carry her into my bedroom. Thank fuck the sheets were changed yesterday and the bed is made. I lower her onto the comforter and follow her down.

Slowly, like time ceases to exist, we strip each other. She covers my skin with kisses from those pouty lips, and by the time I roll her onto her back and slide a knee between her thighs, she's soaked and I'm rock hard.

I slide a finger between her slippery lips and stroke up to her clit. "You need me, baby? Need my hard cock filling this tight little cunt of yours?"

Her mouth opens on a moaned exhalation. "Yes."

"Damn right you do. My cunt. Because you're fucking mine. Not letting you go. No one is fucking taking you from me."

"I love you, Gabriel." The words fall from her lips, and my heart damn near fucking stops.

She loves me.

I squeeze my eyes shut for a beat. "You shouldn't."

When I open them, she's lifting her hand to my face and stroking across my stubbled cheek.

"But I do, and I'm not taking it back. And you're not kicking me out after we have sex either, because you're scared of how I feel."

I dip my forehead to hers. "I'm not scared of how you feel, Scarlett. I just don't deserve it. But I will. Give me some time."

The urge to return her words is so fucking strong that they're practically jumping off my tongue. But I can't say them. Not yet. Not until I'm the man she needs me to be. Instead, I press kisses to her eyelids, the tip of her nose, and her forehead.

"I want you inside me," she says, lifting her hips until the wetness from her pussy slicks across my dick.

"That's exactly what you're gonna get. All of me." I push forward, sinking into her tight, wet heat with her name on my tongue and my chest so fucking full that I think it might burst.

After she screams out *"I love you"* and falls asleep in my arms, it's no one's business but mine that I hold her, listening to her heartbeat, when I should have long since closed my eyes.

I can't fall asleep until I say it, even if she can't hear me.

I pitch my voice low, so it's almost inaudible. "I love you too, ladybug. And I'm going to prove it to you."

FIFTY-SIX

Legend

"I would go with you if I could, but I promise Gunter is super cool. He's the only person I trust in the city to get you set up right in this short a time. I've known him since I was five," Scarlett says as I drop her off in front of Curated the next morning.

Our breakfast conversation consisted of her finally giving in on having O'Halloran drive her and act as discreet security. But, in exchange, I have to go get fitted for a tux that somehow will magically be ready in two days, and I'm not allowed to pay for it. I don't like that she's calling in favors for me too, but she held firm on the bargain.

She even spit on the handshake.

"I'll be fine. I got the address." I give her a kiss. "Go get 'em today, killer. Sell all the shit. I mean stuff. Your stuff's not shit."

I'm tripping over my words like a kid who just got his first blow job, and I know it's because she said those three little words to me last night. I can't help but look at her differently. _She's mine._

It's a great fucking feeling, but that doesn't mean I'm used to it yet.

"I know what you mean." She presses another kiss to my lips. "I'll call you later."

I watch her walk up the sidewalk to the front door of her building and wait until she disappears inside.

She's safe now, and by the time we leave for the gala on Saturday, O'Halloran will be on duty, and I'll finally be able to rest easy about leaving her alone.

After a quick workout at the gym that tells me—loud and fucking clear—I need to start busting my ass if I'm going to be ready for a fight with Bodhi, I shower at the club and then head to the address Scarlett gave me.

It's a black door that has a sign that reads GUNTER and a pair of scissors below his name. *Is this dude like Madonna? Only going by one name?*

I ring the buzzer and wait for a few minutes until I hear footsteps. The black door opens, and a guy I'd guess is in his sixties stands there with perfectly styled silver hair.

He doesn't say anything for a moment as he surveys me. "Only for Scarlett or her dearly departed mother would I do this. Come in. We have work to do."

I follow him inside and up a set of stairs to the second floor. He unlocks another black door and opens it to reveal a pretty bomb-ass loft with a massive bay window over the street. There's shit everywhere, though. Four massive tables are covered in books and fabric and crap. It's like every flat surface has been taken up with more and more shit.

"I'm Gabriel Legend."

He whips a look over his shoulder. "I know exactly who you are, you beautiful brute. Leave it to Scarlett to take a walk on the wild side. You're quite rough around the edges for her taste, but—"

I don't wait for another word before I turn on my heel and head for the door. *Fuck this judgmental asshole.*

"And where do you think you're going? You need a tux, and no one can get you a decent custom one in less than forty-eight hours in this city, except for me."

I look over my shoulder and see him standing with his arms crossed in a beam of sunlight from the window.

"You want to talk shit about me, you don't fucking do it to my face unless you want a busted nose in return. But you never, *and I mean fucking never*, say a goddamn negative word about Scarlett to anyone, anywhere, or for any reason. You hear me?"

His chin lifts in slow motion, and he uncrosses his arms to stare at me like I'm a wild animal in the zoo. "Well, well. I can't say anyone has had the balls to speak to me like that in years."

"Likewise, *Gunter.*"

"Why don't you come back, and we'll start over—with an apology. I shouldn't have been so cavalier with my words. I apologize. And what's more, I would never disparage Scarlett in any way, shape, or form. I've known her since she was practically a baby, and I consider her family. I feel quite protective of her."

I release the door handle and turn around. "I may not have known her that long, but there isn't a goddamn thing I wouldn't do to protect her, and that's all you need to know about me."

Gunter's lips quirk and he smiles. "That'll do. Come in. Let's get you measured so I can get to work performing this miracle."

While he measures what seems like every inch of my body, Gunter never stops talking.

"I started working for Lourdes Scarlett Priest and House of Scarlett when Scarlett was five. You've never seen a happier, sweeter child. She played hide-and-seek in the racks of clothes and spent hours flipping through fabric swatches. Her mother was so proud. She thought Scarlett would follow in her footsteps and take over the house, but high-fashion design has never been Scarlett's passion."

"But Scarlett could've run the business like a boss. She's capable as hell."

Gunter nods in agreement, making a notation on his pad. "Absolutely, but when Lourdes's health was failing, she and Scarlett had the discussion about the future of the business, and both agreed on the sale. It was the right move, in my opinion. And they were both incredibly strong women, which is what it would take to make that kind of decision under those circumstances."

"What about Scarlett's dad?" I ask, because I don't know enough about the asshole whose absence after her surgery made her cry.

Gunter's expression hardens. "I hate that man with the fire of a thousand suns."

"Damn. I figured he was a major prick, but it sounds like I underestimated him."

Gunter clenches the tape measure in his hand. "Scarlett is and will always be Lawrence's finest accomplishment in his lifetime, but he pretends like she doesn't exist."

"I fucking hate that for her." I grit out the words from between clenched teeth.

"You and me both." Gunter pauses, setting aside the tape measure and lifting his brown eyes to mine. "You really care about her, don't you?"

I shift my feet and hold his gaze. "No offense, old man, but what I feel for Scarlett is between me and her. And if I haven't told her yet, I'm sure as hell not telling you."

Gunter's entire expression changes when he smiles widely. "She deserves an exceptional man, Mr. Legend. I truly hope you can be him."

"I don't know about exceptional, but I'm going to do whatever I can to keep her happy and safe."

Gunter nods slowly. "You'll do, Gabriel. Yes. You'll do very well."

FIFTY-SEVEN

The clients I have on the third floor today are enough to give me a total headache.

Two women left without buying a single thing, after each browsing for over an hour. Then Lucy Byers—heiress to a paper company, former prep school classmate, and queen bitch—shows up. Her first order of business is to scold me for keeping her waiting three weeks for an appointment.

"You know, I almost didn't even come. No one makes me wait for anything. It's like you've forgotten who your people are, Scarlett." She lets her words hang in the air, before adding for emphasis, "I guess that's what happens when you start scraping the bottom of the barrel for men. But, tell me, is he really hung like a Clydesdale? Because I've heard rumors."

I stare at her in shock. "Excuse me?"

She turns to her friend, whose name I've already forgotten, because she *didn't* have an appointment, and smiles. "I told you she'd never admit to seeing him. Scarlett has always been too much of a good girl. Worried about her sterling reputation and all."

I have lines, and this bitch just crossed one. "You know what, Lucy? Get the hell out of my store."

Lucy's jaw drops. "What?"

"If you think you can come in here and talk like that to me, then you aren't worth my time. As you're aware, I have a long waiting list of people who'd love to be in here right now, and they wouldn't resort to mean-girl tactics that should've stayed in high school just to feel better about themselves."

Her chin goes up, and it's abundantly clear she's had plenty of work done on her face since prep school. "I don't know what you're talking about. I'm simply making conversation. Did I hit a nerve with my comment about your boyfriend? Or is he just your . . . entertainment? Because no one would judge you for needing a real man after Chadwick. He's an *epically* terrible lay. The worst I've ever had."

Now it's my mouth hanging open. "You slept with Chadwick?"

Her brittle laugh could peel paint. "Only once. You'd only been dating a few months. My husband and I were having a rocky time getting through his affair, so of course I had to get payback. I should've chosen better, though. Too bad you didn't hook up with Gabriel Legend sooner."

This fucking bitch. Bad Scarlett whips her earrings off and is ready to fight, but I stay composed.

"Get out of my store. I won't tell you again before I call security to have you escorted out. I saw some paps out there earlier. I'm sure they'd eat it up. I may even give them a quote."

She looks around the room, decorated with treasures from all over the world. "Like I want any of your secondhand trash, anyway. Come on, Tiffany. This place is so cluttered, it gives me hives." She struts toward the door with her friend trailing behind like an obedient puppy.

I wait until she's out of earshot before I whisper, "You hoity-toity fucking bitch."

Unfortunately, I must not whisper quietly enough, because Tiffany glares at me over her shoulder.

I flip her the bird and sink onto the sofa. Amy finds me a few minutes later with my head cradled in my hands.

"Um . . . Scar? Are you okay? Because Lucy Byers just said some really ugly things as she stomped out of the store."

I lift my head to look at her. "She won't be making another appointment, and if she tries, refuse."

"What happened?" Amy asks.

"She just wanted to run her mouth, and I wasn't in the mood for it."

Amy's eyes widen, but she nods anyway. "Okay. No problem. Losing one client is no big deal."

"She didn't come to buy, so I'd hardly call her a client. She just wanted dirt on me and Gabriel, and to let me know that my ex-boyfriend cheated on me with her, while we were together."

"She *did not*." Amy's hands ball into fists on her hips as she whips her head toward the door, like she's contemplating going after Lucy.

"She did, but I don't even care anymore. She and Tiffany can go buy secondhand trash somewhere else."

Slowly, Amy turns back to me, but the militant expression on her face tells me plenty about her loyalty. She'd definitely shank Lucy for me. That's enough to make me push Lucy Byers and her high-class cheating ass out of my head. At least, for now.

"Who do we have left?" I ask.

Amy lowers herself onto the couch beside me. "She was our last appointment of the day, and your schedule is clear for the rest of the afternoon and evening. Is there anything I can do for you?"

"No, I'm fine. I need to go look through my closet and see what I can find for Meryl's gala on Saturday night."

Amy's eyebrows shoot up to her hairline. "Oh crap. You don't have a dress sorted out already? Do you want me to call that designer back from the other day and see if they have anything that could work on short notice?"

I shake my head. "I think I'm done with people for today, but thanks. I'll find something, or I'll call Harlow. She's always trying to loan me dresses."

"Okay. Just . . . don't let that bitch get to you. You're better than that."

I think about the urge I had to punch Lucy Byers in the face, which was new and different for me. Maybe Gabriel is rubbing off?

I sure hope so.

I'm tired of being the girl who is too polite to stand up for herself. That might not have been fun, but at least I'm proud of how I handled it. I am nobody's doormat.

"I'll be fine. Especially once I see Gabriel." When Amy's gaze dips, I immediately wonder why she isn't meeting my eyes. "Is something wrong?"

"I know it's not my place to say, but . . . are you sure taking him to the gala is a good idea? It's not really his scene, you know."

I rise from the sofa. "Everyone needs to stop assuming he doesn't know how to handle himself. Everything will be fine, Ames. Just wait and see."

FIFTY-EIGHT

I still haven't heard from Bruce and Gerard, and neither have returned the emails I've sent asking for an update on the venue selection. Their radio silence makes walking into the meeting with my investors on Thursday less than ideal.

As Cannon Freeman, Jared Jones-Wyatt, and Lou France file into the office we've converted into a conference room for today, I wish I'd put on a fucking suit to feel more like the CEO I'm supposed to be. I hate that I feel this way.

Q and Big Mike step inside last. At least they won't be surprised to see me in ripped jeans and a hoodie. Some things don't change.

As the men take their seats around the table, I remind myself that I got here without fancy suits, and wearing one now won't change who I am. I can learn to be slick and polished if I wanted to, but none of these guys could have done what I did with what I had. The thought buoys my confidence as I survey our guests.

"Creighton couldn't make it. I'm here as his proxy," Freeman says.

I remember approaching them on the sidewalk one night, both of them looking at me like I was crazy for going legit. But they both ponied up some money, which shocked me. I thought for sure they wouldn't change their minds after they initially shot me down.

Then again, it was Creighton Karas who insisted on this meeting to discuss the future of the club and the disappointing financials, so it's bullshit he couldn't make it. Rather than start the meeting off on a bad foot, I nod.

Jared Jones-Wyatt is a trust fund kid who can't say no to coke or any kind of action he can bet on. He was a regular at my underground club, blowing thousands a night on himself and whatever crew of chicks he brought with him. He always bet on me in every fight, though, and that's why I invited him to bet on me again with Legend. His tolerance for risk is high as fuck, and I don't expect any pushback from him, no matter which way the meeting goes. He's on my side.

Lou France leans back in the leather chair, his short arms crossed over his chest. Lou is a retired bookie who wanted a legit investment to help make his retirement more comfortable. From the frown on his face that strangely resembles Danny DeVito, I'm not picking up a good vibe from him.

Off to my left is Big Mike, next to Q, who both put in their hard-earned cash, even after I tried to talk them out of it. I didn't want their money on the line because I know how fucking hard Big Mike works, and the thought of losing even a penny that belonged to him made me sick. But when it came down to it, I needed every cent I could get, and when they insisted, I caved.

I promised all of them they'd get a hell of a return on their investment. That there was no chance that I could fail. That Legend would become just that—the most legendary club this city has ever seen.

I've failed to deliver, and now I'm being called on the

carpet to answer for it.

Zoe slips into the room and shuts the door behind her. She takes a chair near the wall with a notepad, ready to take notes on the meeting.

I rise from my seat at the head of the table, facing Freeman at the foot. "Welcome back to Legend. I'll skip the bullshit song and dance, if you don't mind, and get right to the reason you're all here."

"Fine by me," Lou says, lifting his chin. "I got chess in the park in an hour. Hoping we can make this snappy."

I take his comment as a good sign and return his chin jerk. "As you all know, the shooting that happened on our grand opening night was a huge blow to Legend."

"Killed it dead on day one," Jared says with a shake of his head. "Total clusterfuck. Still no word from the cops on who did it?"

"I've got new information that we're tracking down," I tell him, thinking of the rumors circling about Bodhi Black's possible involvement.

"Are you going to share that information?" Freeman asks.

"Not yet, because it won't bring the club back to where it needs to be, and that's what you're all concerned about—your money."

"Creighton wanted to make sure everyone is aware that a unanimous vote of the investors would shut the club down and lead to immediate liquidation and return of our investments."

"Whoa, whoa, Freeman. No reason to pull out the big guns yet. Let the boy talk." Big Mike's defense of me keeps me from telling Cannon Freeman to shove his hopes of a unanimous vote up his ass, but I don't lose my cool.

"I wouldn't be too hasty pulling that card, gentlemen. I've got potential action lined up that could bring in enough cash to pay all of you off—in full."

Every man at the table stares at me in varying degrees of shock as they sit up higher in their chairs to listen.

"What are you talking about?" Jared asks, the greed already visible in his posture as he leans in.

"I'm in negotiation to host a fight night—"

Lou interrupts. "Thought you were staying legit, Legend." Accusation underlies his tone. "If you wanted to stick with the fighting, you never should've slaughtered the cash cow."

"A *sanctioned* fight night with a main event that'll sell even more tickets, because Legend's a bigger venue than the one they originally chose and lost."

Freeman threads his fingers together and taps his thumbs. "Tell us more."

"Eight fights. Balcony seats alone will bring in close to half a million. Legend takes fifty percent of the gate. We charge a premium for everything that night, especially the liquor. The place will be packed."

Practically salivating at the betting that'll be going on, Jared's eyes go big. "Who's fighting? What's the main event?"

I scan the table, meeting each of their eyes before I give them the information I hope will sway them back. "Me and Bodhi Black."

Their reaction is a mixture of raised eyebrows, gasps of surprise, and clapping.

"Fuck yeah," Jared says with a fist pump. "I've been waiting for that rematch since you ended the last fight. This is going to be fucking raw. You two are going to try to take each other's heads off."

"You sure putting your neck on the line is the right way to save this club, Gabe?" This question comes from Big Mike. The concern on his face is probably the closest I'll ever get to having a father give a shit about me.

"When you put your money down to back me, I made all of you a promise that I wouldn't fail. And if this is what it takes, then this is exactly the right way to save the club. It could lead to other events. Open Legend up to new opportunities."

Big Mike goes quiet. I know he'll support me, even if he thinks it's a bad idea.

"I'm all for it, as long as I get a ticket," Lou says, looking to me. "You making that happen?"

It's not something I've thought about, but I don't have a choice. "Yeah, you get two tickets if you want them. Might as well come see your investment being protected."

"And you've got this event nailed down? Contracts signed? It's happening for sure?"

I'm not surprised that the hard questions come from Cannon Freeman.

"Next week," I reply with more confidence than I feel. "It's in the works as we speak."

He rests his elbows on the table and studies me. "And what if it doesn't happen? You got a backup plan?"

"Legend and Black have a sanctioned fight, anyway," Jared says with excitement buzzing through every word. "I know a guy on the commission. He and I have an understanding. You don't need an undercard, man. People will pay through the ass to see you two try to kill each other."

It's an option I haven't even considered. I know how to organize a fight. I've watched Rolo do it for years.

"That's right. We'll have the fight anyway. Undercard or not. This shit's happening, and it's going to be one of the most talked-about combat events this city has ever seen."

Freeman's shoulders lift and then fall. "It's your head, Legend. You want to do this, then do it. I won't call for a vote to liquidate if you're still committed."

I don't have a choice.

"I'm committed. You can take that to the bank."

FIFTY-NINE

Scarlett

Kelsey spritzes my face with one last pump of setting spray and steps back to assess her finished work. "You always look amazing, but tonight, you're *glowing*."

I glance at the mirror behind her. I look even more dewy than normal, and I'm digging the look. "Only because you're an artist, Kels."

She leans in to air-kiss me. "It helps to have an awesome canvas to start with. Whatever you're doing . . . keep it up, girl. Your skin is perfect."

"I've made zero changes to my routine, but I am happier. You think that could be it?"

Kelsey beams. "Absolutely. Happiness is about the best complexion booster I've ever seen. Well, that and a good pregnancy glow. You're not knocked up, are you?"

I choke on air and cough. "What? No. Oh my God. Of course not."

But my mind immediately goes to all the condom-less sex I've been having lately. After we skipped one by accident and discussed our mutual lack of risk, we've never gone back.

Last night, after hanging at the club for a few hours, Gabriel came home with me, and we christened my kitchen table. Thankfully, he moved the giraffe salt and pepper shakers, or they never would have survived the ride.

"Well, good, that means you can pour enough wine down your gullet to make tonight fun. Harlow was bitching because I had to get her ready early this afternoon, and she wasn't going to be able to eat anything for the rest of the day. She said she'd make sure to tell you herself how unfair it is that you get my best time slots."

"Harlow can bitch all she wants, but she's too cheap to pay you what I do."

Kelsey nods. "Damn straight. And we all know Mama's got bills to pay. Now, when is lover boy showing up?"

I check the time on my phone. "In fifteen minutes. Shit. We'd better hurry."

I pop out of the chair and walk into the bedroom, where my gown is hanging from a hook in the corner. The shimmering azure-blue silk corset top is exceptionally flattering and forgiving—and my favorite part about the dress. Although, it's a close one, because the skirt's simple lines are elegantly accentuated by a slit to mid-thigh. It's a bright color, but Meryl's events always eschew the traditional black for women. She says color reminds everyone that the charity supports children, and black is too boring.

And . . . this gown is the color of my date's eyes, which made it an easy decision.

Once the dress is securely fastened and my jewelry is in place, I slip on my heels and step in front of the full-length mirror on the back of my bedroom door.

"You think it'll do?"

Kelsey laughs from behind me. "Girl, if this were a fairy tale, Prince Charming wouldn't even notice Cinderella because he'd be too busy staring at you."

The intercom buzzes in the kitchen, and I smile. "He's here."

"I'll go let him up. You stay. I want to see his face when he sees you."

I back away from the mirror so she can slip out the bedroom door. As soon as I hear Gabriel's voice, I take a deep breath and step out of the room, smoothing my hands over my cinched waist.

"Holy shit," Gabriel whispers when he sees me. He stares for a long moment before coming forward, which gives me time to appreciate the clean lines of his tux.

"You look amazing, bossy."

He doesn't say anything about my nickname attempt, which is fine by me because his smile could light up Manhattan. "You look incredible. Holy fuck." He shakes his head and glances at Kelsey, and then back to me. "Goddamn, woman. You're stunning."

I step toward him. "I would kiss you for that, but Kelsey would kill me."

"Shit, that reminds me, you need your clutch. Let me grab it and slip your lippy, mirror, and powder in it. Then you kids can be off to the gala."

Kelsey rushes back into the bedroom, and Gabriel closes the distance between us. He raises a hand into the air near my face and traces the line of my jaw with the back of his fingers without actually touching me. "You look too fine for these hands of mine to even dream of touching you."

"Well, your hands better get over that, because I expect you to touch me *a lot* tonight."

A wicked gleam forms in his dazzling sapphire eyes. "I'll hold you to that."

A few minutes later, we take the elevator down from the fourth floor, through Curated, so I don't have to walk down all the stairs in my four-inch heels. When we reach the black

Escalade out front with a uniformed driver standing at the back door, I shoot a look at Gabriel.

"What's all this?"

"Your new driver and security." He stops in front of the man. "Scarlett, this is Eddie O'Halloran. Hal, this is Scarlett."

"Good to meet ya, ma'am," he says with an Irish lilt. "You can call me Eddie or Hal. I'll answer to either."

I shake his hand. "It's nice to meet you, Hal. Thank you."

"Nah, the pleasure's all mine. Gabe here has done me plenty of favors, and I was happy for the chance to return one. Nothing will happen to you with me around, Ms. Priest. I promise you that."

SIXTY

As soon as we pull up to the red-carpeted stairs, I know I'm out of my element, despite the fancy tux I'm wearing and the beautiful woman on my arm.

Hal hops out of the SUV to open the door, and I climb out first, offering my hand to Scarlett. Cameras flash all around us as she steps out of the Escalade.

Her smile is as perfect as the rest of her, and she knows exactly how to handle the photographers. I take her lead and do what she does, pausing here and there for them to take more pictures of us than I thought were humanly possible.

Leaning slightly, I speak directly into her ear. "Is it always like this?"

Scarlett's smile doesn't budge. "Not always. But Meryl is trying to raise a lot of money tonight, so I'm not surprised she pulled out all the stops. Making people feel important can really help the cause."

"What exactly is the cause again?"

We finish passing through the camera-heavy gauntlet before she answers. "Building project. She needs to expand the center she runs for at-risk youth. It's a huge undertaking, and she needs all the money she can get."

"Got it."

We walk into a ballroom already filled with people mingling. I see plenty of familiar faces, but none who would actually admit to knowing who I am. Rich guys liked to frequent my underground club, but they would never acknowledge me on the street because it would mean admitting where they'd been.

Several eyes lock on me and Scarlett, and you can almost watch the gossip travel from group to group until even more people are staring.

If I thought I was out of place before, I feel like a fish out of water right now. My tux feels too tight, and all I want to do is walk straight out that door, but I wouldn't do that to Scarlett. No fucking way.

I slowly inhale a deep breath through my nose and let it out. They can say whatever the fuck they want about me, but if anyone says a cross word about her . . . I won't be responsible for what happens next.

Thankfully, a familiar blonde comes bouncing in our direction with a man in a suit trailing behind her.

"Scar, you made it! Oh my God, the antique silver tea set you donated to the silent auction is absolutely freaking incredible. I didn't know you even had it! I'm jelly as hell because the bid is already two grand, and the silent auction has only been open for ten minutes."

"Even I was tempted when I saw it," says another voice that comes from the opposite side of Scarlett. *Meryl Fosse*. "Maybe I'll have to rethink my position on Curated, because that tea set is divine."

"Call me next week, Meryl, and we'll set up a private appointment for you," Scarlett says with pride. "I think you'll be quite surprised by what you see and what we can do for you."

The grand dame herself nods. "I'll do that. It'll be my treat to myself for pulling off this gala." She shifts her attention to me. "You look sharp, Mr. Legend. I hope you'll bring your little brother by sometime in the next few weeks. He seems like a truly remarkable individual, and I have several kids who would really benefit from meeting him."

I'm not sure why she wants Bump to come in, and I don't want him being exploited in any way, but I nod. "I'll see what I can do, Ms. Fosse. Nice event you got here. I hope you pry open all their wallets and get the money you need."

Her smile widens. "Me too. And you should all get those wallets out and take a look at the silent auction items. I expect bids from everyone."

She sweeps away, welcoming another group, and Harlow grabs Scarlett by the hand.

"Come on, you have to see this necklace. I swear to God, it looks like it belonged to royalty. I didn't get a chance to bid yet, but it's going to go *nuts*."

Scarlett looks to me.

"Go. I'll get us some drinks."

"I'll come with you, man," Harlow's husband says.

"Oh shit, I didn't even introduce you two yet." Harlow waves a hand between me and her man. "Jimmy, this is Gabriel Legend. Legend, this is Jimmy."

"Thanks, babe," Jimmy says with a kiss to her cheek before we shake hands and Harlow drags Scarlett away. "I knew who you were without the intro. You're as much of a legend as your name suggests."

I shrug. "Not much these days."

Jimmy and I move toward the bar, dodging men in tuxes and women dressed to impress.

"Yeah, that was some shit. Your club getting shot up when it opened. I'm glad to hear you got some new action coming in the door, though. Should be a real help to getting you back to where you need to be. Where you belong."

I stare at the man as we reach the bar. "What are you talking about?"

"Your fight night. I heard Legend got approved as a venue."

I try to smooth my features, but I assume my surprise is all over my face. "How do you know that?"

"I hear all sorts of shit first. Perk of being a sports agent. This city is a hell of a lot smaller than you think, and word in my circle is that your club is about to be the next big thing in MMA venues."

I breathe a sigh of relief. "Well, that's damn good to know, especially since I haven't heard anything. I was starting to think I was going to have to put together my own fight card to make it happen."

Jimmy shrugs. "Doesn't sound like that'll be necessary."

"Well, fuck. Thank God. I'll drink to that." I turn to the bartender. "Three fingers of Seven Sinners. Make that two of them. The lady likes her whiskey."

SIXTY-ONE

Whena we stop in front of the necklace that Harlow is dying to own, what feels like all the blood in my face drains away.

Because I've seen that starburst diamond necklace before . . . on my mother's neck in all her wedding photos. It was missing from jewelry I inherited, and when I asked my father about it, he said it was lost long ago.

"Isn't it just gorgeous? I mean, *damn.*"

I shove forward, not caring that I jump the crowd of people trying to get a look at the piece that's encased in glass. In tiny letters, the placard beneath it gives all the details about the necklace, and then the most damning thing I've ever seen in print.

Donated by Lawrence Priest, Priest Pharmaceuticals.

Oh. My. Fucking. God.

My father had the necklace all along, and he *lied to me about it? Why?*

I grit my teeth together to stop from turning around to find something metal to smash the glass case and take my property back.

How the hell could he do this?

I'm brought back to the here and now when someone jostles me to reach for the pen attached to write a new bid.

"This will look perfect on me. I have to have it."

Lucy Byers. Are you fucking kidding me, universe? How is this right? I pray for a smidge of understanding but come up dry.

"Is something wrong, Scarlett?" Harlow asks, and my name comes out louder than she anticipates, because the crowd around Lucy has gone silent.

Lucy spins around, and I want to smack that perfect pout off her plastic face.

"Oh, Scarlett. Is that your mom's necklace? How charitable of your father to donate it to a good cause."

Harlow sucks in a breath. "Oh my God. Nooo."

Lucy tilts her head to the side. "Oh no. You didn't know he was donating it? That's just *terrible*." The way she says the word, dredged in mean-spirited humor, slices at me.

"You know what, Lucy?" I ask with my chin held high, even though I'm crumbling inside.

"What?"

"You're a mean-spirited bitch, and I don't care if I have to spend every penny I have. That necklace will never be yours."

Her mouth drops open in shock before her eyes narrow. "You fucking cunt. Watch me. I'll bankrupt you if I have to."

"Ladies, ladies. Please, I didn't make a donation to cause arguments."

My father's voice crawls up my spine like a spider dragging its web behind it.

Slowly, I turn to face him. "How could you?"

He shrugs. "I didn't think you'd care. You got everything else of hers. What does one little necklace matter anymore, Scarlett? She's dead, and she's not coming back. Besides, I think it's poetic justice to have the proceeds go to Meryl's charity. Bury the hatchet between them and all, posthumously."

Skeletal fingers of pain wrap around my heart and squeeze. *He did this on purpose. As a way to try to hurt my mother* after her death. *What the hell is wrong with him?*

I have no answers to that question. All I know is that I have to get away from him. *Now.*

"Excuse me. I need to find my date."

I turn around and stride blindly in the opposite direction, not caring where I go, as long as it's anywhere but *here*.

Harlow's heels click behind me as she rushes to catch up. "The bar. They're by the bar." She threads her arm through my elbow. "This way, hon. They're right over here."

I can barely see through the unshed tears in my eyes, reeling like I'm experiencing loss and grief all over again.

Except this time, it's caused by the death of a dream.

My father will never be the man I want him to be. He has never been capable of being that man. I was crazy to hold out hope this long. Why didn't I see it before?

Gabriel's easy expression vanishes the second he catches sight of me and Harlow. He swings his head from side to side as if looking for a threat. But there's no one for him to protect me from, because it's my own fault that I'm devastated.

"What the fuck happened? Are you okay?" he asks quietly, pulling me into his side.

"Lawrence happened. He donated Lourdes's necklace that was supposed to be Scarlett's," Harlow says, filling him in.

"Fuck." Gabriel squeezes me closer to his side. "I'm so sorry, ladybug."

"We'll buy it then," Jimmy says, holding out his hand to Harlow. "Come on. You're going to put your bid down, and we'll get it for her."

I shake my head in Gabriel's arms. "Let it go. Lucy Byers said she'd bankrupt me to keep it out of my hands."

"Who the fuck is Lucy Byers?" Gabriel asks, his tone sharp enough to kill.

"A pretentious bitch who doesn't know the meaning of the word *no*," Harlow says.

"And one I kicked out of Curated this week for being horrendous," I add, dipping my head. "She was saying stupid things . . ."

Gabriel's finger lands under my chin and lifts it until I meet his serious blue gaze. "About me."

I nod. "And Chadwick. And my store."

"Fuck that bitch," Gabriel growls. "She's not getting her hands on your mom's necklace. I don't give a fuck if we have to steal it and pay Meryl off."

"Let me and Harlow worry about the necklace," Jimmy adds in a low voice. "I've got dirt on Lucy's husband too, if we need it."

I haven't spent much time around Harlow's husband before, but I'm liking him more and more with each passing second.

"It's okay. It's just a necklace." I suck in a deep breath, trying desperately to find some calm. "It's fine. Just . . . let her have it." Even as I say the words, a tiny piece of my soul withers.

"Not a chance," Harlow says with a militant expression on her face. "We'll be back, Scarlett. You two . . . go find our seats for dinner."

As Harlow and Jimmy walk away, Gabriel squeezes me against his side again. "I'm so fucking sorry, ladybug. I don't know the whole story here, but your father is definitely a prize asshole for donating something that was your mom's without offering it to you first."

I shake my head. "I don't even know why he would. He doesn't have a charitable bone in his entire body. It has to be for show. Maybe trying to buy some goodwill for something. I don't know, but I really don't want to be here anymore. Maybe we should just go?"

Gabriel squeezes my hand. "We're not letting some asshole and a worthless twat run us out of here. You're stronger than that. Get me?"

I don't know if I am, but with Gabriel holding my hand, I straighten my shoulders and pretend that I don't have a single care in the entire world. "Damn right, I get you."

SIXTY-TWO

Of all the times not to have enough cash on hand to do what I need to do . . . *Fuck.* It kills me that Harlow and her husband are over there bidding on something for my woman, but I'll owe them a huge debt of gratitude if they can manage to snag it from beneath that rich bitch's nose.

"That's Lucy," Harlow whispers to me as a black-haired woman sits at a table next to ours after the waitstaff start moving through the room with salads. "Just in case you need to know who to kill."

Harlow's humorless suggestion knocks an idea loose in my head halfway through dinner. It's not a good one. Scarlett would fucking kill me for even thinking about it. But . . . if it works and no one ever finds out, what's the harm?

I wait for my chance while trying to pay attention to the conversations happening around the table. Scarlett's not too talkative, so no one really notices when I'm not either.

When Lucy gets up and makes her way across the ball-room in the direction of the restroom, I seize the opportunity.

"I'll be right back," I tell Scarlett as I rise and excuse myself from the table.

Before she can ask where I'm going, I'm moving on the same path Lucy Byers took.

Outside the ballroom doors, there are several people talking on cell phones and socializing in the lobby area. I scan around for Lucy, but she's not there.

Fuck.

I spot the bathrooms and slip around the corner to wait. It only takes a few minutes before the black-haired woman emerges.

I charge forward, like I'm heading back to the ballroom, and deliberately knock into her side. "Oh shit. I'm so sorry, ma'am. I wasn't watching where I was going. Forgive me for plowing you over."

Her expression is pinched and bitchy until she gets a look at my face. Then it's a completely different story, just like I was banking on. From the unconcealed hunger in her gaze, Lucy Byers is one of those rich bitches who gets a charge from walking on the wild side with a man they consider dangerous. Her words confirm it.

"Oh no, no need to apologize. I wasn't paying attention either. If I had been, then how could I have possibly missed seeing the infamous Gabriel Legend?"

I flash her a smile that takes every bit of my energy to make it seem real. "I'm afraid you have me at a disadvantage, Miss . . ."

"I would never be at your disadvantage, Mr. Legend." She holds out her hand. "I'm Lucy, and I've been meaning to get out to your club to meet you."

"I don't spend much time on the floor, Lucy. So it'd be a long shot. Better we're meeting here where no one will think twice about you talking to a guy in a suit."

Her gaze drops to my toes and drags up my body, and I

feel fucking disgusting letting her look. *This is for Scarlett*, I remind myself.

"This is a little too public for what I have in mind, Mr. Legend."

"Damn, you're direct."

She flashes me another smile that makes my skin crawl. "I know what I want, and what I want is *you*. I can give you things that Scarlett doesn't even know exist. She's a Goody Two-shoes. Everyone knows it."

"Then what are you?"

Lucy plumps her lips into a pout and leans forward until I'm enveloped by a cloud of her sickly sweet perfume. It reminds me of the time a working girl in Biloxi told me I could make a fortune standing on the corner with her, and I ran the other way as fast as humanly fucking possible. I was fourteen.

"I'll be whatever you want me to be. Scarlett never has to know."

With everything in me screaming in protest, I wink at her. "I like the sound of that, but you gotta do something for me."

"I'll do *anything* for you."

She brushes her tits up against my chest, and I fight the urge to gag as I take her hand and lift it to my mouth like I'm going to press a kiss to the back of it, but I can't make myself do it. Instead, I lower it carefully as I speak.

"Good. Then you'll let that necklace of Scarlett's mom's go, or you and I will never see each other again."

Her eyes narrow. "Are you serious? That's your price?"

I nod slowly, waiting for this to blow up in my face. But it doesn't.

"Fine. I won't bid on it again, but I want your promise that you're going to make me *scream* your name next time we're together."

"Oh, you'll be screaming."

Triumph lights up her blue eyes. "Just wait, Legend. You've never had a snatch as tight and tasty as mine. You'll never go back to that uppity snob once you've had me."

I drop her hand. "We'll see about that."

SIXTY-THREE

"I can't believe she stopped bidding on it," Scarlett says, glancing down at the starburst pendant resting between her perfect tits.

Tits that I don't deserve to be staring at after what I did, even if it was for good reason.

The whole fucking night was a disaster. All I want is to get back to the club, pick up Roux and Bump, get the fuck out of the city, and stay there.

I don't know what the hell I'm going to do about Lucy Byers, but one thing is for sure—my dick is going nowhere near her. *Ever.* I need a shower after touching her.

"You're sure you don't mind staying at my place tonight?" I ask Scarlett to change the subject.

She shakes her head. "Not at all. I like your place."

"Good deal. I'll be quick getting Roux and Bump. Won't take long at all."

"I'll come in with you. Maybe if I post that we're here, more people from the gala will come out because it's still early, they're dressed up, and why go home yet?"

I can think of one bitch who would show up for sure,

which makes it a damn good thing we're not staying. But I don't tell Scarlett that, and I fucking hate that I'm keeping another secret.

I'll give it a few days and then tell her what happened. She'll understand. She has to.

Hal parks in front of the club, and I open the door myself. More cameras flash as Scarlett climbs out with me. It's not quite the same as the entrance to the gala, but this type of publicity will be damn good for Legend, just like Scarlett said.

I give the doormen a nod before heading up the stairs. Once we're inside, I catch sight of Q and Zoe by the bar. Scarlett and I head that way.

"Everything good?" I ask them.

"Busy night. We've blown through way more liquor than I thought we would. We're going to have to start ordering more," Zoe says, beaming.

"Good news. Any trouble?"

Q shakes his head. "Everything's been pretty damn smooth. Except for one thing."

"What?"

Q looks at Scarlett. "Your stepsister tried to get in with a fake ID. I escorted her to the curb."

"Shit," Scarlett whispers, and it's barely audible over the bass. "I'm sorry. She mentioned yesterday that she didn't want to wait to see the place until she was twenty-one. I told her we'd figure something out. I didn't expect her to take matters into her own hands, but then again, I guess I'm not too surprised. Flynn is—"

"A reckless hellion," Q says, and there's something in his tone that I can't interpret. I make a mental note to worry about it later.

"We gotta get Bump and Roux. They in my office?"

Zoe points that way. "Should be. I haven't checked on him

in a couple hours, but last I saw, Bump was watching *Property Brothers* on HGTV again, and he told me you need to buy him a house."

"Fucking hell. That kid." I shake my head. "I'll nip that in the bud quick."

"I love that show. He has good taste. I'll go up with you," Scarlett says as she threads her fingers through mine. There's something about holding her hand that always grounds me.

I lead her to a door that's barely visible from the other side of the room. It opens into one of the hidden corridors that line this building from its days as a Masonic temple.

"Am I carrying you up?" I ask her when we stop in front of a staircase.

"Not necessary," she replies with a wink, and proceeds to show me how quickly she can make it up the stairs, despite her heels.

"Impressive skills. What else can you do in those heels?"

She turns around at the top and flashes me a grin. "Just wait. I'll show you."

I meet her at the top and press a kiss to her temple. "I'd like them digging into my back, if I'm being honest."

"We can make that happen."

"Then we better get Bump and Roux and get the fuck out of here before we cause a scene."

With Scarlett's hand in mine, I reach for the knob on my office door and push it open.

What waits inside is a scene straight out of my nightmares.

No. Fuck. No.

"How long did you really think you could run, Gabe? Did you think I wouldn't find you?"

Bump is on his knees as Moses Buford Gaspard sits at my desk with the barrel of his gun pressed against Bump's temple.

"Don't," I whisper as Moses's finger curls around the trigger.

"Ah, boy. You've forgotten how things work. You don't call the shots. I do. Now get on your motherfucking knees."

Gabriel and Scarlett's story concludes in *The Fight for Forever,* the final book of the Legend Trilogy.

ALSO BY MEGHAN MARCH

Ruthless King

Defiant Queen

Sinful Empire

SAVAGE TRILOGY:

Savage Prince

Iron Princess

Rogue Royalty

BENEATH SERIES:

Beneath This Mask

Beneath This Ink

Beneath These Chains

Beneath These Scars

Beneath These Lies

Beneath These Shadows

Beneath The Truth

DIRTY BILLIONAIRE TRILOGY:

Dirty Billionaire

Dirty Pleasures

Dirty Together

DIRTY GIRL DUET:

Dirty Girl

Dirty Love

REAL DUET:

Real Good Man

Real Good Love

ABOUT THE AUTHOR

Making the jump from corporate lawyer to romance author was a leap of faith that *New York Times*, #1 *Wall Street Journal*, and *USA Today* bestselling author Meghan March will never regret. With over thirty titles published, she has sold millions of books in nearly a dozen languages to fellow romance-lovers around the world. A nomad at heart, she can currently be found in the woods of the Pacific Northwest, living her happily ever after with her real-life alpha hero.

She would love to hear from you.
Connect with her at:
Website: meghanmarch.com
Facebook: @MeghanMarchAuthor
Twitter: @meghan_march
Instagram: @meghanmarch

9 781943 796427